Darcy's Gallant Gambit

A Pride and Prejudice Variation

Jaime Marie Lang

Idle Musings Publishing

Book Cover by Jaime Marie Lang

Editing by Elizabeth Thurmond

Preface

"IF YOU CONTINUE TO refuse to do your duty to your family, I will contact the headman at Oxford to tell them you have acted dishonorably and have you sent down in disgrace. With your brother gone, you must return home to marry and learn how to care for Longbourn and her people." Confident in the power of his position, and the logic behind his reasoning, Reginald Bennet felt assured that his grandson would comply. He did not have many more years in him and he needed to see to his beloved Longbourn. This conflict had to happen. There seemed to be no other way.

"You may choose to force my hand, but you will find, sir, that you will not truly get your way. If you take away my happiness, I will strike at yours. I care not for this plot of dirt or her people. If you require me to marry, I shall choose a woman who will pollute the shades of the home you cherish." And with that, Thomas Bennet turned and exited the room, going off in search of such a woman.

Catherine Bennet had often worried about the bitter attitude of her second grandson, especially after his parents passed. She gave voice to her apprehension. "Reggie, are you certain that this is the wisest course of action? He could do a lot of damage to Longbourn, including selling it when you are gone. Besides, what might happen to whatever poor girl he gets involved in this feud?"

"You always worry too much, Cathy. He is an intelligent young man. He will quickly realize that his future will serve him better with a respectable wife by his side, and a well-run estate. I will prevent him from being able to squander Longbourn by tying it up with an entailment until it passes to his heir. Thomas will see the wisdom of the situation and Longbourn will see multiple generations of thriving Bennet ownership." Determination reflected itself in his grim smile, confident that he would set things to rights even after losing his oldest grandson. Catherine did not smile, for she lacked confidence in Reggie's assurance. Perhaps she worried for nothing, but she had seen the look in Thomas' eyes. He was intent on a destructive rebellion. She hoped her inclination was wrong.

Thomas stomped around the village of his youth. He would find a girl ignorant of the requirements that came with managing an estate. Someone with a splendid figure and an empty head. Someone like that girl laughing too loudly outside the milliners. He studied her for a few moments. Indeed, that loud vulgar girl as mistress of Longbourn would be the perfect revenge on his grandfather.

He was able to deceive Fanny with his honeyed words, leading her to believe he loved her. He doted on the girl with extravagant gestures. Thomas and Fanny's courtship was the talk of the town, and everyone was keenly watching every moment. His only obstacle was Fanny's father; the man never seemed to trust his smiles and compliments. But Mr. Gardiner's distrust was overcome by the power of the town's gossip. Thomas made sure that his attention had been so marked that it would ruin her reputation if they did not marry, and did not care if anyone was happy about it.

The only saving grace that Fanny had in this skewed alliance was the settlement her solicitor father insisted upon. Anthony Gardiner suspected his daughter's suitor's disingenuous, self-gratifying attitude might turn dark with time. He did what he could to shield his daughter financially. He stipulated that Mr. Bennet would set aside a considerable amount of pin money for his daughter. It would also continue to increase upon the birth of every future grandchild. In his loving way, her father was trying to prepare his daughter for the harsher times that would come. Harsher times that were quick to appear.

Sadly, Reginald lived long enough to realize that his plan of coercing his grandson had been flawed. Thomas had malice in his heart, and it seemed virtually certain that Longbourn would fall into a decline. At the time of his death, shortly after the birth of his great-granddaughter Jane, Reggie had become well acquainted with regret.

Chapter One

ELIZABETH SAVORED THE VIEW before her, marveling at the sight and feeling a sense of rejuvenation. A deep azure shade filled the sky, and it seemed to whisper of a future of exploration and wonder. Elizabeth wanted to cling to the hope and wonder that it brought to her heart, at least for the length of her walk home. Reality would intrude on her joy soon enough. She smiled as she looked back at her sister and their young companion, the gentle breeze playing through the trees and stirring her hair.

It had been a pleasure to teach the local children that morning. Despite her hectic schedule, Elizabeth was grateful to be able to commit to teaching at least twice a week. She delighted in the enthusiasm with which the little ones eagerly absorbed all the knowledge they could, and Mary was doing so well with the children that she could not help but feel proud. She had struggled to read aloud and interact with the young ones in the beginning, but had improved so much. Elizabeth had heard Mary's joyous laughter ring out just that morning. It was clear that Mary was really enjoying herself a great deal now.

Mary glanced at the young boy beside her, her face brightening as she observed his liveliness. At ten, he was the oldest of their pupils, and he always insisted on accompanying them as they made their way home to Longbourn. "Kiernan, why don't you go with the other children to play? You know I love your company on our walks, but you don't have to be home so soon. You could play with the others." Mary had noticed for a while that Kiernan never seemed to take advantage of the opportunity to play like the other children did.

"I don't do well with the other kids. I feel out of place and my palms sweat. My words come out wrong and I say the wrong thing. 'Sides, somebody has to walk you ladies home. It's only right. My Mam said it was important for me to take care of my sister because the world isn't always safe for girls. Since you don't have a brother or anything, you're not safe. I only got one sister and we have three brothers, so I figure I can help with some brotherin'." Kiernan beamed up at Mary and Elizabeth, proud of his declaration.

"Why Kiernan, I have never felt so honored. I know my sister and I are privileged to have you accompany us home." Mary smiled at the slight blush on the young man's face. It was rather nice to have someone besides her sister to look out for her.

"I know I would find myself glad to have a brother such as you, Kiernan, and I will welcome your 'brotherin' anytime. You are growing into a fine young man. It's hard to believe you are the same little boy who began our school four years ago. Though actually, I have been wondering if you need more of a challenge. Would you be interested in learning something new?" Elizabeth asked.

"If some learning is good, I think more will be better. My Mam has always said that my learning will take me places. I don't think I want to go very far right now, but maybe it will be fun later on." Kiernan laughed, happy at the acceptance he received from these two genteel ladies.

***

THE SWEET SCENT OF the countryside was like a balm to Darcy, and he smiled with pleasure. He could not help but take a deep breath of the invigorating, crisp air, preferring it to the thick, putrid muck in London. Despite his love of the opera and the museum, he could not abide the city. Between the grubby streets and the condescending aristocracy, he found visiting unbearable. He was glad the pleasant weather had held out. Even the short distance between London and Hertfordshire would have been miserable had there been rain.

The fact that Bingley's carriage had needed some minor repairs had been of significant benefit to him. Without the constant observation and fawning of Bingley's sisters, he could enjoy the ride and survey the area. Darcy was happy to continue to Hertfordshire on horseback alone.

The little town he had passed through had been quaint, much like Lambton, near his home. There were all the typical shops and bustling that one might expect from a small market town. There was even a charming little chapel he could see through the fiery colored trees. He could almost feel comfortable amongst all these unknown people because there was such a sameness. Darcy never liked to think of his struggles when around strangers, but he knew it was the reason he did not travel more. He prayed the visit would not end in regrettable awkwardness.

One drawback of his close friendship with Bingley was being forced to socialize more than he was comfortable with. If he was around too many people, even if he was familiar with them, his hands would shake. His tendency to misspeak when under stress had led him into difficult situations while at Eton, and later Cambridge. Bingley was one of the few people who welcomed him with a genuine smile, despite the clumsiness of his conversation. Whenever Darcy's anxiety got the better of him, Bingley's warm smile and calming manner would save him from making a scene in polite company, at least most of the time.

Darcy hoped that Bingley's first foray into landowning would bear fruit. The property of Netherfield looked promising on paper. He would, however, wait until he saw it to make any judgments. He began contemplating what the difference the warmer climate of the south would have on crops and harvest times. Darcy did not notice the walkers until he had gotten quite close. His sudden arrival took them aback. A young boy was standing protectively in front of two young ladies, each with a load of Horn Books in their arms.

"Apologies for my abrupt arrival. The scenery captivated me." Darcy bowed over his horse's neck and tipped his hat.

"I often find myself captivated by the majestic elegance of the natural world. I cannot begrudge someone else the same enjoyment." A pert smile punctuated the comment made by the taller of the two girls.

Darcy froze, unable to formulate what to say or do next. She spoke with a confident air, which was always something he preferred to the fawning he heard so often in society lately. Though that was not what made him speechless. Her smile was simply arresting, and with that smile, his mind refused to function.

***

THE STRANGER'S BROWN EYES reminded her of the rich chocolate she drank on frosty mornings, and his tousled brown hair made her swallow convulsively. The cut of his coat and the knot in his cravat told her he was a wealthy gentleman but the lack of courtesy in his blank expression and his refusal to answer her left Elizabeth feeling perplexed. It made her old instincts come to the fore despite the way he made the little hairs on her neck stand on end. After a significant pause, Elizabeth glanced at Mary, confusion written on her face. Why would a gentleman refuse to respond to a civil comment?

"Well, we must be going. Do enjoy your ride." Elizabeth made an abrupt curtsy, followed by Mary, and they turned to go on their way. Elizabeth's gait was more of a march than a walk and the other two had to hurry to keep up. Once they were well out of the sight of the gentleman on horseback, Elizabeth began her tirade.

"Just because someone did not introduce us yet, doesn't mean he needs to ignore my attempt at polite conversation. Despite his appearance as a cultured, well-dressed gentleman, I am doubtful of his character." Elizabeth continued to march, her half boots digging into the well-worn path. "And his expression!" Elizabeth swirled around to face her companions; her face flushed with outrage.

"No, Miss Elizabeth, you are looking at it sideways. I have seen that look before. It's the same one Robby Lucas gets when Mrs.

Long's niece talks to him. If she had hit him in the face with a fish, he wouldn't have been more flummoxed. Like his wits had left him dumbstruck." Kiernan giggled at the foolishness of such a smart lady when a gent was involved.

"Robby Lucas is shy. Charlotte speaks of her brother's bashfulness often." Elizabeth paused abruptly as her mind began whirling along a path of new possibilities.

"Not only is he shy, Elizabeth, he is fond of Mrs. Long's niece, but he doesn't know what to say or do when confronted by her." Mary's heart filled with sympathy and understanding for her. Elizabeth was direct and frank, but the world and the people within it rarely followed suit. Mary had noticed that people's emotions were often tangled and difficult to make sense of.

"Really?" Elizabeth responded, this time in a small voice, much different from the tone she had been using. She didn't like admitting when she had a gap in her understanding.

"You struck the gent stupid, Miss Elizabeth. He wasn't snubbing you." It was obvious to Kiernan that the ladies might need more brotherin' than he originally thought.

"Yes, I believe Kiernan is correct. I think the gentleman was quite smitten with you, Lizzie; he could barely look you in the eye." Mary watched Elizabeth struggle with this new information. This reversal of roles was new to Mary, but she was glad to be there for her sister.

"Well, that is not what I expected. If he is truly shy, as you say, I will have to readjust my manner of thinking." Elizabeth felt at a loss. Certainly, reading people was something she was going to have to continue working on. She was still disappointed, but this time it was because of her tendency to jump to hasty conclusions. As she looked at the evidence, it seemed to mock her with its simplicity. As a group, they continued on the path toward Longbourn. Elizabeth squared her shoulders and returned to the issue she had been considering prior to the stranger's chaos.

"Kiernan, would you be interested in accompanying me on my walk in the morning? If you were to join me, we could talk about subjects you are interested in. Also, I was thinking of copying out some pages from a book I have at home for you to practice with."

"Truly on paper an' everything?" Kiernan could hardly contain the hope that was building up inside of him.

"Yes Truly." Elizabeth hid her smile from her young pupil.

"Well, I would love to walk with you most mornings. I already said you needed brotherin'."

Elizabeth and Mary locked eyes, both appreciative that someone wanted to look out for them. They walked on until Longbourn came into view. They had made good time and could wash up before luncheon.

"I wonder if we will see him again?" Elizabeth pondered out loud as she walked under the trellis in the yard.

"He's probably staying at Netherfield," Kiernan spoke while kicking a rock.

"I had heard no rumors that Netherfield was being leased," Mary responded.

"Mrs. Nichols was at the grocer's getting supplies two days ago. She said there was a group of gentlemen and ladies coming soon. She was right excited to get new people coming," Kiernan continued.

"I wonder if they will make it to the assembly this week?" Elizabeth questioned.

"Well, I'm sure they will be told of it, but moving can tire one out." Mary said, always practical.

"You are right. Any time we visit my aunt and uncle in London, it takes a while for me to regain my equilibrium. Though, I would like to think I will see the gentleman. I can only surmise he will improve upon further acquaintance." Honestly, though, how could he get worse?

"No, Miss Elizabeth, I would bet you a book. He will not get any better. Most boys are right stupid about girls." Peals of laughter accompanied them through the yard. The girls promised to see Kiernan soon and said goodbye.

****

ALL THE WHILE, DARCY kept his eyes fixed on where the small group had gone. His horse had tired of his shenanigans and moved to the side of the path, the sweet scent of grass wafting up as he munched. The phrase, which seemed to reverberate in his mind, utterly transfixed Darcy. *What the blazes had just happened?* It was beyond him to understand it at all.

***

ELIZABETH FELT THE INCREASING weight of her many duties as winter approached. Though she and Kiernan walked every morning discussing history and literature, Elizabeth simply did not have the time to ramble about the countryside as she would like. The women of Longbourn were trying to ensure that all the tenants had what they needed to weather the cold, dark months ahead. Elizabeth's duty was to determine the need for any repairs to the tenants' cottages and who were without adequate winter clothing. She carried the facts back to her mother and sisters, and they worked to divide the available funds between their diverse needs. If Mr. Bennet was aware of the hardships his family was confronting, he chose not to help. Elizabeth often thought he would only move to save Longbourn from fire if he thought his books were in jeopardy.

As a child not much older than Kiernan, Elizabeth had realized that there was a problem with the roof of one of the tenant cottages. Afraid that her friends would get sick in the rainy weather, she ran to her father, hoping he would help. She soon understood that her father had no intention of aiding the family that had been working on Longbourn land for generations. Elizabeth had long since learned that her father would only put forth effort for anything if it meant his money for books or port was in jeopardy.

Shortly thereafter, the women of Longbourn had begun diverting some of their pin money into a fund for rainy days and leaky roofs. Thomas Bennet's blatant disregard for human decency spurred the ladies to act on behalf of those who need help on Longbourn land. Mrs. Bennet decided people would recognize the Bennet women as being generous, kind and above reproach, even if Mr. Bennet was not.

And so, the day before the assembly, all the ladies had taken themselves to Mrs. Bennet's private sitting room. A jumble of fabric lay strewn across the floor, creating a multi-colored mosaic. There was a flurry of dresses that had to be altered for the next night's assembly as well as all the of the projects for the tenants.

Elizabeth looked over the list one more time. It looked like they were doing well for the start of October. Seven tenant families relied heavily on the Bennet ladies for their needs, and as of this moment, none of them were in a crisis. They had already reviewed the needs of the expectant mothers. Lydia had developed a great love of babies, so she was in charge of home visits and making baby blankets. She was well along on preparations for the new little ones. They had also discussed the successful completion of the roof repairs for the Sutton family.

Sweet Kitty spoke softly to her sisters and mother. "Mrs. Sutton wanted me to express her gratitude to you all. She was practically in tears, knowing her children will be warm and dry this winter." Her needle and thread moved in and out of two squares of fabric with lovely blue and teal designs. Kitty had a knack for creating beautiful pieces. They decorated much of their house with her paintings and embroidery. Right now, she was making a quilt that would not only be practical, but lovely as well.

"I am glad we could help them. They are a lovely family and have always taken great care of the land. They responded well to the crop rotation you suggested last year, Lizzie." Mrs. Bennet was working with a more delicate fabric than either Kitty or Lydia. Her embroidery skills were quite fine, and she often did up the detailing of the collars and hems on the dresses that her daughters were reworking. Looking around the room at all her precious girls, Mrs. Bennett was proud of both herself and them.

***

WHEN SHE WAS NOT quite seventeen, Fanny had been married to Thomas Bennet for two days before she had her eyes opened to the phrase *Marry in Haste, Repent at Leisure*. Fanny had felt a thrill of pleasure when she realized Thomas Bennet's interest in her. The thrill quickly left her when, after two days of bliss, he bluntly expressed his true feelings. He viewed her as the most witless girl in all of England and was grateful that her stupidity made it effortless to trick and beguile her. He sneered when he said he married her because he knew she couldn't handle the duties of the lady of Longbourn, and it amused him.

It was several days later when her new grandmother-in-law went looking for her after having noticed her despondency. They talked for hours. Mother Bennet told her she was not stupid, and that she felt Fanny could do an admirable job helping run Longbourn. Mother Bennet had been so loving and reassuring, letting her know that everything she needed to do, she could learn with time. The most important thing, she pointed out, was kindness and compassion and the desire to see everyone well cared for. She told her she could either prove her grandson right or she could prove him wrong. All these years later, Fanny certainly felt that with all she had done and still did, she had certainly proven him wrong.

***

Mrs. Bennet was suddenly aware of her surroundings again when Mary's words reached her from the other side of the room. "Mama, the flower design you are doing is just beautiful on Elizabeth's dress. What kind of flower is it?" Mary was working on her own dress for the assembly. It was rather plain, but Mary rather liked the thick forest green ribbon that she was attaching to the high waist.

"Edelweiss. I thought the little white flowers would look well on the pale blue gown." Cutting off a thread, Fanny held her work away from herself to get a better look at the full image.

"The Edelweiss bloom represents courage and devotion. I think it quite suits you, Lizzie." Lydia loved the language of flowers and was happy to share her findings.

"Did Lizzie tell you we heard they let Netherfield, Mama?" Mary was creating small little rosettes of ribbon for all of their hair adornments. It was delicate work, but was something she had learned to love to create.

"I had heard a rumor when I called on Mrs. Long this week. However, I doubt the credibility of the story in circulation. Seven women and five gentlemen seems a bit much," Mrs. Bennet commented.

"We may have met one of the gentlemen earlier this week, on the path from Longbourn," Mary answered blandly.

"Did you?" Mrs. Bennet responded.

"We cannot be certain, but I know of little other reason an unknown gentleman would be on the path that leads to both Longbourn and Netherfield," Mary continued. Glancing over at Elizabeth, she noted the blush gracing her cheeks.

"What were your impressions of him?" Fanny noted Mary's glance, and expected that something interesting would unfold.

"His clothing seemed quite fine. I noticed quality fabrics despite the dust of travel. I would imagine that he was not yet thirty. He seemed quite shy, despite what someone might have thought." Mary could not avoid a snicker. Elizabeth had now covered her face in reaction to Mary's last statement.

"Elizabeth, what could have happened to you to turn that delightful color? You nearly match Jane's dress!" Kitty was agog at this uncharacteristic display.

"I may have jumped to unwarranted conclusions. First, he apologized for startling us, and I responded like a normal person with manners. But then instead of continuing in a normal dialogue, he said nothing." Huffing in frustration, Elizabeth put her fingers to the bridge of her nose.

"After we had gotten away from the gentleman, she ranted about his poor manners. Dear young Kiernan made the cutest speech about how Elizabeth had 'struck the gent stupid,' and it was not his manners in question, but his heart. I think he was so taken with our Lizzie that he lost all ability to speak." Mary did not hide her amusement.

"Oh Lizzie, you do beat all! Only you would conclude that a man who liked you was exhibiting poor manners." Lydia often found the restrictions placed on her too confining and wondered how Elizabeth managed. They had always had similar energy and a love of action, but Elizabeth always appeared to handle it with grace. Seeing that Elizabeth was not infallible was rather reassuring.

"Darling, I love your heart, but sometimes, it not only jumps to conclusions, it fairly leaps." Mrs. Bennet pressed her handkerchief to her eyes, trying to contain her mirth. "Girls, it is fine to giggle, but it is important to remember that not everyone is as they present themselves," Mrs. Bennet reminded them.

"You are correct, Mama. I worry that the first thing I thought about a stranger was negative. I had thought myself a better judge than that."

"I must admit that I am glad I am not out in society yet. I worry I can trust no one's intentions." Kitty was by far the most timid of the girls and did not trust her judgment.

"It will come with time, my dear." Mrs. Bennett had decided shortly after Jane was born that no daughter of hers would come out before her eighteenth birthday. She felt that if she had been more informed of the world prior to taking part in it, she would have selected a different path. She wanted better for her daughters; above all, she taught all her girls that it was essential to know the risks that come with seeking love without first establishing respect.

"Well, though I do not wish to be out either, I wish to see the dancing. All of your dresses are so pretty, you will look like a kaleidoscope of floating butterflies." Lydia fell over backward on her settee and giggled with abandon.

"Then we will spend the morning after discussing our butterfly pursuits," Mary said, her voice filled with warmth.

***

Later, when Elizabeth and Jane met up before bed as they typically did, helping one another ready for the night, they had much to chat about. To ease the burden on their mother, they both took turns spending time with each of their sisters, helping them to cultivate various abilities. But they still committed some time each day to each other.

Elizabeth searched Jane's hair for her last pins and then swept the brush through the locks. "Mary has been doing wonderfully at the school. Her reading aloud seems to have improved and helped her develop more confidence."

"That is wonderful. Lydia seems to enjoy learning how to make lotions and drying the herbs from the garden. She might take over making our scents soon. She has developed quite a fascination for it." Jane felt exhausted, but Elizabeth's gentle brush strokes through her hair were immensely calming.

"What do you think of having eligible gentlemen at Netherfield? What do you think the odds are that they will fall madly in love with one of us?" Elizabeth could not hold back her laugh at the remark.

Soon, they were both laughing. It reminded them of their Aunt Philips, the way she might have commented about eligible bachelors.

"Oh, Lizzie, we can only hope that our beauty will captivate them and help us out of our difficult situation." Jane pretended to joke, but the truth was that she longed to be loved.

"They may adore you for your beauty, dear sister, but I'm looking for someone who will love me for my intellect." Elizabeth giggled as she tied off Jane's braid.

Jane leaned over to kiss her sister on her cheek before she left to go to her own room. Pausing at the door, she grinned at Elizabeth and said, "We can only dream."

Chapter Two

Darcy tried to block out Caroline Bingley's words by concentrating on the feeling of air filling his lungs as he took deep breaths. The slightly nasal pitch of her speech was disrupting his concentration. His position in society required that he attend assemblies and balls, but he had never found a room with over five people comfortable. Assemblies held a good deal more. He felt a crushing tightness in his chest, so Darcy continued taking a series of deep breaths to fight against it. Turning to look out the window, he focused on counting the trees that he could see in the moonlight.

"Really, Charles, how you could ever think settling us in this backwater town was a good idea is beyond me!" Barely taking the time to breathe, Caroline persisted, "It does not even merit the word 'town'. There is no sophistication, no fashion, and no people of quality with which to see and be seen. It is a degradation to even be here!" She did not wait to hear a response. Then again, she never did. "I demand that you have the carriage turned around so that we may leave for London in the morning!"

"We have just arrived. If you do not wish to come inside with us, you may wait in the carriage. If you get cold, there are blankets under your seat." With that, Bingley hopped out of the conveyance and loped up to the building, eager to be away from her.

Darcy scowled at Bingley for not helping his sister. It was not proper, but she made it difficult for anyone to be civil around her. Hurst exited the carriage, helped his wife down, and then assisted Caroline. Darcy descended slowly, trying to delay entering the building for as long as possible. Caroline had held up their departure and now the rooms would most likely be full of people who would stare as soon as he stepped into the building. He steeled himself as each step he took increased the feeling of impending doom.

Upon crossing the threshold, the quivering in his hands increased. Many faces turned and his tension tripled, arresting his breath. Memories flooded through him, halting his progress on the steps. Would the recollections of his mother's rants affect him forever?

"I despair at having so unnatural a son! You are an encumbrance to the family and if you don't stop this shaking, you will never represent your station as you should. If only Tybalt had lived!" The memory of his mother's voice unsettled him, but he fought to regain the present moment. He refused to give her criticism more power over him. At least, that was what he tried to tell himself. While several pairs of eyes followed his movements, he bolted to the corner and placed his back against the solid wall. It grounded him as he attempted to clear his mind.

***

A WEEK AGO, ELIZABETH would have presumed her stranger's refusal to socialize meant he was pompous, but she was trying to look deeper now. He stood with his back to the wall, eyes focused on nothing much at all, and his lips were faintly moving. What struck her the most was that his hands exhibited a tremor visible from several yards away. It was not just shyness; he was nearly terrified. Everywhere she looked, the stares and whispers about his extraordinary wealth were undeniable. That certainly was not helping his distress.

The ladies gossiping by the wall noticed her attention to the gentleman, so she redirected her gaze. Both her sisters were dancing this set and Elizabeth tried to track their progress. The dancers whirled around the room, their laughter and smiles lighting up the atmosphere. Sir Lucas had introduced Mr. Bingley to them, and Mr. Bingley's eyes seemed to sparkle with excitement when he requested Jane's hand in the next dance. Jane and Mr. Bingley were swirling to the rhythm of the music, their faces lit up with joy. They both seemed to be people who looked for things to be happy about. Time would tell whether they were as good a match as their smiles might suggest.

Elizabeth saw Mary amid the crowd, and the smile on her face was as vibrant as Jane's. Mary was dancing with Mr. Goulding's second oldest son, who had recently returned home from Oxford for a family visit. He had always been a bookish boy, and seemed to be an intelligent young man who was hard to draw out into conversation.

Apparently, Mary had found a topic that he felt confident about, as he seemed to be quite enthusiastic about whatever they were discussing.

As the music came to a close, both sisters returned to her side "How did you ever get young Mr. Goulding to talk that much?" Elizabeth was truly curious.

"I asked him what his favorite subject at school was. I think it surprised him that a girl could be interested in any intellectual pursuits." Mary was too polite to roll her eyes in a ballroom, but the way that she scrunched her nose told plenty. "He is interested in structural engineering, by the way. He will be returning to Oxford next week for the upcoming term and he is quite in anticipation." Mary's smile was so large her eyes were crinkling.

"It looked like you were having a good time as well, Jane. What were you discussing?" Elizabeth was delicate, as she did not want to push something that seemed so new.

"Mr. Bingley is all that is pleasant. He seems to enjoy himself in company. I think he is both eager and nervous about managing an estate." He had kept the conversation to only lighter subjects, but that was common for a stranger at an assembly. Jane had enjoyed herself but would wait to make any judgments about his character.

While they had been talking, Mr. Bingley had gone over to Darcy to converse with him. Elizabeth watched his progress out of the corner of her eye, wondering about the two gentlemen and how they interacted. Elizabeth puzzled out their contrasts. The one light and bubbling with energy and the other dark and full of restrained dread.

Maybe they balanced each other out? As they spoke together, the gentlemen moved closer to Elizabeth and her sisters.

Elizabeth felt a sudden pang of embarrassment as she realized she still did not know the man's name. When she heard his voice, she could not resist listening even though she knew it was not polite to listen to another's conversation in a ballroom. They had paused a few paces away from the ladies and Elizabeth could easily overhear all they said. "You know I do not dance with those I do not know. Right now, dancing at this assembly is insupportable." His hands were shaking, though he clenched his fists in what might be an attempt to hide the evidence of his high emotions.

"Come now, Darcy, there are many pretty ladies who are all quite pleasant. I could arrange an introduction to one of them." Bingley's smile was sunny, but it seemed his eyes were trying to convey something reassuring.

"You know, it does not matter how pretty they are. None of them could ever be pretty enough to tempt me to dance. Please, I cannot tolerate it. You have been dancing with a handsome lady; return to her and her smiles. You know you are wasting your time with me." His voice seemed to grow dejected as he encouraged Bingley to leave him. Bingley glanced at the girls and then grabbed him by the elbow and tugged him into the far corner of the room.

"That was a real faux pas," Mary stated grimly. "Jane, did you learn his name?"

"Mr. Bingley stated he is here at Netherfield with his two sisters, Miss Caroline Bingley and Mrs. Louisa Hurst, along with her husband Mr. Hurst, and his good friend Mr. Darcy." Jane conveyed the information with a glance at the women who were across the room. Even when Mr. Darcy said the wrong things, she could feel her compassionate heart go out to him. He seemed to be the opposite of Bingley's sisters, who said all the correct things but in such a way that Jane doubted their sincerity.

Jane had to force her mind from lingering on her introduction to Mr. Bingley and onto the conversation at hand. He had held her hand for longer than appropriate, but the widening of his eyes as he looked at her had done something to her stomach. The dance that they had just enjoyed had made her feel as if she really was a butterfly floating on air. She refused to accept these feelings as they stood on their own, but she was ready to admit that she was interested in finding out more about him.

Elizabeth fiddled with her fan as she pondered the struggling gentleman. "Well, poor Mr. Darcy is certainly not proud as I had assumed previously. Now that I am truly paying attention to more than his words, I can see that the crowd badly affected him. I think he was just so nervous that he bungled his speech. Jane, I wonder if he would be open to trying the tea you blended." She thought he must be miserable frequently, since it was proving to be such a struggle for him to attend an assembly.

"The tea has done wonders for our mother. I am glad I found Grandmother's recipe book in the still room all those years ago. There was so much helpful information." Jane had come into her own when she had discovered her passion for working in the still room. She spent a lot of her time making medicine and lotions for the family and tenants. She had worked for a while to create a palatable tea made with motherwort and lemon balm, which aided in relaxation. It helped their mother when she was suffering from attacks of her nerves.

"Speaking of our mother, have either of you seen her?" Elizabeth asked.

"She is by the punch bowl, speaking with Lady Lucas and Mrs. Long. She seems to be enjoying herself." Mary glanced in her mother's direction, noticing her mother hiding her grin behind a fan.

"I am so glad that she can get enjoyment from these evenings. She has so little enjoyment in her life," Jane said. Elizabeth often thought that Jane would only be truly happy herself if all those around her were happy themselves.

As they had spoken, Miss Charlotte Lucas had approached them with a glass of lemonade in her hand. They had an interesting kinship with Charlotte and the Lucas family. Mr. Bennet had refused to bring a governess to Longbourn, but because Mrs. Bennet was close friends with Lady Lucas, they eventually arranged for the girls to learn certain subjects at the Lucas estate, like French and piano. This led to a very close connection between all the girls.

"How are you fairing this evening, ladies?" Charlotte smiled at her friends.

"The night has been going well. I believe Jane has captured the attention of Mr. Bingley and Mary has gotten Mr. Goulding to smile. Which is a feat accomplished by few." Elizabeth smiled at Mary.

Charlotte looked around the room and stepped closer to Elizabeth before speaking. "I was concerned for you when I heard that Mr. Darcy said dancing with you would not be tolerable. And that none of you were pretty enough." She conveyed the gossip with a reluctant air, and did not expect Elizabeth to laugh.

"Oh, the poor dear is going to be vilified. I am not the only one in Meryton who quickly jumps to conclusions. Please let anyone who speaks of this know that we were close enough to hear his misspoken words and took no offense." Elizabeth smiled at her confused friend.

"Though he used the words tolerable and not pretty enough, he did not mean it in the way it sounded, I do not think," Mary tried to champion him.

"So your understanding is that he was not actually insulting you or the people gathered at the assembly?"

"I fear he does not deal well with crowds, Charlotte. While his words were not kind or well thought out, I sensed no malice in them. There was only fright and frustration at being prompted to dance," Jane added.

"Well, that is a surprise. He is such a tall, wealthy man, one would think he would have nothing to fear." Looking about, Charlotte noticed their mothers coming to join them.

"Have you enjoyed the night, girls? I saw you dancing. You did indeed look to be as graceful as butterflies! I will tell Lydia that her guess was correct." Mrs. Bennet was having a very good evening. She always felt lighter when away from her husband, especially when there was gaiety and dancing.

"Is that your hand I recognize in those lovely flowers embellishing Elizabeth's dress, Mrs. Bennet?" Charlotte kindly inquired.

"You are too kind, Charlotte dear! It was just something I did during one of our recent rainy mornings." Mrs. Bennet was proud of her good work, but had long ago lost her tendency to brag. Mother Bennet had not been around for long after her marriage, but she had been a wonderful model for sincerity and kindness.

***

"Darcy, that was not well done. There were those who could hear you, including the Bennet ladies. The people here have great respect for them and will not tolerate any disrespect." Bingley absentmindedly ran his fingers through his tousled hair. "It is not just that it will look bad. Someone may interpret the things you said as calling those girls not pretty and not tolerable enough to dance with. How would you feel if someone said such a thing about Georgiana?" Bingley questioned whether it was wise to encourage him to attend this evening to begin with. He would have liked to let Darcy stay at home, but then Caroline would have stayed at home and that could have only ended badly.

"That is not at all what I wanted to convey! I cannot trust myself to speak correctly in a crowd. It is very perturbing." Darcy started to walk away, but a hand on his shoulder stopped him.

"Not tonight. You can apologize this week. We can arrange an introduction. If you don't want to make things worse, apologize when you are not in a crowd." Bingley's eyes conveyed his understanding.

Darcy's hand went to his hair, and he wrapped a strand around his finger, the gentle motion calming him as he tried to make sense of his current predicament. "You are correct again. If I try something here, I will end up with my new Hessians lodged firmly in my mouth. Have we been here long enough? Can we go, do you think?" Darcy's expression, which had been glum only moments before, became eager at the possibility of escaping.

"I'm sure leaving now will be fine. Meet us at the carriage. I will gather my sisters and Hurst." Bingley turned, scanning the walls to spot his overdressed sisters.

Chapter Three

The ladies of Longbourn sat at the dining table in a subdued air. The luncheon after any assembly was always a trial to be endured. Mr. Bennet always seemed to feel the need to pull them back from any happiness that they had gained from such a charming time the night before.

Mr. Bennet jabbed a piece of boiled ham with his fork and took a large bite. With a half-open mouth, he chewed it while trying to decide who to focus his attention on next. He had already insulted his wife. Then he had moved on to his oldest daughter Jane; at twenty-one you would think she would have been taken off his hands by now. Neither of them reacted in the way that he wished.

When he looked at Elizabeth, she met his gaze without flinching. "Lizzie dear, have you checked your impertinent remarks lately? I fear you may drive away your sister's suitors with your bluestocking ways. You know that only capturing a wealthy husband will save you girls from the hedgerows on my passing." Elizabeth's dark curly hair and vivid emerald eyes mirrored those of his grandmother. He saw his grandmother's glare of disapproval when he looked into her eyes.

"Yes, Father, it is a fear I have as well. I know having read books is something that will prevent me from finding a husband, but I can hope that the consequences will not spill over onto Jane as well. How else can I spend my days teaching Jane's children how to embroider and play the piano poorly?" Elizabeth returned his denigration with sarcasm.

Frustrated with his lack of headway with Elizabeth, Bennet moved on to someone he thought would be a weaker target. "So, Mary, if Jane's ravishing beauty makes Elizabeth's prettiness seem dull in comparison, you must have no hope of impressing anyone. Were you sure to bring a book for the time you graced the wall with your presence?"

Mary swallowed her last bite before responding. "I have been reading the Proverbs of late and have found many of them deserving of contemplation. Specifically, I am pondering Proverbs 16:8. Though one must also pay attention to Proverbs 17:1." Mary methodically ate her meal, not even looking up at her father. He was not a man who held any appreciation for scripture and would never understand her slight.

"I am glad that you at least have something to ponder while you wait all alone at assemblies." His pious daughter wasted so much of her time reading religious blather. He looked further down the table. Kitty was so cowed that she never raised her eyes when he was in the room. Lydia, on the other hand, was so feeble-minded that she did not realize his animosity. The daft girl put flowers at his spot at the table for him every day. No longer satisfied with the interaction, Bennet threw his serviette down and pushed back from the table. Satisfied that he had at least taken the shine off their fun, he left them to enjoy his books and port.

The ladies, upon his leaving, found themselves able to relax and eat in peace. Habit led the women to regroup in Mrs. Bennet's sitting room after they had dealt with Mr. Bennet. In response to Mr. Bennet's assumption that the ladies were unintelligent and silly, they worked to expand their minds. They would often engage in energetic debates about philosophical topics or read classic literature out loud.

"I feel Voltaire meant that inaction is just as indefensible as a wrong action." Elizabeth often brought up Voltaire when frustrated with her father.

"Yes, I agree with you. It has a similar feeling to a scripture in James that speaks against seeing a need and not caring for it." It had been a while since Mary had branched out in her reading beyond scripture.

"What flowers did you leave for Papa this time, Lydie?" Jane had caught on to Lydia's small rebellion a long time ago.

"Geranium for folly and stupidity. I was looking for an orange lily, but none of them were in bloom. Either way, it works. What is even better is that he leaves me alone because he thinks I am not smart enough to recognize his abuse. After all, I give him flowers." With a clever laugh, she kept on working on the baby blanket she was making.

"How have the mornings with Kiernan gone? Did you bring him the paper so he could practice writing?" Mrs. Bennet had a soft spot for the little boy who wanted to protect her girls.

"Yes, it is progressing well. We have been talking about history as we walk, and I wrote out a few simple sentences for him to copy over. I also wanted to give him something a little more advanced. I remember reading a children's book when I was younger but it is a vague memory but something like that would work. What do you think?" Elizabeth did not want to overwhelm Kiernan, as it might make him want to give up.

Lydia recollected the book her older sisters read to her not too many years ago. "I think there is a book of nursery rhymes on the shelf of the schoolroom upstairs. Is that what you remember?"

"That is it, Lydie! You are brilliant!" Elizabeth got up right away and rushed off to go look for it.

"Who am I to disagree?" Lydia smirked as she left.

When Elizabeth returned, she realized that the subject had changed in her absence. Returning to her spot, she fiddled with the book in her hands. The discussion was about Mr. Darcy and the whispers about his poor showing at the assembly. Elizabeth felt a sense of relief when she heard her sisters defend him to their mother. She tried to maintain a stoic expression, not wanting to show too much sympathy for him, but no matter how hard she tried, she couldn't shake the potent feelings that this gentleman had stirred within her. She was reluctant to delve into the reality of the situation, and the thought of bringing it up to her family was daunting.

"That is unfortunate. I understand the burden of suffering from attacks of nerves. It is kind that you overlook his apparent slight." She knew that if Elizabeth didn't forgive his slight, she would be sure to have voiced her displeasure already. Noticing the book in Elizabeth's hand, she commented. "I think Kiernan will truly enjoy the book, and it should help him along the path of learning."

"Yes, Lizzie, I think it is a great idea," Mary said.

"When will you see him next?" Kitty was still working on the quilt she was making for her Aunt Gardiner. She would go to stay with the family in London this year, as it was her turn, and she wanted to come bearing gifts.

"He still insists on escorting me on my morning walks for my protection, so first thing tomorrow morning." Elizabeth was looking forward to seeing his face when she gave him the book.

***

WATCHING THE SUNRISE WAS one of Elizabeth's favorite pastimes. Before the day had truly begun, it was quiet, everything was aglow, and it held the promise of new possibilities. Somehow, this morning felt rife with potential. The autumn air was crisp, and the leaves were a glorious blaze of color. Elizabeth's lips curved into a grin when she spotted Kiernan skipping down the path. If he was this happy already, what would he do when he saw the book? Elizabeth hopped off the boulder that she sat on, brushed off her dress and went to greet him.

"Good morning, Miss Elizabeth!" Kiernan ran the last few feet with childish joy.

"Good morning, Kiernan. How are you enjoying this lovely new day?" Elizabeth started down their set path, smiling as she went.

"It is a right nice day, Miss Elizabeth. Everything smells fresh an' pure. The trees are sure pretty too." Turning his face up, he took in a deep breath of the clean air.

"Do you remember when you bet a book that the gentleman we met would do poorly at the assembly?" Elizabeth gathered her skirts to avoid a muddy section of the path.

"Yes, Miss Elizabeth." Kiernan did not seem to care that there was mud, as he went straight through it.

"Well, you were correct. The gentleman did not do well at the assembly. He was quite overwhelmed and not up to dancing. Actually, he insulted me and my sisters." Once clear of the mud, Elizabeth smoothed out the wrinkles in her skirts.

"That is a shame, Miss Elizabeth. I hope you're not very upset about it." He would hate to think that a dumbstruck stranger had hurt the girls.

"No, I am trying to be understanding. He seemed to struggle the entire night. I noticed his hands shaking, and he seemed overwhelmed." She moved to pick some flowers along the path, wondering what Lydia would think of them.

"I'm glad you're not hurt." Kiernan was glad she realized that there was more to the situation.

Elizabeth smiled at his concern. "No one had their feelings hurt, but we were all concerned for the man. Either way, I have brought you your winnings." Elizabeth brought out a brown paper-wrapped package.

"What?" Abruptly stopping, Kiernan looked up at Elizabeth in shock.

"Did you not bet a book, Mr. Kiernan?"

His reaction did not disappoint Elizabeth. "But that was just a joke, Miss Elizabeth. I did not mean fer you to get me a book. They are far too precious for the likes of me." Kiernan did not want her to think he wanted anything material out of their friendship.

"It is not so precious, a book. It is only a small one of children's tales. We used to read it when we were little, but none of us girls are of an age to read it anymore. I had hoped that you could use it to practice your reading, and eventually read it to your siblings. I have also brought some paper and a pencil for writing practice." Elizabeth held them out to Kiernan.

"Oh, Miss Elizabeth, Oh my! I promise to take such good care of it!" The awe on his face made it all worthwhile for Elizabeth.

"As long as you enjoy it, I will be happy!" They walked away in companionable silence before Elizabeth continued their previous conversation. "Last time we were talking about a ruler named Julius Caesar."

"He lived in Rome, right?" Kiernan enjoyed talking about history. Their conversation was quite captivating, and they continued for a while in such a manner, until Kiernan spotted someone on their path. "It is that gent. I think he is looking for something." Mr. Darcy was standing in the path, his steed following behind him placidly while he paced.

"It appears so. Let us see if we can help him." Elizabeth silently wished that this exchange would be more successful than their prior meetings.

"Are you looking for something, sir?" Kiernan took his brotherin' job seriously and moved slightly in front of Miss Elizabeth.

***

Darcy's eyes widened when he saw the two figures coming down the path. It was a little boy and one of the Bennet sisters he had accidentally insulted. The one with the smile from the other day. "I was on the lookout for one of the Miss Bennets, but I am only now realizing that no one has introduced us. Not to worry, I will handle this muddle which is entirely of my making." He took off his hat and played with the brim while he tried to decide what to do.

"Hello sir, I am Kiernan Anderson, and who may you be?" Kiernan had seen many introductions and figured it could not be so very hard.

"Thank you, good sir. I am Fitzwilliam Darcy of Pemberley in Derbyshire. It is a pleasure to meet you." Darcy was relieved that the pint-sized gentleman at the lady's side was a quick thinker. He wondered who the little boy might be. His clothing implied that they were from different stations, but they seemed quite close. He felt himself wanting to know more about both of them.

"Miss Elizabeth, may I present Mr. Fitzwilliam Darcy? Mr. Darcy, may I present Miss Elizabeth Bennet, of Longbourn of Hertfordshire." Having completed his task, Kiernan grinned widely and bounced on his toes.

"It's a pleasure to meet you, Mr. Darcy." Elizabeth gave a graceful curtsy. She was proud of the wonderful job Kiernan had done, both in the introduction and in helping Mr. Darcy find his way out of the hole he had dug for himself.

"The pleasure is all mine, Miss Elizabeth, truly. Ever since I saw you on the path, I wanted to know your name." With those words, Darcy wondered why he ever opened his mouth. Would he be able to have a civil conversation if he kept saying the wrong things? His hand made its way back up to his hair, fidgeting with a curl at his nape.

"Well, um, thank you." Elizabeth bit her lip. It would not do to laugh at his struggles.

"I must thank you, Kiernan, for helping me amend my oversight." Mr. Darcy turned from the exuberant boy to the delightful lady beside him. "Miss Elizabeth, I have come before you to apologize for my abysmal behavior at the assembly. No matter my distress, I never should have spoken in the manner I did." Darcy found it entirely impossible to look Miss Bennet in the eye.

"I wholeheartedly accept your apology, Mr. Darcy. It is not everyone that would put forth the effort to apologize in the manner that you have. I doubt most people would continue to go to assemblies if they struggled as mightily as you do." The sincerity of his actions was palpable, and it affected Elizabeth.

"So you noticed?" He whispered the words, almost inaudibly. Darcy knew his idiosyncrasies would eventually come to light. Her cheerful acceptance of his apology warmed his heart, yet the fear of rejection was ever-present.

Kiernan recognized the fear he felt in the man before him. "You don't need to worry, Mr. Darcy. I'll not think any less of you, nor will Miss Elizabeth. I say the wrong things sometimes an' my hands shake when I try to talk to people sometimes, but Miss Elizabeth still helps me with reading an' my sums. She's never made me feel less than any

of the other kids. She is not that kind of person. You're safe with her."
Maybe everyone had fears, even adults. Kiernan would have to think
about it later.

"Mr. Kiernan is quite right. I appreciate those who strive to
transcend the hardships they face. Is it the crowds that are difficult?"
Elizabeth had always felt the need to champion people who could
not do so for themselves. Maybe she could help protect him from
himself?

Darcy paused before responding. He would not normally reveal so
much to a veritable stranger, but something told him it might be safe
to do so. "Yes, it is the crowds and being outnumbered by people that
I do not know. It becomes a sea of faces that I cannot read and there
seems to be no safe island of friendship to shelter me." It was a novel
experience for him to confide in someone else. Maybe not being able
to keep his mouth shut would help him this once.

"Maybe knowing that someone in the crowd is friendly and not
judging you will help? Also, my mother has a tea that she likes when
she has what she calls 'attacks of her nerves'. She claims it is quite
soothing. I could get you some if you would like to try it." Elizabeth
thought she recognized the look on his face as hope.

"I will try almost anything. This is a malady that has haunted me
since I was a child." Could a new tea possibly help him?

It would not be so hard to gather a small amount for him to try. "I
will get some to you. What are you doing today?"

"I would be very grateful. I am on my way to town to mail a letter
to my sister back in London." Darcy tried to remember where it was
in town that he could post his mail.

"If you come back this way, I could have some tea ready for you to take back to Netherfield with you. Kiernan, do you think that your mother could do without you for a while longer? Maybe you could get a bite to eat while I gather the tea and then pass it on to Mr. Darcy?" Elizabeth pondered out loud.

"My Mam would be fine with it. An' your Mrs. Allen makes the best scones. I would love to have some." Kiernan's mouth watered at the thought. He was so enthralled with thoughts of breakfast that he completely missed when Mr. Darcy said goodbye and rode off towards Meryton.

Chapter Four

Kiernan swung his legs back and forth while sitting on top of the fence that bordered Longbourn land. It had been the very best morning. The air was crisp. The clouds in the sky were white, puffy, and happy. Best of all, he had a book of his very own, something that he had only dreamed of possessing. He saw Mr. Darcy coming and leapt down from his spot to greet him.

"Hello again, Mr. Darcy. Were you able to get your letter mailed alright?" Kiernan tried not to stare at Mr. Darcy's horse. He moved with a powerful grace, showing off his glossy and distinct coat. His mane and tail were a jet black, and his body was a deep mahogany brown, yet when the sun shone on him, his coat was almost as dark as coal. Its regal presence was captivating, and Kiernan felt like he'd stepped out of a fairy tale.

Mr. Darcy smiled at the boy as he dismounted. "Yes, I did, Mr. Kiernan." He found it was much easier to converse with children, and this boy had been a delight already. If he didn't miss his guess, the boy was quite fond of his horse. Kiernan's gaze seemed to be transfixed on his steed.

"I am glad. I would hate for your sister to miss her letter from you. Mine would be rightly upset." He could not stop staring at the horse with admiration. He kept hands firmly clasping the package he held to keep himself from reaching out to touch it. It would not do to go touching the horse without permission.

Darcy spotted the desire in the boy's eyes. "Thank you for helping me get the tea Miss Elizabeth spoke of. I have nothing to offer you in thanks at the moment, but maybe you would like to give my horse some sugar. He has a sweet tooth and would quite like a treat." Children who lacked fear of his horse always made Darcy smile. The stallion was over 16 hands tall and was a bit much for even some adults.

Kiernan reached for the sugar lump after handing Mr. Darcy the package of tea. "I would love to, Mr. Darcy, as long as you do not mind." He thought to himself that this was the very best of days indeed.

"Of course not. Cadmus is a friendly animal, for all that he is a stallion. When my little sister met him, she quickly realized how sweet his nature truly is. She said Cadmus was too stuffy a name for such a sweet animal, and she's taken to calling him Crumpet ever since." It was a very dear memory, and it brought a smile to his face.

Kiernan giggled but did not take his eyes away from the dark beauty in front of him. He let the horse eat the sugar lump and lick his flat palm. "What kind of horse is he, Mr. Darcy?" When Cadmus began snuffling around his face and blowing at his hair, he snickered.

Darcy was quite curious about the Bennet family and the town he had come to. It was possible that he had a ready source of information. "What if I answer your questions if you answer mine?"

"That would be fine." Kiernan only minimally paid attention to Mr. Darcy. Most of his attention was on the velvet perfection of the fine animal's nose in his hand. He felt the softness of the horse's muzzle as it lipped his skin, the sensation of its breath tickling his tender flesh.

"It is only fair that I answer first. He results from a shire horse and an Arabian. My head groomsman has been experimenting with cross breeding the two. His coloring is called Mahogany Bay. Now my question: how do you know the Miss Bennets?" Darcy's inner conflict was strong. His methods may border on bribery, yet the allure of curiosity was powerful. Those who were aware of his deficiency normally sought to exploit it or humiliate him. Even his own family joined in the words they spoke like ice, cold and cruel. Miss Elizabeth's beaming smile and sympathetic words had had a mesmerizing effect on him. She cared, and his curiosity about her consumed him.

"Well, my family has been tenants of Longbourn land near on two hundred years. Almost as long as the Bennets themselves. Four years ago, Miss Elizabeth and Miss Mary started classes to teach the local kids sums an' reading twice a week. I have been learning from them since the beginning, an' lately they have been giving me harder work. Miss Elizabeth has even started telling me about history and people like Julius Caesar." Kiernan smiled, happy to rub under the horse's chin. It surprised him when the horse pressed his head up against his chest without knocking him down. It was almost as if he was returning his affection. Kiernan was certain that the horse was more a Crumpet than a Cadmus; the horse was all sweetness.

"Few landowners support a local school like that. Mr. Bennet must be very generous." It astounded him that a young woman would give so much of her time to teaching children. Her opinion that Kiernan should explore Julius Caesar as part of his education revealed her wide-ranging knowledge.

Kiernan took a moment to look at Mr. Darcy and shake his head. He spoke up. "No, not Mr. Bennet, it is the ladies. Now it's my turn. How long have you known you have a problem with crowds?" Kiernan sometimes wondered if he would outgrow his own similar problem. Though it seemed Mr. Darcy had not gotten better with age.

"I think I was slightly younger than you when I first noticed it." Darcy grimaced, recalling and promptly banishing the memory of what had started his difficulties.

"I have had a few problems like yours, but my mam says everyone is different with different strengths and weaknesses. Miss Elizabeth has said that I can practice, an' she will help me. It's your turn, Mr. Darcy." He tried to reach the horse's mane, extending himself as far as possible to see if it was as luxurious as it seemed.

Darcy smiled, amused at Kiernan's love of his horse. "You said that Mr. Bennet was not generous. What kind of man is he?" His first thought was that a life of ease and harmony would inspire Miss Elizabeth to be compassionate and considerate.

"I guess I would have to say he was a bad one. Mr. Bennet refuses to pay for anything that the tenants need. The Bennet ladies normally take care of things with their pocket money. Miss Elizabeth had to save for a year to get the supplies for the school. It's supposed to be a secret, but Mrs. Allen, their cook, told me about that one. He is also very mean. I have heard how he talks to Mrs. Bennet an' his daughters. If I talked that way to my sister, my Pa would tan my hide. My Pa said the world is mean enough. You don't be mean to family an' never to girls." Kiernan's voice had dropped to nearly a whisper when he talked about how mean Mr. Bennet was. He felt guilty, but the whole town knew that Mr. Bennet was a bitter man and had been cruel for a long time. Kiernan's voice brightened as he asked, "So, how old is your sister?"

"How regrettable that Mr. Bennet acts in such a way." Darcy would consider this information later. "My sister is fifteen. She is supposed to join me with my cousin in a fortnight. I will be glad to see her. How old is your sister, Kiernan?" Darcy thought about Kiernan's sister as he recalled the soldiers he had seen in town, his worry growing. She could draw unwanted attention from the soldiers, depending on her age.

"I have three brothers and one sister. Kayleen is the youngest of us all, at nine. I told the Miss Bennets it was not fair that my sister has four brothers to protect her and they have none. So I told them I would stand in and take care of what brotherin I could. They are twenty-one, twenty, nineteen, seventeen, and fifteen. Where else would Crumpet like me to pet him?"

"Practically anywhere, though he might like his neck scratched. Kiernan, when I was in town, I noticed some militia men moving about. I wanted to warn you that though they might appear gentlemanly, they are not always what they seem." Kiernan was too young for any kind of further explanation. His sister was thankfully too young to be a concern, but the Bennet ladies might need a watchful eye.

Kiernan turned to face Mr. Darcy, looking him in the eye before speaking. "Thank you for letting me know. I will keep an eye out. I will also make sure Miss Elizabeth brings me on her walks an' such. The other ladies, too. Mr. Bennet refuses to allow a groom to accompany any of the ladies unless they have permission to take the carriage." Kiernan knew that most men would ruffle his hair and laugh him off when he said those kinds of things. The fact that Darcy recognized his desire to protect the ladies meant a lot to him.

"I had better return to Netherfield before I worry someone. I have truly enjoyed our talk, Master Kiernan. Maybe we shall have time to talk again soon." Darcy would need to think about how to proceed with the information he had collected.

"Miss Elizabeth put instructions on the bag for you, sir. I enjoyed talking to you and getting to meet Crumpet. Thank you for the warning. I will take it to heart." With that, he ran towards home to tell his Mam all about the great dark horse named Crumpet and his new book.

***

Darcy was less carefree on his ride back to Netherfield than young Kiernan. Though he had apologized, which had been his goal, it did not settle his mind. Hearing the kindness and understanding in Miss Elizabeth's words was making him pause and reevaluate how he saw things. As if she brought a candle into a dark room, everything looked different. Disregarded by teachers, classmates, and his own family, his life had been a dark place and now there was light. In the past, he avoided meeting new people because of the risk of them discovering his weakness and shunning him for it. But what if he was wrong? What if the things his family had taught him about himself and the world were wrong? The even greater question was: What would he do about it?

Quite distracted by his pondering, Darcy arrived back at Netherfield in what seemed like no time. He dismounted his horse and nodded at the approaching stable hand.

"I will brush Cadmus down and get him some breakfast, sir. Did you enjoy the ride?"

Darcy tried to remember the stable hand's name. "Yes, I did. Thank you, was it Jonah?"

"Yes, sir. Jonah Moore, sir. Just let me know if you need anything." Jonah rarely got an acknowledgment from any of the gentlemen whose horses he cared for. Mr. Darcy seemed to be a good man, if a little remote.

He made his way through the house and into the dining room. His heart sank when he realized how much time he had been away from Netherfield. There would be consequences when he returned. Darcy was already bracing himself for the unpleasant breakfast he would have with Caroline Bingley. The mere thought made his stomach turn sour.

***

"OH, MR. DARCY, IT is so good to see you this morning. I take it you slept tolerably well." Caroline had been lingering over her coffee for a while, hoping to happen upon him over breakfast so they could converse. She desired to show off her refined tastes and skills as a hostess.

"The bed was most comfortable, and I slept reasonably well." Darcy always struggled to interact with Miss Caroline Bingley. How was one to be polite without leaving room for an interpretation which might lead to unfounded hope? He may struggle with some things, but the decision to never marry Miss Bingley was never one of them. The smell of his breakfast filled the air as he worked through it as quickly as possible, attempting to block out the noise of her chattering. He was only moderately successful.

Chapter Five

Elizabeth tuned out the world and embraced the stillness of the moment. The birds were silenced, the breeze no longer plucked at her hem, and she brought her breath under her control. With her thumb at her ear, Elizabeth waited for a moment and then released the arrow to fly toward its destination. The thunk was barely audible from thirty yards away. She always got a rush of satisfaction when she heard the triumphant sound of success.

"No matter how hard I try, I can never hit the target as accurately as you." Kitty's melancholy and lack of confidence dwelt just under the surface of her words.

"You only just took up archery less than a year ago, Kitty. Though you do not see it, you are improving. Your grouping is well-clustered and you have fewer outliers when you shoot. Your form is excellent. Besides, hitting the bull's eye is just the icing on the cake. Archery is about being able to settle yourself and focus on a goal. I have found that archery helps my balance and awareness of the world around me, which helps me look graceful on the dance floor." Elizabeth strode across the field, the wind blowing against her skin as she went to collect her arrows.

Kitty trailed behind, fiddling with her bow. She bit her lip as she considered what Lizzie said. "Do you think I will learn those things from archery?" She gathered her arrows from their target.

Elizabeth and Jane were teaching their sisters various skills, so they would be prepared to navigate the world with confidence. She still spent time with Jane, but her growing relationships with all of her sisters made Elizabeth exceedingly happy. She knew how much Kitty struggled with confidence, and she hoped that learning archery would help her. "Yes, I think we can learn a lot of things from archery. You have already learned patience. You used to release the arrow before you had aimed effectively and would miss the target completely. Confidence will come when you recognize that you have improved and continue to do so. You will not only have confidence in archery, but in all areas of your life because you will know you can work toward a goal and succeed." Elizabeth collected the remaining five arrows and gestured for Kitty to go first.

Kitty took a few deep breaths, feeling the tension in her shoulders, then let her arrows fly one after another. One of them hit the bull's eye, but all the others were close. Kitty's joy was palpable as she let out a triumphant squeal, jumping up and down after taking the last shot.

"That was marvelous, Kitty. You are coming along well." Elizabeth let her first arrow fly after steadying herself. "I am working on things myself, you know. When Father is at his worst, I find it almost impossible to keep my emotions in check. I know that lashing out will not be to anyone's benefit, so I have to push the vexation inside me down. But if I do not let it go, I will explode. Instead, I come down here and remind myself that I am more than his opinion of me." A thud sounded in the field as she released her arrow, punctuating her point. "Father is not as superior as he would want us to believe." Thud. "Mother is neither foolish nor silly to care for our futures." Thud. "There are good people in the world and we can make things better." Thud. The arrows were all tightly grouped in the center of the target.

Kitty watched her sister's skill with admiration. "I never thought about doing anything like that. I will admit that I rarely know how to cope with my sensitivities. It feels like I am always afraid when he is there. I feel so powerless." Kitty rubbed her arms as she spoke, as if she had experienced a chill.

"I think you are forgetting about something, Kitty. For as smart as Father thinks he is, or as much power that he has over us, he is far below us in some things."

"What do you mean?" Kitty asked.

Elizabeth put her bow down and faced Kitty. She needed her sister to hear her. Gripping Kitty's hands, Elizabeth looked into her eyes, willing Kitty to see her sincerity. "Father has never been fond of physical activities. He has never even attempted archery. He would never have the patience to work at something as you are. More than that, you have more compassion for people and put more heart into the things you do. In everything that counts, you are a better person. It is not the money or property we have or the things we know that are important. It is how we love those around us."

"Oh, Lizzie." Kitty laid her head on Elizabeth's shoulder as she hugged her, tears wetting her cheeks. It had been a bad day yesterday, wrought with so many big emotions. Fear of her father weighed heavily on her, and she felt a constant need to shrink into the background. She never thought much of herself and always focused on her failures. To know that this was how Lizzie saw the situation they were in meant a lot. That this was how Lizzie saw her meant so much more.

Elizabeth gave Kitty one last squeeze before whispering to her, "You mean so much to me, dear girl. I just hope that someday you will see the great things in yourself that I see in you." Leaning back, she checked the time and grimaced. "I don't mean to end our time so soon, but it is Mamma's at-home today. We are already running late, but I would love to help you dress and fix your hair. It will mean that we can chat more." Elizabeth walked across the field to retrieve their arrows.

"You are right. We have little time to change."

***

DARCY LOOKED AROUND THE parlor he sat in. Had this been a week ago, he would have stood and looked out the window to better protect himself from having to interact with people he did not know. However, his recent revelations had changed him. He was noticing things he would not have before. On closer inspection, he saw that the furniture he observed was perfectly polished despite being worn and out-of-date. It was a restful room. The chairs were both visually appealing and comfortable. The paintings on the walls were not by famous artists, but the colors were all soothing and went well with the natural theme of the space.

He paused and scrutinized what he saw, forming an opinion of Mrs. Bennet. Though she couldn't afford the latest fashion, she kept the room tidy and gave it a cozy feel. She also cared a great deal for the comfort of her visitors. The knowledge that she did this while under the strain of her husband's apathy and antagonism strengthened his regard for her.

"How do you take your tea, Mr. Darcy?" Mrs. Bennet was presiding over the tea service. The Netherfield party had come to call, and she hoped it would go smoothly.

"Cream and sugar, Mrs. Bennet." Though he was readjusting the way he thought, Darcy was still fighting to get words to come out of his mouth on command.

Mrs. Bennet could recognize Mr. Darcy's struggles from where she sat across from him. His hand trembled, a faint but noticeable sign, and the tension in his jaw was unmistakable. The poor boy was attempting to be polite and take part in the conversation, but she could sense his discomfort. "How do you like Hertfordshire, Mr. Darcy? Do you find it much different from Derbyshire?" She gave him a supportive smile as she passed him his cup.

"It's both different and the same," Darcy began, but was cut off before she could finish.

"Oh, you are so droll, Mr. Darcy." Caroline's annoying titter abruptly halted Darcy's attempt at conversation. She was adamant that Mr. Darcy would not fall into the clutches of the insignificant family before her. If there was one thing that she had taken away from the dreadful school she had attended, it was how to school people in the art of humiliation.

Caroline went on. "How you could find anything in this village in the back of beyond comparable to Derbyshire, the location of your grand estate of Pemberley, is beyond me." Caroline forced a smile calculated to charm. How her brother had convinced Mr. Darcy to come and rusticate here and visit these nobodies, she would never know.

Mrs. Bennet watched her guest's behavior with a blank face. If her guest was going to act like a petulant child and insult people, she would treat her like one. "You were saying, Mr. Darcy?" Mrs. Bennet attempted to make Mr. Darcy feel welcome, despite Caroline's lack of etiquette. She peered over to make sure her daughters were content. She saw Jane was in an animated conversation with Mr. Bingley and Mary was working on getting Mrs. Louisa Hurst to converse. Mrs. Bennet felt a sense of ease knowing she could manage until Elizabeth's arrival.

Darcy had to look away from Caroline to avoid smirking at her stunned expression. She had obviously never dealt with anyone like Mrs. Bennet. The matron's ability to make him feel relaxed while ignoring Caroline left him in awe. "Yes, I was going to say that the hills of Derbyshire will always be home. However, I am fascinated with the agricultural possibilities of having flatter fields. Everything I have seen while on my rides has been quite picturesque. As for similarities that some cannot see, the town of Meryton is quite similar to Lambton, which is the town I frequent near my home.

I believe it results from communities having the same fundamental needs."

"My sister-in-law has often commented on the similarity of Meryton to Lambton," Mrs. Bennet disclosed.

Eyes lighting up with curiosity, Darcy sat up straight in his chair. "Is she from the area?" He never would have thought someone here would have a connection to his home.

Mrs. Bennet was happy to have hit on a topic that seemed to bring some cheer to Mr. Darcy's normally solemn face. "Her father was the rector there. She said that exploring the surrounding hills and dales on picnics was one of the best parts of her childhood." She was very fond of Mrs. Gardiner, nee Wallace. Matilda was a sweet girl who had married Fanny's brother for love. She gave Fanny hope that her daughters could find their own fortunate outcomes.

Mrs. Bennet heard approaching footsteps and observed her daughters as they came into the room. They both had pink cheeks from being outside on the cool fall day. Kitty, the daughter that she sometimes worried about, appeared to be benefiting from her time learning archery. Her smile did not seem as timid today. Elizabeth always seemed brighter after having spent time outside. Her eyes twinkled with laughter, and her tousled hair only added to her cheerful aura.

Fanny noticed Elizabeth pause, her smile widening slightly as she saw Mr. Darcy in the room. It appeared the quiet gentleman had her daughter enamored. How delightful.

"I am sorry to arrive late, Mama. We quite lost track of the time while practicing." Elizabeth took in the guests scattered around the room and moved to sit near her mother and Mr. Darcy. Kitty moved to sit near Mary. She was not out but would come out soon and had joined the at-homes as an observer.

"How was archery today, darling?" Fanny Bennet was always happy when her daughters could enjoy themselves.

"I always enjoy being outside, and Kitty is very much improving." Elizabeth looked at her sister, noting her blush.

Still trying to gain the upper hand, Caroline laughed derisively. "Oh, do not tell me you practice something as archaic as archery. Can you not spend your time on something more refined, such as painting or practicing an instrument?" Caroline stared at Darcy, her face full of contempt, as if to say 'Can you believe how provincial these people are?'.

Elizabeth often wished that she had Lydia's skill at lifting one eyebrow at a time. This would be the perfect moment to display such a skill. "Well, with five girls and only one piano, we take turns. Mary and Jane will practice today. As for painting, I have found no skill at it. I fully understand your skepticism about archery. My aunt's cousin suggested I take it up when I was fifteen. I hesitated myself, but she insisted and I noticed that as I worked at it, I truly enjoyed myself. I have passed the skill on to any of my sisters who care to learn." Elizabeth held her head high, her smile unwavering as she refused to back down. She had grown up listening to her father's cutting remarks. Caroline Bingley would have to become far more skilled at this if she wanted to ruffle her feathers.

"Well, since you have no chance of being accepted into high society, you may as well take part in a rustic activity; it's not like you have any prospects." Caroline's smirk faded as she saw her brother's thunderous look. It disappeared altogether when she saw Mr. Darcy's.

Elizabeth saw the expressions shift around her and intervened. "It is disappointing to learn of my lack of prospects. I had such hope." Elizabeth punctuated her point with a dramatic sigh. "I will just have to become your very closest friend and live vicariously through you. You simply must tell me about all of your prospects. As the daughter of a man of trade, just how many proposals have you received from the men of the Ton? I know this is not the time, but you will have to tell me all about them when we have a moment alone together." Elizabeth's eyes crinkled when she brought her napkin up to her lips to hide her smile when she saw the woman's expression. Nearby, Darcy burst out in an unfortunate coughing fit.

Jane could not hear what Caroline Bingley said to Lizzie, but she recognized that look on her sister's face. There was a need for a change of scenery. "Mama, what do you think of Lizzie and I showing our guests around the garden?"

"I think that would be lovely. The rain we have had recently has cleared up and the paths have dried out nicely." Mrs. Bennet smiled at her peacemaker daughter, who always sought to make everyone around her comfortable.

Darcy jumped at the opportunity to escape Caroline Bingley's oppressive presence. "Miss Elizabeth, it would be my pleasure to explore the garden with you."

He extended his arm to the woman he was eager to get to know better. Elizabeth's eyes drew him in. They were aglow with a captivating spark that had not faded since her verbal sparring match with Caroline.

Nodding her thanks at her mother, Elizabeth stood and moved to take his arm. The rush of sensation that flooded her when they first touched surprised her. A shiver ran down her spine when she took his arm, and she bit her lip to mask the feeling as they walked out of the room. "And it would please me to show it to you. We have put a lot of work into it." She hoped they would have a moment to talk without the antagonistic presence of Miss Bingley.

Bingley eyed his sister suspiciously. She looked ready to chase poor Darcy down. "Caroline, you look rather flushed. Stay inside. I would not want you to feel poorly." Bingley passed his sister with Jane on his arm. He knew Darcy needed some time away from her and was happy to help. Following Darcy and Miss Elizabeth out of the house, he wondered at how comfortable they seemed to be together.

"Mr. Darcy, I was happy to see you in the drawing room when I came down. Seeing you converse with my mother was reassuring. I fear I had the thought that you were one for staring gloomily out windows." Elizabeth peeked over at Darcy and became dismayed to notice his slight blush. It was not her intention to embarrass him.

"Well, in most cases, you would be correct. However, today several things are different." Darcy replied, his fingers twined in a lock of his hair.

"How so?" Elizabeth asked. She noticed Darcy was not looking her in the eye and was instead inspecting the garden. She accepted it was easier to talk about hard emotions without gazing at each other and, in addition, it was a wonderful patch of wilderness.

"Well, first off, I tried the tea you gave me. Not only does it have a pleasant taste, but my distress feels as if it has decreased in magnitude. And second, our recent conversation has stirred something in me to look at the world in a more positive light. It did not hurt that your mother is also very good at making me feel at ease." In a reflexive action, Darcy stretched out his arm to remove the low-hanging branch from Elizabeth's path.

She smiled up at Mr. Darcy in appreciation. "I will have to tell Jane that you enjoyed the tea, and it has given you a beneficial outcome. She stumbled across a book of recipes left in the still room by my great-grandmother, and has been carefully recreating them ever since. Jane makes up teas for the tenants' various ailments, along with the usual ointments and treatments found in still rooms. My mother, for example, has a nervous disposition, and the tea she drinks regularly helps to soothe her anxious thoughts." Elizabeth felt immense pride for her sister's tireless work in providing comfort to others.

Darcy glanced back and saw the woman they were discussing, her kind expression radiating as she spoke with Bingley. "It is a very noble undertaking to use her skills to succor those around her."

Elizabeth reached over to rub her fingers along some sage, enjoying how the scent permeated the area. "Yes, my sister Jane is a veritable angel. Most only see that she has a classic beauty and an outward appearance of serenity, but overlook her inner strength. More than the tea, I am curious about how you saw the world in a more positive light." She looked up at the tall man beside her.

Darcy hesitated, trying to decide what exactly to tell her. As he looked into her eyes, he knew she would not use it against him, but was he ready to let her into his past and make himself vulnerable? Deep down, he wanted to say yes, though he could not understand his own impulse. "Ever since I was a young child, my parents made me aware that I was a disappointment and that I would never gain genuine approval anywhere. I had a lifetime of fear and apprehension anytime I had to interact with people, but then you and Kiernan came along and gave me a more hopeful outlook. I'm trying to take a fresh approach and see things in a more positive light." Darcy looked to the ground, feeling exposed after such a speech.

Elizabeth wished she could not so easily imagine how a small boy would struggle under a parent's disapproval. "I am sorry that those closest to you did not seek to aid you as they should have. I know from experience that those who are supposed to shelter you can fail in that regard." Elizabeth gently squeezed his arm, her touch radiating warmth and comfort.

Darcy rubbed at the warm ache in his chest, and the feeling of his heart swelling from her sympathetic words. It was too much, too quickly. Eyes moist, he knew he had to change the subject. "Kiernan told me you and Mary teach the children of the area twice a week. I have myself thought of instituting such an endeavor at Pemberley, but have not known where to begin." Darcy shifted his weight, hoping she would not perceive his change of subject as impolite.

Elizabeth understood how difficult it was to discuss painful subjects, so she took the change of subject with grace. It intrigued her to think that Mr. Darcy might want to do something similar on his estate. "It took me a while to gather what I needed and coordinate things so that we had use of the parish church on Tuesday and Thursday mornings. I think it would have not taken so long had my father been willing to help. Would your family be willing to help you set something up?"

"I have neither impediment nor support from family. It is only myself and my much younger sister at Pemberley. Both of my parents passed on some time ago: my mother passed some ten years ago, and then my father passed shortly after I reached my majority. I think it was harder on my younger sister. She was only four when we lost our mother," Darcy explained.

"Taking control of your estate and a young sister must have been very difficult at such a young age." Elizabeth commiserated. Gifted with an amazing imagination, she could picture his suffering all too well.

Darcy was happy to have someone he could talk about these problems with. "The first few years were extremely hard. The daunting size of my newfound responsibilities seemed like an impossible burden to bear. To learn the intricacies took quite some time. Now that I have, I am struggling to bring about changes, like making sure the children get an education." He had a few people he could talk to, but none of them truly understood the matters of assisting his estate's families and children. His aunt and uncle had not taught his cousin Theodore estate management because they thought he would not need that information in the Regulars. Bingley, to whom he was almost as close, was from a family in trade and was himself asking for guidance on estate management.

Elizabeth had enjoyed learning how to help the seven tenant families on Longbourn land. Mr. Darcy, however, worked alone, and she guessed he might have a great deal more tenants. "I can only imagine how hard that was and continues to be." Elizabeth noticed Jane's gesture and nodded. They had run out of time for this lovely conversation. She turned onto the path that circled back home.

Darcy noticed they were heading back to the house and realized how long they had been outside talking. He realized that, for one of the first times that he could remember; he did not want his call on someone to end. "What time do you teach the children, Miss Elizabeth?" Darcy hoped she would not mind if he walked with her and her sister in the morning. He told himself that he still had quite a few questions to ask her. Yes, that was the only reason.

***

THE JOURNEY BACK TO Netherfield made Mr. Darcy promise himself that he would ride Cadmus to Longbourn next time. Perhaps then he could avoid Miss Bingley and her rudeness altogether. How she thought he would ever be interested in a screeching termagant was beyond him.

"The self-serving country chit! Who does she think she is, insulting me?" Caroline was so exceptionally upset, but confined in a carriage, she had no other option to channel her rage except to shout.

Whenever Bingley was in company, he felt the shame of his sister's behavior weighing on him. He was done waiting for her to take initiative and improve on her own. "Caroline, this pattern of misbehavior must stop. You cannot go into people's homes and insult them. If Miss Elizabeth was curt with you, she was only responding in kind. I am surprised Mrs. Bennet did not have you removed from her home. Your behavior today was not acceptable."

Caroline narrowed her eyes at her brother and inhaled deeply, readying to unleash her wrath. "Not acceptable? I went to a prestigious ladies' seminary in London. I would know better than you what is acceptable!" Caroline tried to regulate herself, but it was not working and now she felt her face flushing. She hated when that happened, for it clashed with her hair.

Bingley was tired of giving way to his sister's wrath to keep the peace. It was going to end. "Hornswoggle! I could not care less about the artificial manners you learned at that waste of money of a school. I will not tolerate such behavior from someone who lives under my roof." His parents and brother had been gone for a year now and he was gaining his bearings. They may have allowed his sister to put on airs, but this would not be how the rest of his life went. Charles would demonstrate to his sister that he wanted her to stop her cruelty.

"That girl was rude to me. How can you defend her?" Caroline had long gotten her way and was determined not to let anything change now.

Wilting under her sister's glare that demanded her support, Louisa spoke up. "You must agree, Charles, that it sounded discourteous." Louisa never felt comfortable being cruel like Caroline did, but she also did not want to be the target of her spite. She often would take her side just to protect herself. Louisa sent an apologetic look to

Charles, and he grimaced in response. He recognized the challenge of overcoming Caroline's tremendous force of will.

Caroline changed tactics. "Are you not angry that she treated me with disrespect, Mr. Darcy?" Her lips curved into a pout she had perfected as she glanced at the man she was pursuing.

Darcy's eyes narrowed in disgust at the sight of Caroline's rehearsed expression. Pointedly ignoring her, he looked out the window. How did her personality diverge so dramatically from that of her kindhearted brother? Maybe it was that school she always talked about? At least the carriage ride was going to be brief.

Chapter Six

Darcy allowed Cadmus to munch on the grass that ran along the path where he waited for the Bennet ladies to appear. He found his mind drifting back to last night, which had been a dramatic frenzy worthy of the stage. He witnessed broken vases, screaming, and recriminations. Darcy was deeply concerned for his friend as he watched Bingley struggle to keep his sister in check. An excited voice called out, pulling him from his thoughts.

"Mr. Darcy! How are you an' Crumpet this morning?" Kiernan was pleased to see his newest friend and favorite horse.

It surprised Darcy when he realized they had come upon him without notice. "Miss Elizabeth, Miss Mary, Master Kiernan. A good morning to you all. We are both doing well today, Kiernan." Darcy bowed to the group.

Elizabeth bit her lip. She did not want to discourage Mr. Darcy, but it was just too funny. "Crumpet, Mr. Darcy? I would have thought he would have been something more like Agamemnon or Zeus." She restrained her laughter with effort.

Darcy smiled at the expressions on Miss Mary's and Elizabeth's faces. "Well, I told Master Kiernan that my sister decided when she met my horse that he was too sweet and she renamed him Crumpet.

It is now a bit of a joke between us now that she is older. I do still use his other name, which is Cadmus."

Elizabeth remembered two likely references for the name. "So, did your noble steed get his original name from the fact that he excels, or are you fond of the tale of the Phoenician prince?"

Darcy halted in surprise at her query. "I found he excelled at everything which I asked of him and so I chose that name. Though, I will admit that he also has a princely air about him. I must profess that I have rarely come across anyone who knew the references of which you speak." The more he learned about Miss Elizabeth, the more he wanted to know.

"I am rather fond of Greek and Roman legends, and I have dabbled with learning Greek. I would have loved to learn more, but my father has refused tutors." As soon as she spoke, she started doubting herself. Should she have disclosed such information? Elizabeth continued along the path, wondering if gentlemen really disliked women who read. Doubting herself was something that she did not do often and she never appreciated having to muddle through the feeling.

Kiernan had been waiting for Mr. Darcy and Miss Elizabeth to end their conversation. He noticed his opportunity and quickly spoke up to ask his question. "Mr. Darcy, may I pet Crumpet today?" He had politely kept his hands behind this back lest he pet him before he had permission.

Darcy smiled at the boy but looked after Elizabeth as she hastened down the path. "I would be happy for you to pet Cadmus, or, if you wish, you could ride him into town."

"You don't think he would mind?" Kiernan had never even dreamed of riding such a wonderful horse.

"No, I am quite certain he would be happy to have you ride him." Darcy helped the boy put his foot in the stirrup after he shortened it and swing his other leg around. All the while, he kept glancing up the road at Elizabeth. Had he given her a dislike of him? Had he once again said the wrong thing?

Kiernan's smile knew no bounds. "I am so very tall!"

"Are you comfortable up there, or do you want to come down?" Darcy wanted to make sure Kiernan felt comfortable atop the very tall horse before he led the horse forward.

Kiernan felt as if he could conquer the world from this high up. "I am fine where I am, Mr. Darcy." He was not holding the reins but was proud.

Darcy tried to keep his attention on the overjoyed boy before him. "You have a very good seat, Kiernan. You will ride by yourself in no time." He clicked his tongue to get Cadmus to follow him. Darcy walked down the path, the smell of damp earth and pine surrounding him, desperately searching for a way to make it up to Elizabeth. But what was he trying to make up for?

Mary had watched all the previous interactions with curiosity. There was definitely something developing between her sister and Mr. Darcy, but it seemed as if neither was aware of it yet. She whispered a silent prayer that whatever it was would end up bringing them both joy. "Mr. Darcy, my sister said that you were interested in setting up classes for the children at your estate. How many families do you think might be interested?" Mary wondered how a gentleman who cared for his tenants might go about fulfilling the needs they would have.

He was happy to explain things to Miss Mary. "We currently have thirty-two tenant families with several vacancies on Pemberley land. I am trying to decide how to identify which children are interested in learning and which can be exempted from their family's responsibilities."

Mary responded to Mr. Darcy's question with some of her own. "Do you visit the families yourself, or perhaps your sister? How do you check in to make sure that they have all they need? We found it was easier to bring up the plan for lessons during one of those visits." Mary watched Lizzie walk slightly in front of them on the path. She was definitely ruminating on something.

The thought that he might go visit the tenant families himself was something Darcy had never contemplated. "I have little direct interaction with the families. My steward has all the direct contact. My sister is only fifteen. She does not have much contact with them either, at least that I know of. Is that something that the woman of the estate might do? I know my mother found any dealings with the tenants to be far below her."

Mary did not want to offend him, but found that he did not know this odd. It was possible that things worked differently in the upper echelons of society. If that was the case, Mary was happy to remain on the periphery. She enjoyed interacting with the tenants of Longbourn. "I can say nothing about the larger estates like yours, but here in Meryton, the ladies at the estates visit all the families regularly. They see if the homes are in repair and if they need food and clothing.

In small communities, they also check to see if they need remedies for various ailments."

This thought caused Darcy confusion. "Would not a competent steward see to all those things? I often talk with him about certain needs, such as when there is damage after a storm." Darcy was fairly confident that he was taking care of all those families at Pemberley. But what if he did not know the right questions to ask?

Elizabeth had not walked so far that she could not hear what Mr. Darcy was discussing with her sister. She found herself drawn back into the conversation. "What you are overlooking, Mr. Darcy, is that a someone else may not see what you see. A family maybe too proud to tell your steward they are struggling, but is he noticing the ragged clothes and wan faces which might tell a different story? Does he speak with the woman of the homes? A mother will get what her children need where a husband may not care or be too proud to do so. I know you are not married, but it is important to know that a woman may confide in another woman what she will not to a steward or the master of the house. She may speak to a woman about the difficult time she is having with her pregnancy or the baby that will not get well." Elizabeth was still questioning how Darcy may view her reading habits and felt less charitable than usual. She knew she was getting heated, but she had spent so much of her life in the company of someone who was indifferent to anyone's needs, she couldn't help but express her feelings.

The bottom seemed to drop out of Darcy's stomach. He had never thought about any of those scenarios. "That is not something I had ever considered. I hope no one is suffering from my lack of foresight." Darcy started thinking of ways he could amend the situation.

Darcy's quick reaction, paired with his regret that he had not been more knowledgeable, was palpable. It filled Elizabeth with a deep sense of guilt for assuming the worst of him. "You have been following the same customs as your parents, unchanged since their time. It is possible that someone was seeing to the things that your mother was not. A housekeeper, perhaps? Regardless, maybe you should contact your steward or housekeeper to see if those kinds of things are being taken care of."

Darcy was glad that Elizabeth was once again talking with him. It almost distracted him from discovering he might have problems back at Pemberley. "That is a good idea. Do you feel that at fifteen, my sister would be too young to help? And how do you organize such an endeavor?" Darcy felt that his problems were now multiplying.

Mary felt the need to speak up, as Elizabeth seemed to struggle with something. "Mama had us helping by twelve or thirteen. We try to see every family twice a month. We all go in pairs and everyone has their day to go out. You might find it best if your sister goes with a companion and a groomsman. We always bring something for the family, whether it is a treat for the children or something we know the family needs. I would imagine it would be different with as many families as you have, but in principle, it would be the same." Mary eyed Mr. Darcy and Elizabeth. They both seemed to be confused. She hoped that if there ever was any kind of attachment between herself and a gentleman, she wouldn't look so lost. She felt a warmth in her chest when she thought of Mr. Goulding, but she forced herself to push the feeling away.

Darcy recognized the opportunity before him and, inhaling deeply, posed the query that he had been considering. "My sister will visit soon. Would you mind if I introduce you? I fear she is much in want of female companionship and she could learn a lot from the women of your household." He was talking to both Elizabeth and Mary, but he was looking Elizabeth in the eye, wanting her to be willing despite whatever his blunder might have been.

Elizabeth's heart sank as she felt even more guilty. He thought highly enough of her to want to introduce her to his sister. She would have said yes even without looking at Darcy's expression, which was filled with hope. "I anticipate meeting her with delight and I am sure that we will enjoy one another's company." Elizabeth looked at Mary, and with a simple series of facial expressions, conveyed many things. It was a language between sisters that had existed for centuries.

Mary's smile widened as she looked at Elizabeth and then Darcy before turning away and hurrying further the path. Mary was more than happy to give them enough time to talk. She would be sure to remember this. It would be helpful to bring it up if she needed the favor returned.

Darcy had watched the two converse without words, marveling at how close they were. Mary was far enough ahead that he was not worried about her overhearing. Darcy hoped that Kiernan's focus would remain elsewhere and not on their conversation. "Miss Elizabeth, I know I often say the wrong things and offend sometimes without meaning to. I think I might have said something that upset you and I would like to apologize."

Elizabeth spoke without her normal joviality. "It is not your fault, Mr. Darcy. It is mine. You said that you had been contemplating new things and I am finding myself doing the same."

"I am relieved that I have done nothing to upset you. If you find need of it, I am here to help." The relief that Darcy felt was unwarranted for a relationship of such a short duration. However, it was extremely important to him that the woman that had brought light to his world was not upset with him.

"I have a question, but I'm not sure it is appropriate." Elizabeth knew propriety did not allow her to ask a gentleman his preferences, but just now she questioned the sense behind propriety.

Darcy found he did not like the doubt he saw in Miss Elizabeth's face. "Please ask your question. I am more than willing to help."

Elizabeth gazed off into the distance, putting off her statement as much as she was able. She could feel the warmth of the sun on her skin as she gathered her courage to speak. "How do you feel about well-read women who do not fit the mold encouraged by society?" She could not bear to glance at him. It seemed to be an eternity before he responded.

Darcy gave the question a lot of consideration, as it seemed to have great importance to her. "Well, I do not fit into the mold encouraged by society. Why would I want anyone else to?"

"My father often speaks of how I damage my sisters' prospects by reading as I do. And I so often hear that my thirst for knowledge is unattractive and unnatural. When I realized I had revealed my erudite tendencies, I worried you must have thought dreadfully about me. I have been trying to fight my inclination to assume the worst of people and situations. I have not been entirely successful."

Darcy disliked the idea of Miss Elizabeth being diminished by her father. "I understand the pain of having a parent disparage you. He is entirely wrong in his words and actions. I am struggling to deal with my mother's disappointment in me and she has been gone for many years. As for being a reader, I enjoy talking about what I read and the fact that you are female makes no difference to me. I know some men may find it off-putting, but I am sure that is only because they lack the intellectual fortitude to finish a book." He was pleased to see her smile peek out after the melancholy expression from earlier.

Elizabeth found it humorous that Mr. Darcy held such a view of unread gentlemen. "I know you often say the wrong thing, but just now you may have said the kindest thing I ever heard." Elizabeth liked the thought that he would value discussing books with her. More than that, that someone outside her immediate family felt her father was wrong appeased something inside of her.

"I know you will teach until closer to noon, but would you be willing to allow me to accompany you home? I find the thought of spending time with you and your sister most enjoyable." Darcy felt he could go over some things with Bingley about the running of his estate and have time to return. He aided Kiernan in getting off Cadmus when they reached the church.

Kiernan's voice rang out with gratitude and joy. "Mr. Darcy, thank you so much for letting me ride Crumpet." He attempted to get his legs to do what he wanted and eventually bowed.

"You are entirely welcome, Master Kiernan." Though Kiernan was delightful, Darcy felt his attention pulled toward Miss Elizabeth.

Elizabeth felt his eyes on her and quickly answered his question with a gentle tone. "I will plan on seeing you at noon, Mr. Darcy." With a curtsy and a smile, Elizabeth went into the building. It was probably a good thing that she did not know what her pert smile did to Mr. Darcy.

***

LOOKING AROUND THE TOWN, Darcy went into the booksellers. Bingley had no literature remotely useful in learning how to run an estate. Perhaps he could find a treatise on crop rotation or animal husbandry. Paying for his choices, he started walking out the door and froze. There, down the road, flirting shamelessly, was the fair-haired lothario who had caused so much pain wherever he went.

Bitter memories of the corrupt man quickly overpowered Darcy. When they were boys, he was always charming and endearing while Darcy had been mute and awkward. Darcy's parents used Wickham's poise to try to improve him, though their belittling tirades never seemed to help him socialize. Later, when they were both sent to school, Wickham became a bully and a cheat who had learned how to manipulate the adults. By Cambridge, he had fine-tuned his manipulation to get his way with women. He left a trail of broken hearts and debts wherever he went. The number of base born children being supported on the Pemberley estate was disturbing.

Most recently, Georgiana narrowly escaped becoming his latest victim. He had received a letter from dear Georgiana imploring him to come visit her sooner than they had originally discussed. She implored him to hurry, as Mrs. Younge's odd behavior caused her to doubt that she had her best interest at heart. Hastening to his beloved sister, he overheard Mrs. Younge telling Georgiana she did not need to keep her maid in the room when "dear Mr. Wickham" showed up. The ensuing chaos was an overwhelming and tiresome experience.

Coming out of his memories, Darcy stepped back into the shadow of the doorway to watch Wickham flirt. It dawned on him that his sister would be arriving soon. He would have to do something both to protect his sister and the people of this town. If he did not, there would be debts and dishonored daughters by the new year. It looked like he had joined the militia, judging by his red coat.

Darcy had a conversation with a few of the shopkeepers. Bingley could wait until later. He had people to protect. Over two hours later, Darcy had bulging saddlebags but had spoken with most of the proprietors in the town. Store owners seemed more willing to listen after you bought things with hard coin. He had let them know that he had had problems with a militiaman in the town near his home in the past, specifically regarding debts and the daughters of the town. It comforted him he had alerted the shopkeepers, but he still had one more thing he had to accomplish. Approaching those he sought, he smiled and gave a bow.

"Ladies, Master Kiernan. I was wondering if I might ask you ladies to wait a few moments before we head back to Longbourn. I have a task that I hope Kiernan might help me with." Darcy hoped they were not under a time constraint.

Mary spoke up when she saw Elizabeth looking at her questioningly. "Oh, that would be fine. We can stop by the haberdashers until you are ready to go. I have heard that there are new ribbons." Mary was curious, but felt there was no rush.

Kiernan was grateful to be moving about after sitting so long to learn. He was more than happy to help the kind man who had let him ride Crumpet. "What do you need help with, Mr. Darcy?"

"There is someone I would like to show you. We will have to be quiet. I do not want to be noticed." They walked down the street towards where a group of men in red coats stood outside the pub laughing. "Do you see the one at the end? He is blond with blue eyes and has his hand on his saber?" Kiernan remembered Darcy had spoken of being careful around the soldiers but still wondered what this was about. "Yes, he has shifty eyes looking at everybody. What about him?"

"That man's name is George Wickham, and he is not to be trusted. He lies, cheats, and does not pay his debts, but worse, he is not good to women. I hoped you could let me know if he tries anything with any of the girls from town." Darcy had already warned quite a few people, but he liked the idea of Kiernan being there to warn the Bennet ladies if it became necessary.

"You can trust me, Mr. Darcy. Is it all right If I tell my brothers?" Kiernan felt certain they would help. They all took Mam's words to heart about protecting girls.

Smiling down into the earnest face, Darcy reassured him. "That should be fine, Kiernan. I am trying to figure out how to make sure he stops hurting people, but it may take a while." He was working on a plan. Hopefully it would work out.

"Let's go back to the girls and make sure they get home safe." Kiernan wanted to hurry back. Who knew if any of the other soldiers were bad men?

Chapter Seven

Elizabeth stood near the entrance of the Lucases' home. She knew the Netherfield party would come at some point and wanted to be there to ease the way for Mr. Darcy. They had discussed the upcoming gathering at the Lucas home on the walk back to Longbourn a few days ago. Elizabeth knew though he was trying to alter how he handled crowds and strangers, he was still not anticipating the event with pleasure.

Charlotte Lucas had never seen Elizabeth so discomposed. "You are not paying attention, Eliza. What has you so distracted?"

"I am sorry for my inattention, Charlotte. I know the Netherfield party should arrive, and I am worried about Mr. Darcy. He is not at all good with crowds of strangers." Elizabeth spoke to Charlotte, but her eyes kept drifting off to the entrance.

Watching Elizabeth's eye line shift, Charlotte wanted to probe the subject further. Why would she be interested in the insulting gentleman from before? "Is the redoubtable Eliza developing a tendre for someone?"

Elizabeth knew that admitting such a thing was out of the question. She valiantly fought against the sensations of her skin flushing. "Absolutely not. I may develop a friendship, but nothing more." Elizabeth had too many things to do and too many people to look after to get distracted by a gentleman.

Charlotte's jaw clenched as she tried to keep her frustration out of her voice. "You would do well to set your cap for him. There are rarely any eligible gentlemen in the area and you will not be getting a season in London." Charlotte found it irritating when her friend didn't appreciate the gravity of her situation. Charlotte had no desire to be a drain on her family's resources and was even now desperate to find a situation, any situation.

"They hound the poor man enough. Do not you start as well." On the surface, Elizabeth understood why people talked of visitors' eligibility, but it ignored the people that they were where it counted.

A commotion by the doorway alerted her to the arrival of the Netherfield party. Mr. Bingley was in the lead, gregarious as always, his smile bright and kind. His sister Caroline followed him through the crowd. She wore an ostentatious peacock headdress, and a sneer of disdain. The Hursts were next, and both looked bored. Elizabeth noticed Mr. Hurst seemed to perk up when he saw the punch bowl across the room. Then Mr. Darcy entered, his clothing fine but his face a stoic mask. With a polite smile, Elizabeth left Charlotte and headed in Darcy's direction.

Elizabeth waited to get closer to Mr. Darcy before speaking up. "This simply will not do, Mr. Darcy. You will meet no one standing over here." She noticed his eyes were scanning the crowd and, though he was standing by a wall, he did not appear to be shaking.

"Miss Elizabeth, I did not see you." Darcy felt himself relax the smallest bit when he recognized her. He became assured that hostile strangers did not surround him. He reminded himself that he had friends in this sea of faces.

"Yes, I gathered that. How are you faring, Mr. Darcy?" Elizabeth eyed him, trying to analyze how he fared.

Darcy looked up at a laugh across the room. He did not recognize the group and had to fight the feeling that they were laughing at him. "I am well enough. Better than last time, certainly. I drank some of the tea you suggested before we left, and I cannot tell if I am feeling better because of that or because I know that there are people I know and trust here."

"Well, let me point out the people you know so you feel more at ease. Over towards the piano is my sister Mary, who is talking with Maria Lucas. I think we will have some music before long. My mother and Jane are talking to Bingley close to us. Mrs. Hurst and Caroline Bingley have taken up a position on the wall. Mr. Hurst has found the punch bowl and I think he is now looking for the card room." Elizabeth began looking around to see if there was someone that might not be intimidating to introduce him to.

He let out a soft chuckle, unsurprised by what he saw. Darcy knew that to escape the pain of his marriage and his sister-in-law's caustic remarks, Mr. Hurst often sought refuge in various vices. His marriage to Louisa had not been a love match, but they had been doing well before Louisa's parents died and they inherited Caroline. "Yes, it would not surprise me to hear that Mr. Hurst found the punch bowl or the card room." Darcy spoke with a hint of concern for the man.

"Would you mind being introduced to Sir William Lucas? He is quite harmless and will most likely spend all of your introduction talking about being knighted." Elizabeth hoped that if she introduced him to a few benign individuals, he would eventually enjoy his time in Meryton.

"I think that is something I could do. It is heartening to have a basic understanding of the person before engaging in conversation." Somehow, he felt himself relaxing. Darcy felt as if this evening could very well be not entirely horrible.

As the evening progressed, he noticed himself enjoying it. He found that Sir Lucas was a jovial man who, though not a deep thinker, was kind. Mr. Goulding was an older gentleman who proudly talked of his son, who had just returned to Oxford. He also met Charlotte Lucas, a close friend of the Bennet women. She seemed sensible and attentive to the needs of those at the party. He might not have developed a talkative demeanor in one evening, but he found himself able to interact without losing his breath or having his hands shake. On the carriage ride back to Netherfield, he contemplated how grateful he was to all the Bennet ladies for their support and kindness.

***

AFTER SEVERAL DAYS OF showers had confined the Bennet ladies indoors, the sun finally came out and dried up the puddles. Jane and Elizabeth had decided to treat their sisters to tea and confections at the tea shop in Meryton. They had been very diligent in their various projects while confined by the rain, and a satisfying stroll would do them all good. Kitty and Lydia walked arm in arm, leading the way while stepping carefully to avoid the puddles. Jane, Mary, and Elizabeth chatted softly about the gathering which had happened the night before the rain had descended.

Jane glanced over at Mary, proud that she was wearing brighter colors than usual lately. "You did a lovely job playing that new piece of music. I think everyone quite appreciated it, Mary." Jane was also proud of how far her sister's musical abilities had progressed. Since she had spent those months in London with their Gardiner relatives and had the music master, she had advanced as a pianist.

Mary's face lit up at the compliment, pleased to be acknowledged for her improved ability. "Thank you. I have been working on the things that Master Giovanni told me to focus on, the pauses as much as the notes, and I can tell the difference. I am looking forward to working with him again in the new year."

Once the girls had reached a certain age, Mrs. Bennet determined they would need to take lessons from masters and had devised a plan to make it happen. She had expressed her irritation with her sister-in-law's repeated appeals for her daughters to lend her a hand. Knowing how much it would hurt his wife, Mr. Bennet felt content to have them leave. So every year, two of the girls spent two months with their Gardiner relations. It gave them the opportunity to take lessons and see some of the wider world. It excited Mary that Kitty would join her this year, as they had arranged for a painting master to teach her.

After a brief interlude of silence, Elizabeth posed a question to her sisters. "How did you think Mr. Darcy handled the gathering?" She was proud of his progress, though she knew she might be too close to the situation to be completely objective.

Mary felt for the man who struggled with his interactions with people. "He seemed to hide behind a mask of indifference at first, but it slipped the longer he interacted with someone. I see improvement."

Jane was always one to look for the positive. "He did not offend anyone by misspeaking and he spoke more than he did before."

Elizabeth scanned the area as she spoke, looking for her younger sisters. "I think that though he still has more ground to cover, he has already come a long way." She realized they had fallen quite behind and she could not see the girls at all, so she quickly picked up her pace.

***

Lieutenant George Wickham looked down at his current marks and smiled in his most trustworthy manner. The girls' simple dresses spoke of their not being out in society, but that had never stopped him before. It was a pity that the cut of their gowns was so high, otherwise he would get a pleasing eyeful. Turning back to his fellow officer, he smirked. He loved how easy this always was. "I would have joined the militia sooner if I had known that you two lovely ladies would be here to welcome me." Wickham chose a pose that seemed casual and yet showed off his new red coat to its best advantage. "I am sure that knowing you will be the only payment I will need to endure any suffering I experience as a soldier."

Across from him, Kitty and Lydia looked at one another, startled at his forward behavior. Though he was flattering, it was also somehow unsettling.

Social rules dictated they should not talk to a gentleman to whom no one had introduced them. But they could not simply walk on because he was also blocking their way. Hopefully their sisters would catch up to them soon.

Slightly out of breath from rushing to her sisters, Elizabeth spoke up with determination. "I am so sorry we fell behind, sisters. Now that we are here, we can continue to our destination." She watched as Mary looped her arm through Kitty's and Jane did the same with Lydia. Elizabeth took up a defensive position, her body blocking her sisters from the soldiers' view. When the gentlemen did not move back, Elizabeth looked the leader in the eye. "Excuse me, gentlemen, we have somewhere to be. I am sure you have somewhere to be as well." The soldiers all moved aside, the leader bowing low, and the Bennets continued on their way. They all walked silently until they reached the tea room and had gotten settled in their seats.

Kitty was wondering if all the soldiers would be so ill-mannered. "I was unsure what to do with him blocking the path, but I knew you would catch up with us shortly."

Elizabeth was trying to maintain her dignity in a public place, but it was a struggle. "Well, really, the nerve! Blocking the path and trying to talk with girls who are obviously not out yet."

Jane was trying to figure out how someone might behave so poorly to young girls not yet out in society. She gazed at Lydia, but the younger girl appeared to be bouncing back. "Maybe they did not learn proper behavior growing up? Maybe being a soldier will help the leader learn proper behavior?"

Elizabeth chewed at her lip pensively. "I feel that lead soldier was completely out of line, but last time I felt this way, I was sorely mistaken. I dislike questioning my instincts so. What do you all think?"

Mary, though not as lively as either Elizabeth or Lydia, felt a deep-seated need to protect. "They were certainly trying to ingratiate themselves with Kitty and Lydie. By blocking the path, they put the girls in an uncomfortable situation, which is not gentlemanly behavior." Her voice was firm as she spoke to her sisters.

After smoothing her skirts and squaring her shoulders, Lydia declared. "I no longer want to think of those uncouth soldiers. My lemon tart and tea are calling my name. I was looking forward to this and I will not let some stupid boys prevent me from doing so." With that, Lydia stirred the sugar in her tea and swirled it around. A moment later, she took a sip and sighed with contentment.

"I think you may very well be the smartest of us all, Lydie." Elizabeth took her own sip of tea and endeavored to think of more pleasant things.

***

ACROSS THE STREET FROM the tearoom, Wickham stood in
contemplation of the situation. He had brushed off his fellow officers
and stated that his failure was part of his plan, but the situation was
perturbing. Those girls should have at least giggled, even if they did
not speak to him. They were young and naïve. They should have been
puppets to be manipulated by his greater expertise.

More than the girls not bending to his will, the older sister was
also a conundrum. She spoke to him with an unflinching confidence,
without a single blush. Her eyes narrowed in a menacing glare, acting
as if she could see right through him. Her voice had a cutting edge
that spoke volumes. That never happened. He always caught women
unawares until he left them to pick up the pieces. Yet somehow
the emerald-eyed Valkyrie had glared, her eyes sparking fire and
contempt.

Wickham considered that he might have been resting on his laurels.
It was too easy to take advantage of innocent maidens. Maybe he
should move on to the Valkyries of the world. It certainly would
be more satisfying to bring down someone with more spirit. To be
successful, he would need to do some research and lay groundwork.
He was going to be busy.

***

MRS. BENNET RODE IN the carriage on the way to her sister's card party, fighting a certain amount of trepidation. Her sister had always taken strongly after her mother and liked to throw parties with as many people as possible. Constance Philips tried to show that she was better at throwing parties than her younger sister, Mrs. Bennet. She never understood why Fanny did not throw lavish parties as the mistress of one of the largest estates in the area. Fanny Bennet often wondered why she went to her sister's gatherings and in the end, she decided she did not want to create more drama by refusing to go. There was already so much discord in her family; why give rise to more when she could avoid it?

She surveyed the carriage and wished her girls didn't have to attend the card party. She had reason to believe that her sister would invite the officers. After what the girls had told her of their experience in town, she did not want to expose Kitty and Lydia to their presence again. But at least with Lydia and Catherine coming with them, they could all return home early and would not have to linger.

***

ELIZABETH SIGHED AS SHE looked around the room. Though she would normally enjoy such a gay evening, she was hesitant to let herself go. The experience with the soldiers in town had made her wary of all of their smiles and compliments. There were so many red coats in the room that she felt there was nowhere she could relax. If this was anything like what Mr. Darcy felt, she needed to apologize for underestimating the feeling. Across the room, she noted that the plan to stay in pairs seemed to work. Jane stood with Lydia and Maria Lucas talking softly, and Mrs. Bennet was talking with Kitty and Mrs. Long and her niece.

Mrs. Philips bustled up to her niece, sitting by herself in a corner. "There you are, Lizzie dear. I wanted to introduce you to one of the newer officers in Meryton, Lt. George Wickham. Lieutenant Wickham, my niece Elizabeth Bennet. She may not be as pretty as her sister Jane, but she is quite the conversationalist." Mrs. Philips, having performed her introductions and her slight, felt free to leave the two together and be on her way to stir up more fun elsewhere.

Mr. Wickham executed a perfected bow before beginning his siege. "Miss Elizabeth, it is truly an honor to meet you at this splendid gathering. It seems your aunt is a remarkable hostess." Wickham looked at the lady before him, the one that he had spent so much time trying to find out about. Everyone, privileged and pauper alike, respected her. It had not taken long to find out that she would be at her aunt's gathering this evening, so he got himself invited. He would start on his plan this evening and hopefully soon there would be delectable results.

"Lieutenant Wickham, I am sure that my aunt will be happy to hear that you admire her abilities." Elizabeth caught sight of Mary coming back with her lemonade. With Mary beside her, she felt confident she would not confront Wickham on his blatant lies in an unladylike manner.

Mary handed her the glass while evaluating the situation. "There seemed to be more than a few people waiting to get lemonade. I am sorry it took so long."

Wickham directed his cerulean gaze at Mary and increased his flirty behavior for the plainer sister. "I was keeping your sister company. I would hate for any lady here to feel neglected." Compliments and attention seemed to go farther with girls who got less attention regularly. He had no intention of settling for the younger sister, but it could not hurt his chances with the older sister if he was nice to the other.

"Oh, is that so?" Mary replied.

Not being able to ignore him, Elizabeth was determined to understand who he was. She sensed the possibility of deception in her immediate future. "Mary, this is Lieutenant Wickham. From what I understand, he is new to the militia. Lieutenant Wickham, what has brought you here to Hertfordshire?"

"With my sense of duty to society, I knew I had to make a difference. So when the church was unavailable, I sought to keep my home country safe from any dangers." Wickham's eyes glinted with satisfaction at their obvious interest.

Not liking the look in his eyes, Elizabeth continued. "Did you not feel the need to join the regulars? With the war on the content and the battle against the tyrant, there would surely be a noble effort." Elizabeth felt sure that this would not have suited the well-groomed man before her.

"Yes, it was something I thought of, but found that I could not be so far away from my home soil." What ladies spoke of the war? Wickham did not understand why it was so hard to direct the women from this family.

Mary doubted Mr. Wickham's motives, but it would not do to roll her eyes at him. "Are you able to earn your way in the militia? I have heard that the pay is much less than that of an officer in the regulars." Maybe if he felt he was not being held in the best light, he would leave.

"Had things gone the way they should have, I would have a much better situation now. But being as ill-used as I have been, I must work to support myself." Being careful to look woebegone and yet brave, he waited for the questions to begin.

"How are you finding Hertfordshire, Lieutenant Wickham?" Elizabeth looked at Mary out of the corner of her eye. This might be fun.

Startled by the lack of attention to his prompt, Wickham persisted. "I am finding it differs from Derbyshire, where I grew up. Though being honest, being here away from my troubling memories will probably be good for me." Looking into the distance, he continued to display an almost despairing attitude. Were these girls simple minded? Did they not get his obvious hints?

"How do you find the landscape to be different?" Mary continued with their game.

These girls were impossible. He fought to keep up his downtrodden facade, attempting to hide his annoyance at their feather brains. "The landscape? I suppose there are more hills back in

Derbyshire, where someone who was once my friend dashed all my hopes."

Elizabeth noticed that his veneer was slipping. "Mr. Wickham, how were your hopes dashed?" She figured if she did not ask what he wanted her to, he would become apoplectic.

"My father raised me on an estate in Derbyshire called Pemberley. He was the steward and close friend of the estate owner. As Mr. Darcy's godson, I received many benefits. He encouraged me and helped with my education by sponsoring my going to both Eton and Cambridge. My memories of our time spent together and the conversations we had are some of the brightest recollections I own. The only dark note among so many bright ones was the animosity of his only living son. The son was a haughty and prideful boy who was above talking in company. As we both grew up, I grew closer to his father, and he resented me for how much his father loved me. Sadly, shortly after I finished Cambridge, Mr. Darcy Senior died, and I lost a remarkable mentor. The son used this opportunity to seek his petty revenge. My mentor had left me a valuable living as the rector in Kempton. I would have enjoyed such a peaceful and meaningful life. But it was not to be. He went against his father's wishes and refused me the living and left me to shift for myself. I can only be grateful his poor father was not alive to see such villainy." This having concluded his tale, Wickham looked to the lights near him, trying to get his eyes to water. He had never learned how to cry on demand, but this method worked well enough to garner the sympathetic response he was after.

"Such a tale of woe, Lieutenant Wickham. I can scarcely credit it," Mary spoke, determined not to roll her eyes at his fabrication.

Elizabeth spoke with an enthusiasm she did not feel. "How anyone could go against their parent's desire in such a way is beyond me. Was it not in the will that they granted you the living? You must surely have recompense even if they granted the living to another." It would not do to have him know she was onto his game yet.

Wickham fought to keep a smirk off his face. The sympathy would lead to caring and from there, they would be in the palm of his hand. "You are too kind to think of me so. Alas, they worded the will in such a way that Mr. Darcy could avoid following through as he should have. Had he had any desire to honor his father as he should, it would have been mine."

Mary countered his preposterous comment with a comment of her own. "Lieutenant Wickham, I know I am only a simple uneducated female, but something is confusing me. Once you became ordained, you could go to any rectory, and perhaps you should investigate other areas to see if you can find one elsewhere. I understand the need for security and familiarity, but you should not ignore such an important mission." She spoke with an earnest conviction, belying her thought that the weasel before her would soon be stuck in his own trap.

"Well, that is to say, um..." Wickham found himself stuttering like Darcy when he was a schoolboy. What had just happened? How did two county nobodies poke so many holes in his well-rehearsed story? He cleared his throat as he tried to decide what to say.

Elizabeth hoped he would simply leave their presence without a confrontation. "Oh, dear Lieutenant Wickham, you sound parched. Go get yourself some lemonade. Do not let us keep you."

"I would never suspend your pleasure in our conversation by withdrawing from two such gracious ladies." Wickham remained flummoxed.

"Do not worry your compassionate heart, Lieutenant, we will not pine for you in your absence. I am confident your tale of misuse will keep well enough. Go seek some lemonade for yourself. My sister and I are quite content to see you go."

Mary was relieved when he finally turned to go.

As Wickham walked to the refreshment table to get himself a drink, he tried to sort out what had just happened. That two country maidens managed him with ease was flabbergasting. Ladies were never happy to see him go. They longed for his presence and begged him to return as quickly as possible. If only his creditors had not been so relentless, he would not have had to flee London. He had joined the militia to blend in with the crowd and gain the respect of the community. Maybe he should try for someone who would prove to be more susceptible to his many charms. There had been something intrinsically wrong with those girls, and that was why things did not work out. That had to be it. The information he had gathered on Miss Elizabeth implied an insignificant dowry. So she was not a long-term plan, anyway. He surveyed the area, musing over how to uncover any knowledge about an heiress in the area.

***

MARY'S EYES SHONE WITH laughter. She could not help but express her thoughts to her sister. "At least the weasel has left our vicinity and we no longer have to deal with his blathering." She tittered behind her fan.

Elizabeth, startled at her pronouncement, burst into peals of laughter that were not at all appropriate for the current setting. "Mary, you endeavor to get me into trouble. Weasel, really? Even now Mama is looking this way." Elizabeth tried to center herself and move past the nervous energy that filled her veins. She did not know the Lieutenant's goal, but it was not good. More than that, he obviously had something against Mr. Darcy. It would take her some time to sort through what he said and implied. She would have to seek Mr. Darcy to warn him. Maybe they could pay a return call to Netherfield tomorrow?

Chapter Eight

Darcy would have to advise Bingley to invest in better chairs
for his study, or at least some cushions. The room wasn't all that bad
on the whole, only mostly bare and missing the books and maps that
Darcy was fond of in his own study. He looked to where Bingley sat at
the desk, trying to muddle through the reports on the harvest yields.
He felt his heart go out to him. It had not been so long ago that he
had inherited with no notice and little preparation. The feeling of
an overwhelming weight pressing upon him that never seemed to let
up. The weight of all those lives in the balance of his decisions. It had
taken a while to get his bearings.

"Bingley, how does it look?" Darcy knew what he thought of the
paperwork but was curious to see what Bingley noticed.

Bingley frowned at the papers spread across his desk. "If I am
interpreting this correctly, the yield from the crops has decreased
since last year. Further, it looks like this has been a diminishing trend
for the last three years. Only I cannot see a reason?" Bingley leaned
back into his leather chair. He was glad that Darcy had come along
to explain things.

Darcy shifted in his seat uncomfortably as he tried to explain some
minutiae of estate management. "There may be a reason I do not

see, but I know that a property that is up for lease often loses the oversight that it needs to stay gainful. Unless, of course, there is a very good steward in charge of things. Tenants left on their own are less productive if they have no one to apply to about a broken plow or flooded field." It was fascinating how much of the estate work was information that either had to be passed down or muddled through. Trying out a chair in the corner, he found the padding lumpy and arms too high for comfort. He would definitely need better chairs or to invent a game of finding one that worked.

"If that is the case, why lease out what could be a very profitable estate?" Bingley's mind was still used to seeing the world through the eyes of a businessman. It was sort of nostalgic looking over papers at a desk. He almost heard his father's voice questioning the efficacy of something. The wood paneling was even remarkably similar to that which had been in his father's study.

"Not everyone has the same situation. Maybe a widow is holding the property for her son but hasn't the wherewithal to have an effective steward and does the best she can. Or it is a fourth or fifth estate and the owner has become overwhelmed. There are many reasons." Darcy himself had two satellite estates where a steward oversaw the daily issues but that he visited every year. They both had better chairs than this room, Darcy complained silently to himself. The last chair he tried was uneven somehow, and he kept having to shift to keep from tipping out of it.

Bingley tapped on the ledger with his fingers distractedly. "I must admit that I had not expected the amount of oversight needed at this small estate. What I do not understand is how all the men at White's never seem to worry about anything like this." He had half thought owning an estate was all garden parties and big houses.

"That is where a good steward can come in. If you have someone reliable, you do not have to worry overmuch. However, you risk them swindling you and running your estate into the ground if you do not at least check in regularly. I hesitate to spend too much time away from those who I am responsible to oversee." Darcy tried to be mindful of his friend's autonomy, but he felt the urge to warn him away from activities that would bring dissipation. That and these chairs were distracting.

Bingley may enjoy having a good time, but he was finding the need to have meaning in his life. "I can see how that holds true. A businessman needs to make sure his managers are honest or he can go bankrupt." He was also enjoying Darcy trying to find a comfortable chair. His facial expressions were hilarious.

"How are you enjoying the endeavor on the whole? Do you feel it suits you? Also, why are all the chairs so absolutely horrible?" Darcy wondered if his happy-go-lucky friend would take to the hard work necessary for estate management. He also wondered who designed these chairs.

Bingley could not respond to his friend's query because of his hysterical laughter. After a few moments, he managed a gasping stop. "My father once told me that a gentleman needed to have uncomfortable chairs in his study so that he has the upper hand in any negotiations." His laugh let Darcy know he had found his predicament entertaining.

"Can you at least get me one comfortable chair? Unless you want me to stand anytime we are in here." His pleading tone signaled his desperation.

"I will have one found and brought in here for you, old chap. As for running the estate, I find it is a lot of work, but I am enjoying the challenge. It has been frustrating having to put up with my sisters harping about good people. I have enjoyed the society here despite their complaining." Bingley was still trying to figure out how to get some freedom from his sisters.

"Would the society you are enjoying have blue eyes?" Darcy grinned.

Bingley's focus shifted, and he seemed to get a goofy look on his face. "You know, Miss Bennet is the most beautiful lady I think I have ever seen, but she is unlike any lady I have known. We had an entire conversation about the benefits of crop rotation the last time we spoke. That night I was trying to think if I had ever had a serious conversation with a woman before. I do not think I ever had. She even asked me what I was doing to aid the tenant families on the property. I am ashamed to admit I could not even remember how many tenant families lived on Netherfield land." The shift in his reality confused Bingley.

Darcy recognized the look on his face as the looks he would get when there was a new lady in his life. "Miss Elizabeth similarly questioned me. I have written to my stewards to see if some things she questioned were being provided for, as I had assumed." Darcy looked at his thoughtful companion, thinking that Miss Bennet may be the making of him. Darcy stood to go gaze out the window and contemplate how a different Miss Bennet had affected him.

He came out of his pondering when he spotted a carriage coming up the drive. "It looks like we have callers. Shall we head down?" Ready to leave the room, Darcy still found time to glare at the uncomfortable chairs, which seemed to mock his indignation.

"Yes, we have been working long enough. Let us head down." Bingley stood and straightened his attire before he headed for the door.

***

IN THE PARLOR, CAROLINE Bingley could barely withhold her glee at being able to prove to Darcy her superiority to the country chits that had come calling. Mrs. Bennet had arrived, accompanied by her two oldest daughters. They were obviously sniffing after her brother and Mr. Darcy and would have to be put in their place.

"I am glad to host you in my parlor. It must be a treat for you to see a room in the latest style." She swiveled her gaze to the maid in the corner and requested the tea service. She glanced around the room, admiring the way the light caught the gold of the furniture and the intricate details of the statues.

Mrs. Bennet looked around the room, noting both the needless opulence and uncomfortable furniture with little to no padding. The color scheme relied heavily on a mustard yellow and a kind of faded salmon color that almost made her lose her appetite. "I see that you have put a lot of effort into this room." She had been on the receiving end of too many cutting remarks, so she refused to respond with her own. Fanny felt she had managed her response fairly well.

Caroline smirked at the comment. The lowly family who had come calling obviously had no notion of style. Their dresses were a stark contrast to the fashion of the Ton. "Yes, these colors are quite the thing right now. My close friend Mrs. Stanford told me that the combination was all the rage and even Lady Jersey was redecorating with these hues this season." It had been a tremendous feat of hers to befriend Mrs. Stanford, who had the most singular style in the Ton.

"I see that you thoroughly embrace the shades, Miss Bingley." Jane eyed the odd salmon-colored dress with rows of lace on the bodice.

Elizabeth knew she would never desire to be seen as fashionable if these were the colors she would have to embrace. "How have you been enjoying your time here? Do you find living in the country to suit you?"

"It has been a trial, I tell you. You do not know how I suffer. As you do not live in London, you do not understand the pain of being separated from high society. How I miss the entertainments and calls, the ability to see and be seen. There is simply nothing to do in the country!" Caroline was even more put out that her sister had been staying in her room most mornings. To make things worse, Darcy had not adequately fawned over her abilities as a hostess.

Jane frowned, hearing the upset in Caroline's voice. "Such a shame that being here keeps you from engaging in the activities you like. If you are looking for activities to take up here in the country, we would be more than happy to help you find something you fancy. You are more than welcome to come to join us when we practice archery, and

I am certain that the tenant families could use some caring oversight."
Jane's joy was never complete without the people around her being
content. Their sadness was a burden she could not shake. Maybe
she could help the newcomer to the community find her footing.
Country living differed from town living and big adjustments took
time to become accustomed to.

Everyone heard Caroline's huff of disgust. "It is so quaint that you
would invite a cultured lady such as myself to your paltry activities.
It is certainly not something I will be attempting. Genteel ladies do
not lower themselves by mixing with other classes." These pathetic
girls may wish to spend their time with dirty people, but she did not!
Really, how dare they ask her?

It always astounded Darcy at how condescending Miss Bingley
could be. "I am sorry to contradict my host's sister, but that
statement is false. I have it from a very credible source that great
estates offer succor to those that live on the estate they own." He
looked down at her from where he stood by the door. How did she
come up with what she spoke about?

Caroline swallowed the comment she wished to make. "I think
providing aid when needed is entirely justified. I only question how
one would dispense it. Would you like tea, gentlemen?" She changed
the subject before she would have to backtrack any further. Belatedly,
she realized Darcy had gone to sit near Miss Elizabeth. That simply
would not do.

To this event came Mrs. Hurst, looking wan. When she sat down,
Mrs. Bennet moved to sit near her and Bingley went to sit next to

Jane. As Mrs. Bennet and Mrs. Hurst began whispering, the rest of the gathering settled into their own conversations.

"Miss Bennet, Miss Elizabeth, do you think you would mind helping my younger sister when she visits soon? I think she would enjoy the activities you mentioned as I came in. She is very shy and has no genuine friends to help encourage her." Darcy loved how close and sincere all the Bennet ladies were. He thought Georgiana would do well to be exposed to that kind of relationship.

Caroline Bingley had just taken a sip of tea when she heard Darcy's comment. She had been trying to be that insipid girl's friend for years. Such was her outrage that she inhaled her tea and started sputtering. Bingley jumped up and hit her on the back to stop her choking, concerned about the color her face was turning. By the time Caroline was breathing normally, her hair was in disarray and she had spilled tea on her lap and down the front of her dress. Beyond that, she was livid.

Louisa knew how awful Caroline was about to get and realized she had to get her out of that room. "Oh, Caroline. Let me help you upstairs so that we can take care of all this. Please excuse us." Mrs. Hurst gave a quick curtsy before propelling her sister up and out of the room.

Bingley decided they would be best far away from his soon-to-be-screaming sister. "Would you ladies like to go for a stroll in the garden?" he suggested.

Jane readily took the arm that he offered. "It is a lovely day out and that sounds splendid." Across the room, Darcy offered his arm to Elizabeth, which she took.

Jane glanced back at her mother sitting on the chair by herself. Jane did not want to leave her mother by herself. "Mama, do come with us. The weather is beautiful."

"I think I will join you all. If I remember correctly, there is a bench I could sit on and enjoy the autumn air." Mrs. Bennet did not want to intrude on anything, but felt she should be a chaperone for both couples.

Elizabeth had intended to suggest a walk, but things worked out without her interference. "I am glad we got the chance to speak, Mr. Darcy. It was my primary goal in coming here today." Looking around, she took in the peaceful park. Even without flowers, it was tranquil. A gravel pathway ran in curving loops around fountains and statuary.

"It was quite convenient that circumstances arranged themselves thus." Darcy found he enjoyed walking with her in the sunshine. They had so many days of rain this time of year, it was nice to be at peace in the sun.

Elizabeth hesitated momentarily before bringing up the interaction she needed to talk to him about. She did not want to disrupt the pleasant walk, but felt she must warn him. "Last night I attended a card party with my mother and sisters that was thrown by Aunt Phillips in Meryton. She invited the officers from the militia and one specific officer quite unsettled Mary and myself."

Darcy found it a struggle not to glare at Miss Elizabeth when she spoke of someone causing issues. The idea of anyone bothering her or her sister was upsetting; the thought that it might be Wickham was almost infuriating. "That would not have been someone who goes by the name of George Wickham, would it?" Had the snake already raised his smarmy head?

When she noted a dark expression on Mr. Darcy's face, she hoped he was not upset with her. She was trying to read him better and felt that she knew him enough to assume that he would not be upset with her, but maybe the situation. "Yes, a Lieutenant Wickham, so you know him? He was rather forward... I guess that might be the way to say it."

"I hope he did nothing unpleasant, Miss Elizabeth." The gravel crunched under Darcy's boots, his agitation a counterpoint to the sound. He was even more determined to put an end to the reprobate's misdeeds.

Realizing that Mr. Darcy was, in fact, upset with Mr. Wickham, Elizabeth seemed to relax. "Mary and I were both perfectly fine, in full view of everyone. He was desperate for us to inquire about the mistreatment he had endured. I think he was quite upset over our lack of capitulation." A giggle escaped her despite the serious topic. He had been attempting to be smooth and persuasive, but he had fallen completely short of the mark.

It surprised Darcy to note her giggle. Watching her carefully, he tried to understand how she had not fallen for Wickham's lies and came away laughing at the interaction. "Then he wanted to tell you how I refused him a living. He has swayed many people to his side with that story."

She kicked a pebble with her half boots and watched it bounce down the path. "Do not fear that either Mary or I were one of those people. There were so many obvious holes in his tale. If ordained, he could get another rectory or even work as a curate; either would earn more money than a lieutenant in the militia." Elizabeth huffed at Wickham's presumption that they would not be logical enough to think things through.

"Why is it that no one else questions that? He refused to become ordained. Which I was fine with because I could never in good conscience put forward such a disreputable rector. He received three thousand pounds plus his inheritance of one thousand in compensation for giving up the living. It was only a few years later that he came back, having lost it all in a debauched lifestyle, requesting that I turn over the living. I have the paperwork where he signed away his rights to it for the money and could turn him away." Darcy ran his hand through his hair in frustration. It hadn't kept Wickham out of his life for long.

Elizabeth's eyes widened in shock. It amazed her to know Mr. Wickham's character. With that much money, she could overhaul the tenant farms with updated practices and equipment, plus have enough put aside for a rainy day or year even. "I suspected his character when I caught him leering at Kitty and Lydia in Meryton, but to have lost four thousand pounds in a few years is remarkable."

"I hope his actions did not affect your sisters too negatively. He is not one to be trusted in the company of women or girls." Thinking of how many of Wickham's inclination leaned toward young girls not even out made his stomach roll.

"I think they came through the experience fairly well. Jane, Mary, and I had been only around the bend, so we were not far away."

A wave of relief washed over Darcy, and he let out a long breath. He decided in an instant to recount Wickham's entire story to her, down to the last detail. "He is a man not to be trusted. Recently, he seduced my sister's companion and tried to get my sister to elope with him for her dowry."

"Do tell me your sister is well," Elizabeth spoke, urgently concerned.

"My sister knew something was wrong and got a letter to me asking for help. I arrived in time to stop anything untoward."

Elizabeth was reassured at least that his sister was safe. "How did he convince her companion to help him? I cannot see how there would have been any benefit for her."

"He had lied about me to her. She was also under the impression that he was in love with her and they needed to take advantage of my sister in order to be together."

"I know it is no excuse but to be so deceived by the man you thought loved you is a horrible blow to any woman."

"It was eventually discovered that she was with child. He had promised to keep her as his mistress once they had got Georgiana to the altar and taken her dowry." He felt an intense need to make sure Elizabeth was safe and knew she was intelligent enough to guard herself and those around her, if given a warning.

"Your sister is the true victim here; the woman she was supposed to rely on betrayed her. How is she recovering?" Elizabeth found her anger rising at Wickham's presumption. She had to restrain herself from kicking the artfully arranged topiary that lined the path.

"It was a shock, but I think the fact that she was suspicious and reached out to me helped her confidence. She has a new companion, Mrs. Ansley, who has been good to her. Our cousin Colonel Theodore Fitzwilliam is with her now in London and they will head down to stay here until the holiday season." He would need to give his cousin a warning about Wickham. Darcy added that to his list of things that he needed to do later in the day that would help him avoid Caroline Bingley.

"I hope their visit goes well, though I am concerned about his presence here affecting your sister." Elizabeth's maternal instincts were coming to the fore.

"Wickham Is terrified of Theo, so it should be well enough. I will ask him to bring two of our bigger footmen, who are ex-soldiers. With someone to escort her, I think she will feel safe enough. I also spoke to the shop owners about not giving credit to the officers, as he does not pay his debts." Darcy ran his fingers through his hair again.

Tilting her head, Elizabeth studied Mr. Darcy. "It seems like you do well with socializing in some settings. Do you find it easier to communicate with fewer people in the vicinity? Or is there some other reason, do you think?" Elizabeth questioned.

Pausing, Mr. Darcy considered her question. Did he do better with some people than others? He felt an interesting gladness when he considered he was doing well in some of his interactions. "When I took over my estate, I had to interact with many people to make sure things started running smoothly. I found that if I felt that the interaction was part of my duty, it was fine. If there was a reason behind my words, if someone needed something, I had no problems.

I do not know why that worked, but I was glad it did," Darcy answered.

Reaching out, she ran her hand along the hedge that marked the edge of the garden. It separated the pretty from the useful, as the kitchen garden graced the other side. "That must be very helpful for getting everything taken care of. I know this is a change in subject, but I have a question that may be out of line and do not answer if you do not wish to. One thing Lieutenant Wickham said was that you were your parents' only living son. Did you have a brother?" Elizabeth knew it would devastate her to lose any of her sisters.

Darcy did not always think of his lost brother as it was so long ago. "Yes, I had a twin brother. He was older than me by twenty-three minutes. He was not born healthy, and it was only a matter of days before he died. It affected my mother that she had lost him, as it had been a difficult pregnancy, I am told." He was happy to have his sister but had not known his brother to regret him as a person, though he regretted the idea of him.

"I am sorry for your loss. I am sure that even though you do not remember, it affected your life." Elizabeth spoke with compassion.

"That is very accurate. All my life, I was being compared to Tybalt, my poor dead brother who would have been so much better than me, by my mother. Of course, my father was no better. He was comparing me to Wickham, who seemed to be born with the ability to speak pleasantly and persuasively." It appalled him that some people had a knack they would only exploit for their own dark intentions.

"Did he never see his baser proclivities?" Elizabeth had a hard time comprehending a man approving of any such activities.

Darcy had a hard time considering the relationship his father had with Wickham. He hoped his father did not know how bad he was. "I cannot be sure, and I do not know what feels worse. That he never paid enough attention to see what was happening, or that he did not care about what was happening. My father placed great value on appearances and Wickham can appear to be all that is genuine and good. While I have always struggled not to appear taciturn and judgmental."

They continued along the path together, contemplating their own issues and lost in their own thoughts. Despite their inattention to one another, they still moved in sync, their movements mirroring each other. Their stride matching unconsciously. Gaining warmth and comfort from the presence there willing to support them.

"We both have reasons to regret our parents' choices. So now that we have discussed all the serious matters, we should let us move on to brighter topics. What do you think of Mr. Bingley and my sister?"

Darcy was glad to change the subject. "He has always been a cheerful person, and would sooner jump out of his carriage and help someone than pass by a person in need. Yet despite that, he has taken nothing completely seriously. When a carriage accident took both his parents and older brother, his opportunities and future changed. He had begun the process of obtaining his own estate, as his father had asked, but it had not transformed him. I think to him it was just another lark. But meeting your sister has been different. He told me he does not remember having a serious conversation with a woman before he met your sister. She is making him think, which is an excellent thing."

"Well, that is reassuring. I know my sister deserves a great many good things in her life. She spends most of her time trying to help people. Though being honest, I think making Miss Bingley think about her color choices would be more beneficial to us all than making Mr. Bingley think. Sadly, I do not see anyone being successful in that endeavor."

Elizabeth's thickly lashed eyes widened when Mr. Darcy did the most remarkable thing. He laughed. He laughed so hard that it drew the attention of everyone in the garden. Remarkably, when Elizabeth witnessed Mr. Darcy's great booming laugh and dimples, her brain ceased to function. She tripped over her own feet and landed in a heap on the path. Powerful hands helped to pull her to her feet and Jane brushed off her dress. Her eyes had a glazed, dreamy look, and the only word that floated through her mind was "dimples".

Chapter Nine

"I ASSURE YOU, MY good man, I am a gentleman. I pay my debts." Wickham gazed at the pudgy proprietor before him, his endearing smile masking his perturbation.

Martin stood his ground, the old wooden counter between them creaking beneath the pressure of his palms. Despite its smaller size compared to those in bigger cities, he was proud of his store. The shelves on the walls were polished, and they kept the goods in order. He would not let this soldier before him try to take advantage. "I do not doubt that, sir, but I have to run my business profitably. Rumor has it that the troops got paid yesterday. You have more than a pound on your account. Until you pay off your current tab, I will not be selling you anything."

"It is merely a few trinkets and a bottle of whiskey. I would think you would prefer my continued patronage over whining about such a paltry issue." Maybe a little pressure would sway him. Wickham found his winsome smile could convince many a person to do his bidding.

"I am sorry if you feel that way, sir, but this is my policy for all the soldiers. Everything should run smoothly as long as you pay off what you owe after they pay you." Martin glanced into the angry eyes of the red-coated man before him and was grateful for Mr. Darcy's wisdom. This man would never pay a penny piece if he thought he could get away with it.

Eyes narrowed, Wickham spoke with a hint of his malice seeping through his facade. "I had not thought that you would treat me in such a style this day, so I have not brought my money with me. I will, of course, pay you what I owe next time I am here." Wickham tugged his red coat into position and contemplated his next move. His anger translated itself into his boots, striking against the hardwood floor even if the smile never left his face.

Martin gathered the handkerchiefs and bottle of alcohol from the counter to put back on his shelves. "I will look forward to seeing you then, sir." The man's footsteps were like thunder as he left the room, and Martin shook his head in disbelief. He doubted he would return, but did not regret losing the soldier's business.

Wickham became more harried as the day progressed. Though he had thought the grocer's attitude would be a singular event, it did not prove to be so. The cobbler would not make him the new boots he wished for without payment upfront. The haberdasher would not give him the cravat he wanted without payment for the waistcoat he had ordered already.

Even the tavern had held an unwelcome surprise. They did not permit him the meal he had asked for without first paying off his tab. He refused to eat the swill available to the soldiers unless forced, so he had to hand over the three pounds and two shillings. It was nearly all he had left after the sergeant had found him this morning and demanded his winnings from the card game last night. At least the tavern owner generously put two bottles of whiskey on his tab after he had paid off everything else.

Worse, he had made no progress with the local girls. Even forgetting that horrible blunder with Miss Bennet, he had made little progress where it mattered. Though the tavern girls had smiled and blushed at his advances, he had gotten no further. The grocer's daughter always seemed to have her brother or father about, so that had gone nowhere, and it was the same story wherever he looked.

There was nothing for it. Since joining the militia, every decision he made seemed to backfire. Not only was he required to follow the orders of the buffoon of a colonel, they made him rise at a truly ungodly hour to do drills. All those years of bowing and scraping to that old nabob had not been worth it if he had ended up here. He thought he would have an estate, at least, for his efforts. A living and a thousand pounds, how ridiculous. He would just have to find his way, as he always did. He could surely convince someone to fill his pockets by their own will or otherwise.

He cautiously made his way back to the camp, the bottles in his satchel jostling against one another with each step. Maybe he would have better luck at a card game. As he crossed the street, he saw a familiar figure in the distance atop a great, dark steed. Suddenly, everything felt still and clear. Darcy was in town and was once again meddling in his affairs.

The implication was clear: the sanctimonious prig had protected the poor people of Meryton from the unscrupulous soldiers that had come calling. He had probably warned everyone about giving credit and protecting their daughters.

Why had Darcy always cared about the people who were no better than the dirt beneath his feet? They deserved no notice or concern. It was their lot in life to serve those who mattered. Darcy foolishly attempted to help people, even the women whom Wickham had jilted and the brats they had produced.

Well, his time here was a wash. There was no way he could get out of the town what he needed, not with everyone wise to his ways. It would take more work than he wanted to put into it. He would leave and find another way to gain his fortune, but first, Darcy would pay for interfering.

***

MR. THOMAS BENNET LOOKED around the dinner table in satisfaction. He gained something to see all of his family so cowed. The atmosphere was one of quiet reverence around the table, as they respected his wishes and intelligence. They knew that anything they would say would be drivel and so kept silent. He had been keeping a secret from them all and he felt now was the time to reveal all and reap his reward for being so patient. "Mrs. Bennet, I wish to inform you of a guest that will arrive soon. You will have the great pleasure of failing as hostess for my cousin, Mr. Wilberforce Collins." His sneer spoke of his cruel intentions.

Mrs. Bennet tried to gain more information as she thought. "Your cousin, Mr. Bennet? I do not believe I have met him yet." She began going over preparations in her head. The guest room would need to be made up, but it would not do to have Mr. Bennet see her flustered.

"No, you have not met him. He is the man who will inherit this ruinous heap on my death and cast you all into the hedgerows before I grow cold in my grave. I would think you would try to be on his good side for all that he holds over you. Yet he arrives in mere hours and you have nothing prepared for his visit. It does not bode well, my dear." His chuckle was grating on all of their nerves, for they knew it held no joy, only malice. He caused a stir at the table and sat back, pleased to observe their wide eyes and quick glances, excited by their panic. That should do it. He would be quite content in his library for a while. Then he would come out and see what more he could do once his odious cousin arrived.

Once he had left, Mrs. Bennet reached over and held Kitty's trembling hand. She wished she could take her girls far away from here, but that was not to be, so she had to stay strong.

Mrs. Bennet began by clearing her throat. She attempted to loosen the anxiety that was coiling in her chest by breathing slowly. "I will talk with Mrs. Allen about food and Mrs. Hill about the room. Lydia, could you collect something nice from the garden for his room? I believe that the best option would be to put him in the green room. It is the farthest away from you girls and we can say that is because we thought he would appreciate the quiet. I may ask you girls to share while he is here. We will come through this as we always do. Now if you will excuse me, I need to talk to the staff." If her voice wavered as she spoke, no one pointed it out.

Jane's hands moved to smooth the fabric of the plain linen tablecloth. "Maybe he will be a kind gentleman and it will be a pleasant visit." Jane's optimism brought such thoughts to the fore.

But even though she tried to keep her emotions in check, she could not deny to herself that this new situation made her uneasy.

Lydia's mind had been cataloging the garden and the need for flowers. She did not want to donate her flowers to the cause of a cousin many times removed with plans to make her homeless. "There are few blooms in the garden this time of year. Do you think a bundle of fragrant herbs would be acceptable?" Lydia thought over her herb garden plots to consider options.

Mary took a bite of her toast, her anxiety having soured her stomach. "I am sure that would be acceptable. I know I am fond of both rosemary and sage in a sachet."

Elizabeth looked down at her plate with an uneasy stomach. The poached eggs had sounded lovely before her father spoke. Now they just seemed congealed and inedible. "I know I may regret this, but I find I cannot finish eating. I will go see if I can help prepare the guest room." Elizabeth slipped from the table, leaving her cloth serviette by her plate. As she walked out of the room, she gave Kitty a hug. The poor thing was not handling the issue well.

***

"I AM SO THANKFUL for your magnanimity in allowing me to visit, Cousin Bennet. I look forward to familial unity and the rectification of the former breach." Proud of his practiced greeting, Wilberforce Collins attempted a grand, sweeping bow. It was a rather bunglesome display because of his lack of coordination and unhealthy proportions. On regaining his footing, he surveyed what he viewed as his domain.

The building was not nearly as magnificent as the grandeur of Rosings, and the grounds appeared to be merely adequate. Moving his gaze to his relations before him, it gladdened him to see that the women who would be under his control were very comely. Their clothes lacked the ornate style of Lady Catherine De Bourgh or her daughter; it pleased Wilberforce to find that they naturally recognized and maintained the differences in their social rankings.

Mrs. Bennet saw he was not paying attention to the introductions, but instead had been ogling her daughters' figures. Yes, the girls would share rooms for the duration of his stay. "Mr. Collins?" She got his attention, this time at least.

"You are too kind." Mr. Collins relied on this phrase whenever he became lost in a conversation and found it worked all most every time.

"If you would follow me, good sir, I can escort you to your room myself. I am sure that you would like to rest and refresh yourself after a lo ng journey. One of the staff will bring up your trunk." She twirled around and gestured to the house, encouraging him to follow her and leave her daughters behind.

"Yes, that would be acceptable." Mr. Collins followed the matron into the house, looking around with a calculating air.

From his spot in front of the house, Mr. Bennet observed his cousin's covetous demeanor and smiled. This was going to be an enjoyable two weeks. He had not been blind to the leering stare Collins ran over his daughters. That made room for some interesting possibilities. He would find much gratification from the coming interactions. Mr. Bennet felt no one would be comfortable until his cousin departed and that suited him just fine. He had long ago decided that if he could not have what he truly wanted, no one else need to get what they wanted either. Over the years of his exile from the shining halls of intelligent society, he learned to find diversion where he could. It was often in the flinches and unhappiness of those around him, and his cousin would provide great fodder for his amusement this fortnight.

Mary was trying to have some kind of conversation at the dinner table. The nervous silence was maddening. "As a clergyman in charge of a parish, how do you go about composing the sermons you give?" She knew that speaking might benefit whatever her father's plot was, but at least it was no longer silent.

Choking slightly when he attempted to speak with food in his mouth, Mr. Collins swallowed. He then began talking about one of his favorite subjects. "I have the immense benefit of having Lady Catherine de Bourgh as my patroness, and she, in her beneficence, allows me to present the sermons she chooses. She occasionally will even write a sermon if she feels a subject would be of benefit to my parish, such is the magnitude of her bountiful supremacy. Last week I presented her sermon on recognizing one's betters." Finally stopping for breath, he shoved another forkful of meat into his open maw. Proud of his patroness and his ability to help her, he smiled broadly around a mouthful of ham.

It astonished Mary to see the arrogance with which Mr. Collins celebrated his violation of canon law. "Oh, that is not something

I would have predicted." How could a man with schooling and ordination still be this ignorant?

Mary Bennet's derision went unnoticed as Mr. Collins beamed at her with a delighted grin. He had a large piece of something green stuck between his teeth. Unperturbed, he continued on with the glories of his patroness. "Lady Catherine's determination to intervene and oversee the lives of those beneath her has been a surprise to many. She has, even in her wisdom, suggested that I put shelves in all my closets." He extended his arm across the table and scooped up a helping of kippers and onions, piling them atop his ham. Whenever onions were served, he would dig in, relishing their strong flavor. At home, he required them at every meal, as his saintly father had often spoken of their healthful properties.

Elizabeth feared she might start wasting away if she faced Mr. Collins' habits at every meal. "Shelves in the closet, Mr. Collins? I do not see how that would not crease all of your clothes." She goggled at the foolery.

"Very much so. Lady Catherine is of the belief that it ensures your servants are caring for your clothes as they should. They must scrutinize the outfit while ironing out the creases." He brought another forkful to his mouth so overloaded by the onions that he left a trail across the tablecloth. Smacking his lips in enjoyment, he belched loudly, thoroughly satisfied with the meal.

Frowning, Mary spoke up against the absurd notion. "That would be a tremendous amount of extra and unnecessary work." She continued to be aghast by his appalling table manners and the interference displayed by Lady Catherine.

Mr. Collins had finally noticed the upset and confused expressions on his cousins' faces. He felt it was his duty to reassure them. "That is what they are there for, to do my bidding. I get to choose how they spend their time, just as Lady Catherine chooses things for me. It is the divine order of things. I do not expect a young lady such as yourself to comprehend the correct order of things. Do not worry, it is not your place to understand, it is simply your place to obey." The teachings of Lady Catherine always made him feel powerful. Realizing that the ladies had ceased to speak, he refocused on his meal, only pausing to breathe and wipe his mouth occasionally on his sleeve.

Across the table, Mary and Elizabeth sat, both thunderstruck. The repugnance of the man before them was astounding in every way. His inability to eat with any decorum coupled with his views on the world made having him at the table something that would prove difficult to endure. Further down the table, Jane sat with her serviette covering her nose and mouth, trying to manage her reaction to the display. At the foot of the table, Mrs. Bennet spent her time coming up with plans to protect her girls from the creature sitting next to her husband.

Mr. Bennet spent his energy trying not to laugh and ruin the current display. This was better than he had hoped. He was a sycophant who was both servile and pompous. How was that even possible? He did not know how, but it was hilarious! From the man's rambling letter, it sounded like he wanted to unite the two branches of the family back into one by marrying one of his daughters.

But who to choose? Jane's beauty was too exquisite for the small parish, but her tranquil attitude would keep her from becoming too disheartened. Lydia would be so young and incompetent that things would be in shambles, but who was to say that the buffoon would even understand that? Elizabeth was intelligent enough to understand just how incompetent he was and yet she could not counteract his dictates. In return, she could make his life as miserable as possible.

The thought of Elizabeth marrying the foolish nincompoop filled him with a strange excitement.

In Mrs. Bennet's sitting room, they gathered to devise strategies to counter any problems that might occur. They all agreed that spending as little time as possible with their cousin would be for the best. She had warned the girls from a young age that material comfort was not always a guarantee of safety when choosing a man. There was more to life than the quality of the table one set. Being able to hold one's head up at home and living without fear was better than any china set or opulent seating.

Mrs. Bennet thought her daughters would be safest far from the house. Elizabeth and Kitty would go out visiting Charlotte and Maria, while Jane and Lydia would visit the expectant mothers. Mrs. Bennet and Mary would be going into town to get supplies, freeing up some servants to deal with the extra work that Mr. Collins brought. Hopefully staying out of his way as much as possible and always in pairs, they would stay sane. There were only ten days until he returned to his parish.

"But what are we to do the next day and the next?" Fretted Kitty.

Fanny hugged her daughter close. She understood that it was not what happened now that worried her. It was whatever Mr. Bennet planned. He feasted on the minutiae of people's misery, the very antithesis of Jane. Mrs. Bennet worried about her second youngest child, so fearful by nature. She could only give her love and support and hope she would find her way. "We will take it one day at a time, my dear. Even if we must, by necessity, spend time with Mr. Collins, it will never be alone. You will always be with one of us." Kissing her daughter's brow, she prayed Kitty would one day find her fire.

***

CHARLOTTE SMOOTHED HER HAIR back from her face as she greeted her unexpected guests. "Oh, it is always a pleasure to have you visit, no matter the time. How are you, Kitty?" she inquired. As she glanced around, she felt a sense of satisfaction that everything in the room was as it should be. Although it was not as grand as the Bennet family's parlor, it had its own unique touches of charm and style. Even though the Bennet sisters were practically family, she still wanted to maintain her dignity. She would not want to be seen in an unpleasant light.

Kitty's smile was not as bright as Elizabeth's, but she seemed to have become more relaxed the further from Longbourn they got. "The walk was rather nice. Even though it is fall and the trees are becoming bare, I find the lack of foliage might inspire a sketch or painting. It was all picturesque." Kitty's mind, though timid, was also artistic, and she was ever looking for the beauty in the world around her.

Maria Lucas lamented her ability. Slumping into her well-stuffed chair, she became the image of defeat. "You are ever so accomplished with paints and drawings. I despair of even making something recognizable. I attempted to paint Father's horse Jupiter recently and Robby told me it was a very tolerable cow."

Kitty made sure not to laugh, though she found the situation funny. She saw how bothered Maria was; she seemed to be beside herself. "Animals are ever so hard. I find painting nature so much easier. Trees and fields do not move around nearly as much. I would be happy to show you a few techniques I use whenever you wish." Kitty's grin lit up her face. Art was one of her passions, and it was not quite a secret.

"Charlotte, may we go practice in the morning room?" Maria clasped her hands together in a beseeching motion.

"That would be fine." Charlotte smiled at both of the girls' joy. "Try to keep the paint off the furniture," she called after their rushing forms.

Elizabeth was happy to see her sister with some enthusiasm. She needed a problem that she could work on and conquer, preferably not her own problem. This would do nicely. "Thank you for indulging them. Kitty really could do with some distraction."

"Maria could use the practice. She is not nearly as skilled as Kitty, though I know she tries. Is there something that has you escaping Longbourn?" Though fond of a call from Elizabeth, it seemed something had prompted this excursion. She had not just happened by.

Elizabeth did not dare voice what she truly thought of the man. Ladies did not speak aloud words like those. "My father's cousin, many times removed, has come for a fortnight. He is the heir presumptive and will inherit Longbourn on Father's passing. He is not a man any of us would choose to spend time with."

"Did he come with his family?" Once the tea arrived, Charlotte busied herself with preparing cups for her guests.

Elizabeth shuddered. She could not picture sitting across from the man at the dinner table for longer than she had to. The thought of Mr. Collins fathering children was nauseating. "The man is quite single." The woman who married that man would have her eternal pity.

"What are his prospects besides Longbourn?" Charlotte inquired.

"He is the clergyman who holds the living at the Hunsford parish. Lady Catherine de Bourgh gave it to him." Elizabeth worried for the people of Rosings, if the woman in charge chose Mr. Collins.

Charlotte felt brittle at the news of an eligible gentleman staying at Longbourn. She had no hopes or prospects and yet her friend somehow had many opportunities and too many principles. "If that is the case, I question why you are spending time here and not at home trying to promote yourself to a highly eligible gentleman. I do not understand how you can overlook an opportunity such as this. You could be the mistress of your childhood home!" Charlotte found at times like these it was difficult to be Elizabeth's friend. She had so many things going for her. She was intelligent and beautiful, and her family had held Longbourn for two centuries. Yet she did not use what she had to reach for the one thing all single women sought: a husband.

"Charlotte, he is not a man that I, or I believe any woman, would be comfortably married to. His attitude toward people under his power is disturbing. His thoughts about women are infuriating and his table manners leave me without an appetite. He reeks of onions even when bathed. In short, I can only assume that marriage to him would be a misery despite any benefit derived from prestige or situation." She knew Charlotte could never understand the torment that existed in a home with a husband and father who did not respect or even care for you.

The clatter of her tea cup slamming into its saucer punctuated Charlotte's upset. "You are younger than I, so maybe you do not understand the fate you are tempting. To be a poor relation or being forced to find some employment are the prospects I now face. The opportunity to be the mistress of my own establishment is a prospect I would do almost anything for."

"Charlotte, he is an utter buffoon. He blathers on without end, using more words than necessary in every sentence. I doubt he fully understands half the words that come out of his mouth. He has deified his patroness Lady Catherine and holds her opinion over the Holy Scripture and canon law." It pained Elizabeth to think that Charlotte, an intelligent woman, would put herself under the power of such a man.

"Not everyone is as intelligent as you are, Elizabeth, and I stand by my former statement. As neither of us is likely to change our opinions, perhaps we should choose a new topic of conversation?" Charlotte's voice took on the prim tone it sometimes took when upset.

"I noticed Lady Lucas was not here to greet us. Is she suffering from another one of her headaches?" Elizabeth could never imagine the desperation that Charlotte felt, but Charlotte could never comprehend the oppressive weight of living under her father's tyrannical rule. Elizabeth had long ago decided to never marry a man who she could not respect and who would not respect her in return.

Chapter Ten

Elizabeth relished her walk with Kiernan this morning. The air was especially crisp, and she was grateful for the ability to walk off some of her frustrations. "How are you enjoying the book, Kiernan? Has it been giving you trouble?"

"I think I have been doing well. My little sister likes the stories and because I read them often, I get to practice." Kiernan puffed out his chest, his pride in his progress clear. He looked around and noticed they were almost back at Longbourn.

Elizabeth derived so much joy from her time with Kiernan that she felt he deserved a treat. "You know, Kiernan, Mrs. Allen was starting a batch of scones before we left. I do not think she would mind if you tried one to make sure it meets her standards. I think she was worried about the quality of the apples."

Kiernan's mouth was already watering at the thought of a nice warm scone. "I would be delighted to help with that, Miss Elizabeth. I am fond of apples, but sometimes you can get a bad one."

In no time Kiernan was back at Longbourn and accepting a scone fresh from the oven, the aroma of spices tantalizing his nose. He thanked Mrs. Allen before he went outside to enjoy it in the cool morning air.

Kiernan strolled along the exterior of the building until he found a cozy spot to sit beneath a window. He took his first bite while gazing out at the tranquil garden. Warm and flaky, the flavor of cinnamon and spice burst onto his tongue, followed by the reassuring sweetness of the apple. Mrs. Allen was the best baker.

***

MR. COLLINS LOOKED AROUND the room that would one day be his domain and smiled. The scent of leather and port permeated the room and books lined the shelves floor to ceiling. "Thank you for inviting me to speak with you in your library, cousin." He found reading laborious and aggravating, but that did not mean he did not know books were expensive.

"Not at all, cousin. You stated you had a reason of some importance to discuss?" Mr. Bennet saw the covetous glance, but it did not disturb him. He was welcome to this heap when he was done with it. Longbourn would likely be in a dilapidated condition, but it would be his at some point.

"I want to reassure you of my desire to heal the breach between the branches of our family. The most honorable Lady Catherine has advised me that to provide for my female relatives after your demise, I should marry one of your daughters. I have decided that, of course, your eldest daughter will have her rightful place as my bride." Wilberforce became captivated by his wanton imaginings.

Mr. Bennet waded through his laborious speech with annoyance. He might find it entertaining to watch the buffoon with his daughters, but he would be happy when Collins was not here to yap at him. "I must inform you of the fact that she has already begun a courtship with one of our neighbors before your arrival. I would hate to diminish your standing in the community by encouraging you to steal a woman another man had spoken for. That, however, is not the case with my second eldest daughter." It was a blatant lie, he vaguely recalled that there was a few new gentlemen visiting in the area but he was not aware of any courtship. He wanted Elizabeth to be stuck with the bumbling buffoon, not Jane, and his cousin was too stupid to understand his manipulations.

"I would never want to be so disrespectful as to claim a lady another gentleman had prior claim to. Your daughter Elizabeth, though nowhere near her sister in comeliness, has her appeal. I shall endeavor to request her hand, as I assume I have your permission?" One woman was just as good as any other to Mr. Collins. He heard the creak of the chair as he settled back into it, running his hand over the polished wood.

Mr. Bennet could not help the grin on his face as he spoke. His plans for his daughter were so eminently satisfying. "You have my permission, however, asking my second oldest daughter may not get the result either of us wants. Sadly, my wife encouraged an independent streak in her I cannot approve of. However, I feel there is an opportunity that might work to cure her of it and have you happily married." His smile widened as he watched his cousin try to work through what he had said.

"Independence, you say, that is quite concerning. What are you suggesting?" Mr. Collins was not unaware of his authority, yet he was lazy at heart and did not relish the effort it would take to enforce his authority as needed with such a wife.

Mr. Bennet often found himself unsatisfied with the amount of respect his second daughter directed toward him. She was too much like his grandmother. Her eyes spoke of her disdain, even if her words did not. This would see her brought down if not broken. He would find great satisfaction in that. "Though my daughter would certainly incorrectly refuse your hand, she could not do so if you compromised her. Once such a thing happened, I am sure she would recognize her place in the world and you being there to guide her would reinforce it."

Collins' mouth fell open in reaction to the suggestion put forward by his cousin. "Compromise, sir? I am a clergyman; no one can see me acting inappropriately. How could we arrange this so that it appears honorable?" Wilberforce refused to be seen acting in any way that would bring dishonor. It never occurred to him that the appearance of honor was not the same as being honorable.

"We could keep it all completely innocent. You are staying here and if you were to get lost in the dark and accidentally enter her room and get in bed with her, no one could see it as your fault. Once they discover you together, a quick wedding will surely follow. I am sure you could say your vows and be married by the time you need to return to your parish." This was going to be something he could look back on and smile about when he was bored.

"You would wish such for your daughter, sir?" Sometimes his cousin confused him.

He was becoming frustrated with Collins' lack of immediate compliance. "Sadly, this is a hard lesson about obedience that she needs to learn. You will one day understand that as a parent you have to make the hard choices for the betterment of your child, no matter the pain that it gives them." That was a phrase his grandfather had used, though Thomas doubted he had pictured the plans being put in place.

Collins had a shred of conscience, yet his father had ingrained in him the need to obey those in power from a young age. "When do you feel we should go about the plan? I think I would like to return home married." He was already envisioning a triumphant return to Lady Catherine, his mind conjuring the praise and adulation that he so rightly deserved.

"I suspect that if we draw it out, something might come up to circumvent you. Tonight should be well enough." Mr. Bennet had long waited for a way to bring the daughter that so often reminded him of his grandmother down. His grandmother had disapproved of his actions and had made it clear when she took his wife under her wing before her passing. She had endeavored to stop the enjoyment he was finding in a life deprived of intellectual stimulation and challenge. She spoke to him passionately about making changes and becoming a better man. Despite this, he never grasped why it was necessary to change if one was content with their current state.

"That will be fine, I'm sure. How do I find her bedroom?" Mr. Collins had been cataloging all the things of worth in the home, but had not tried to figure out where people slept.

***

Kiernan had known that Mr. Bennet was an awful man and that Mr. Collins was an idiot, but he had never suspected how wicked they could be. The scone, which had been so delicious not five minutes earlier, now tasted like ash in his mouth. He set such a store by Miss Elizabeth that someone wanting to do such a thing to her made him very upset. How would he save her? He had to find a way. There was no other choice but to save her. He dropped the scone into the dirt at his feet and took off running.

***

Night had fallen at Longbourn and, after waiting for all the servants to retire, Mr. Collins left his room and made his way to the family wing. As he stumbled and bumbled, blindly running into furniture and banging his toes against walls, his attempts to remain quiet were futile. He hunted through the dark hallway, counting the doors on the left. He finally found what he had been seeking. The third door on the left with an embellished letter E was his destination. Opening the door, he tripped into the room.

"Miss Elizabeth, I wish to reassure you we will hold our future marriage with all due honor, as is required by the clergyman of Lady Catherine De Bourgh. Your father has informed me you must recognize my ultimate power if you are to rid yourself of your inappropriate streak of defiance." He crept across the floor and then stopped to catch his breath. The still figure under the blankets drew him. As they would be married, it would hurt nothing to see her in an undressed state. Perhaps he would only take a peek.

His trembling hand reached out to draw back the blankets from around the prone shape. Only the blankets did not want to be drawn, so he leaned against the bed and pulled harder. On his second tug, a hand reached out from behind him and grabbed his wrist, clamping down so tightly he had to release the blanket.

Rich brown eyes narrowed in disgust at the portly man before him. To sneak into a lady's room was a disgrace, and for a clergyman who spoke of honor, to do so was an abomination. "You would not be intending mischief towards Miss Elizabeth, would you, sir? I feel that would be a bad idea." His grip on the man's wrist only tightened. Knox, like his little brother Kiernan, did not agree with the mistreatment of women.

"You are interrupting something that is beyond your understanding. Leave this room and leave me to my business." Mr. Collins turned and tried to stand tall to impress his importance on the young man before him, but had to look up to meet his eyes. Dark brown eyes looked down at him with animosity and his dark hair was long enough to brush his collar. His garb was plain and spoke of rough work. He was a nobody and thus should obey.

Knox was neither impressed nor fooled. "I fully understand that you think you will get away with evil this night, but I am here to ensure that you do not. Miss Elizabeth means a lot to my family and we will not see her hurt by the likes of you." His hard-earned muscles strained under his shirt, ready to act as necessary.

Collins took a deep breath and tried to stand as tall as possible, hoping to gain a few inches. "I am the future owner of this estate and I act with the support of Miss Elizabeth's father. Her father has deemed her too independent for her own good and we are ensuring her good marriage and her eventual understanding of her place in life. You are nothing to me and shall obey my command, or I will seek to ensure that you will regret it. You need to follow the directives of your betters." Feeling confident in his speech, he attempted to pull his arm free. If the person before him did not let up, he would permanently damage his wrist.

"Are you foxed? Miss Elizabeth is an angel and you are no more than a bracket-faced widgeon. She's better than you. Confound it, I'm better than you, you maggot pie. Sneakin' in ta a girls' room at night?" Finally letting him go, Knox stepped back and readied himself for the expected explosion he was sure would come.

"How dare you, you lout! I shall teach you a lesson here and now!" He pulled his good arm back and attempted to punch the peasant in the face. Only he ducked under his swing and retaliated with a swift smack to his nose. He heard something crack and a tremendous agony distracted him from the amount of blood pouring from his broken nose and down his face and clothes. "My nose! How dare you strike your better!"

Tired of talking to the horrible buffoon, Knox pulled back his fist and punched him twice more. Looking into the eyes peeking out from under the blankets, Knox smiled reassuringly at his little brother. When Kiernan had come to him for help with protecting Miss Elizabeth, he had been eager to help, though he had not fully grasped the severity of her family's cruelty. He sort of wished Collins had not passed out so quickly. Men like this needed to learn a lesson. "Don't worry, Kiernan, he is out. What a horrible pig. How could he be a clergyman?" Knox wanted to wipe his hands on his trousers. He almost felt dirty just touching the creepy man.

"I think this man is what Mam was talking about when she said girls were not always safe." Kiernan came closer to look at the bruised and bleeding man and scowled. How would anyone want to hurt a good person like Miss Elizabeth?

"I told Mrs. Allen we would leave him in his room in the other wing. We will have to carry him between us." Reaching down, he gripped the man under the arms and waited for Kiernan to grab his feet before moving away from the bed. His muscles, though strong from working at the blacksmith's shop, still strained to carry the overweight man.

"Thank you for helping me protect Miss Elizabeth."

"Of course. Men like this need to be stopped. The only thing I don't understand is why he smells so bad." Looking down, Knox thought he looked fairly clean. He just could not understand the stench that followed the man around.

"Miss Elizabeth told me he eats a lot of onions at every meal. I think it is coming out of his skin." Wrinkling his nose, Kiernan tried to breathe through his mouth. They would both need to bathe and wash their clothes.

"No woman should ever have to marry this smelly brute. Where is Miss Elizabeth? Did Mrs. Allen say?" Knox was glad she was safe elsewhere.

"She said that she has been sleeping with Miss Mary and Miss Kitty. They thought it was wise in case there was talk. I think it was a wonderful plan. It certainly made this easier." Kiernan decided he would have to tell Miss Elizabeth what happened in the morning.

Chapter Eleven

It had rattled Elizabeth to the core when she heard what her father and his cousin had plotted the night before. That Kiernan had recruited help from his seventeen-year-old brother and the servants to protect her meant so much to her. Despite that, the malicious intent from someone in her home was appalling. She was on her second cup of calming tea.

Charlotte had come calling, and Elizabeth was having difficulty acting normally. It was not the time to discuss what had transpired the night before and Elizabeth had trouble coming up with topics of conversation. She could not stop considering last night. Charlotte knew her well enough to know something was wrong, and she was not discussing it, making things a little awkward.

Charlotte viewed her friend with a critical eye. "I do hope you are not coming down with something. You are quite pale."

"I had some distressing news when I saw Kiernan this morning and I am trying to make sense of it." Elizabeth put her teacup down with a slight rattle.

"I am sure that you will tell me when you are able. In the meantime, please know I am here for you." Charlotte was pragmatic, and she tried not to ask anything of anyone that they could not do.

"Thank you, I will. Would you like a biscuit or more tea?" Elizabeth offered. She observed the room, checking for any signs of distress from Maria, Kitty, and Lydia. Jane and Mary were in the still room working on a lotion they were both fond of. Mama was meeting with Mrs. Allen to plan meals for the week. It was a nice day, but she dreaded her father or Mr. Collins showing themselves.

***

Mr. Collins walked into the room moving stiffly and feeling the results of the night before. It had been quite a while since he had experienced such intense pain. He had impulsively ridden a horse around his parish, but the horse's wild movements resulted in him being thrown to the ground. Thereafter, he never attempted to ride and had the ill-mannered horse sold. If only this situation was so easily handled.

He had tried to tell his cousin of the disrespect he endured, but what was his reaction? He laughed! Bennet's laughter erupted from his mouth, spraying his desk with the port he had been drinking. Now Collins was at a loss for what to do. More than that, his face and chest ached.

***

CHARLOTTE WAS NEVER AVERSE to being introduced to a suitable gentleman. "I have not had the privilege of being introduced to your cousin, Elizabeth. Would you mind doing so?"

"Certainly. Miss Lucas, may I present my cousin Mr. Wilberforce Collins. Mr. Collins, my good friend Miss Charlotte Lucas." Elizabeth could not understand the desire of her friend to know such a dreadful man.

Eager to receive some recognition, he joyfully bounded forward to cater to the new woman. She did not hold a candle to his cousins, but they had fallen out of favor with him. "It is a pleasure to meet you, Miss Lucas." Mr. Collins tried to bow respectfully but found this exacerbated his broken nose and made his head throb. He blindly groped his way to his chair, and with a heavy thud, he plopped down into it. Charlotte watched with worry as the chair creaked and groaned in response to his action.

Charlotte softly inquired, "I hope you don't mind me asking, but it seems like you're injured. Whatever happened?"

He was in no position to tell the truth. "I, um, I ran into something in the dark last night." Mr. Collins was happy about her respectful form of questioning him.

"Maybe you should have stayed in your room and not gone exploring where you do not belong," Lydia spoke up from across the room. She had no warmth for the man that had wanted to commit her sister to a life of degradation.

The door opened and Mrs. Hill announced that the Netherfield party had come calling. She curtsied as they passed her, Mr. Bingley and Mr. Darcy in the lead, with Miss Bingley sullenly following. Standing, Elizabeth invited them to sit and asked Mrs. Hill to bring more tea and refreshments. While Elizabeth was performing the introductions, Kitty excused herself for a moment as she went to fetch Jane and Mary.

Mr. Collins couldn't believe his eyes when he saw his noble patroness's nephew arrive at his cousin's house. "Mr. Darcy of Pemberley?"

"Yes, do you know it?" Mr. Darcy looked at the overly stout man before him. Two black eyes and a broken nose marred his face.

At his servile best, he bowed and scraped even while seated across from Darcy. "Not so you would say, but my esteemed patroness Lady Catherine de Bourgh speaks of it and her nephew regularly. Let me assure you that as my taking leave of her not six days ago, she was in perfect health, as was your cousin Miss Anne de Bourgh." Pausing for breath he noticed that Mr. Darcy had sat next to Elizabeth on the settee. "You should not be sitting next to my cousin. What would your fiancé the Rose of Kent think?"

His words took Darcy aback. He had felt comfortable with the Bennet ladies, and they accepted him. It was rather surprising that someone in their home would behave so. Seeing the upset faces around the room gave him the courage he needed to counter the imbecile. "Who told you such scurrilous lies? I will have you know, I am engaged to no one. I am not and have never been engaged to my cousin Anne. As for where I sit, that is my choice and Anne may think what she wishes, as I have no connection to her beyond the ties of blood," Darcy exclaimed.

"Why, your esteemed aunt Lady Catherine speaks of it often. Everyone in Kent is aware of your engagement. It is of long standing. An arrangement made between your mothers at your birth. Do not let my impertinent cousin distract you from your duty. She is comely enough but does not even have her sister's beauty. She also has an independent streak her father and I are trying to rid her of." Wilberforce was beyond confused. Why were things not going as they should? His cousin Thomas laughed at him when some unknown lout injured him. His cousin Elizabeth showed him no respect, even though her father had agreed to their marriage. The only person who had shown him genuine regard since he got here was the woman who must surely be nearly on the shelf. And now his patroness's nephew was challenging her dictates. What was the world coming to?

Mrs. Bennet was very glad Mrs. Hill had alerted her. To be witness to that man disparaging her daughter stirred her ire beyond what she could tolerate. "Mr. Collins, I fear your head injury has made you irrational and you are saying things you do not mean. I am sure you never meant to insult my guest and my daughter. I ask you to leave this room, sir." Her voice stern, she brooked no room for disagreement. She had long had to put up with her husband, but she would not allow a man visiting her home to insult her daughter so in company.

Mr. Collins had never been so upset and confused. Standing, he gave no bow to the matron of the house as he passed her. She deserved no respect; none of them deserved respect. If his beloved Lady Catherine had not commanded him to return married or, at the very least, engaged, he would have returned to his parish already.

Charlotte Lucas quietly excused herself and followed him out of the room. She saw an opportunity and took it.

Darcy witnessed the trembling in Elizabeth's hands and wanted to separate her from the group and make sure she was alright. Something in him demanded that he help the lady who had already helped him so much. "Mrs. Bennet, I was just thinking that I would love to stretch my legs. Would it be too presumptuous of me to request to walk with Miss Elizabeth in your garden?"

"That would be superb. Be sure to get her to show you the bench under the arbor. It is quite charming." Her smile was quite maternal as she watched him offer his arm to her distressed daughter. Observing Jane and Mary's presence, she grouped everyone to converse and served tea, thwarting Miss Bingley's attempt to follow the couple.

***

DARCY DID NOT MISS how tight Elizabeth clutched at his arm. How could a man who was her relative treat her so? It was not right. "Miss Elizabeth, tell me if I can do anything to help you recover your equanimity." He placed a reassuring hand over hers, resting on the crook of his right arm, to provide her with comfort.

"Just walk with me for a time. It has been a very trying day." Elizabeth was eminently grateful for Mr. Darcy's support. Time passed nicely as they walked in companionable silence. Once having walked enough to return to her naturally curious state, Elizabeth wondered at some of her cousin's statements. "Mr. Darcy, I know my cousin is a fool, but I am curious about the things he was spouting. Is your aunt trying to get you to marry her daughter?"

Though Darcy had no involvement in the plot, its annoying existence kept rearing its head. "Yes; after my father died, she started prattling about it incessantly. I have never agreed with her plan. I do not agree with cousins marrying each other." Darcy had often wondered why so many people supported the practice as they did.

"Is it just that you do not want that sort of connection with your cousin, or is that based on another principle?" Elizabeth certainly did not want to marry her cousin.

"I have worked with animals long enough to know you do not breed animals that are closely related without risking significant issues arising in the offspring. My cousin suffers from very poor health and I think it is the same thing that brought my mother to an early grave. I would not want to pass the illness on to any children of mine." People had often told Darcy that his opinions were ridiculous, and he was curious to know what Elizabeth thought.

"That is very logical. I am struggling with a similar problem and find myself just as opposed to marrying my cousin." Elizabeth did not know why she felt comfortable sharing this with Mr. Darcy, but she did.

"Please tell me you are not being encouraged to marry that presumptuous fellow I just met." That would be a truly uneven match. Darcy could not even stomach the idea.

Elizabeth felt an irresistible urge to tell Mr. Darcy of her troubles. She had a feeling that he could provide her with the solace she longed for. "My father and Mr. Collins have been conspiring to force my hand. In fact, young Kiernan saved me only last night. He had heard their plotting to have Mr. Collins sneak into my room. They know I will refuse an offer and are seeking other means." Elizabeth resented that her voice was not the confident and assured one that she was used to hearing when she spoke. It sounded small and lost, and she hated that her father still had that power to affect her so.

"What happened? Are you alright, Miss Elizabeth?" His dark, coffee-colored eyes widened in shock.

"I have been staying in one of my sisters' rooms since he arrived. I had thought it was a foolish precaution, but I was wrong. Kiernan got his older brother Knox to hide in my bedroom with him, and when Mr. Collins showed up, it did not go well for him. Knox has an apprenticeship with the blacksmith and tolerates no disrespect to women of any age or kind." As affected by everything as she was, Elizabeth still would have liked to be witness to the goings on. Seeing the sniveling man taken down a peg would have been nice.

"That would explain his broken nose. I applaud young Kiernan's actions and those of his brother." Darcy could not fathom being so unsafe in one's home. His own home had not been happy, but he had the best of everything and had certainly never worried about his safety.

Elizabeth was just as glad that Kiernan had acted as he did, maybe more so. "Yes, between Kiernan and his brother and Mrs. Allen, they handled everything last night without my knowing. It was a shock to learn about it this morning. I know my father is not a good man, but to find out that he suggested to Mr. Collins that he sneak into my bedroom at night has been too much."

"Are you and your sisters safe? With him staying here?" Darcy questioned.

"We have been staying in pairs and now we have even arranged for the maids to stay in our rooms at night. It should not be this unsettled for long. He must return to his parish and your aunt in less than a fortnight." They were all counting down the hours and Elizabeth was thinking of figuring out the minutes.

"I fear for you, Miss Elizabeth. This is a lot to handle." Darcy wished there was some way he could protect the Bennet ladies, but society and the law were against him. Women were basically property, and husbands and fathers could decide how they were to be treated. He could not even offer them refuge, as Mr. Bennet had the right to demand them back. Maybe he could discuss this with his cousin when he arrived.

"I grew up in an uncertain environment and it has taught me the power of resilience. My courage always rises to the occasion." Elizabeth hoped at least it would continue to hold true.

Chapter Twelve

With a sigh, Wickham tried to adjust his position against the rough bark of the tree where he was sitting on the forest floor. He took his frustration out on a handful of fallen leaves. He felt anger bubbling up inside as he cursed, unable to comprehend that he had committed to five years of service in the militia. He had signed papers when he joined, but never figured they would be so serious about his sticking around. When he had brought up the fact that he was tiring of it all with Lieutenant Denny, Denny warned him against trying to leave before his five years were up. Wickham opened a bottle of whiskey, the taste of the cool liquid burning down his throat as he took a swig.

Denny explained they caught someone trying to slink out of camp and they flogged him. It was a punishable offense to leave without permission during a time of war. They labeled it as desertion. They hung people for that.

As someone who had avoided punishment for his crimes for most of his life, this brought him up short. He took a deep gulp of his drink, thinking about the outcome of his actions. He would either need to leave the country soon after he fled this drudgery or he would have to stick with it. But how would he stick around without the luxuries he deserved in his life? It was all that prude Darcy's fault. He destroyed more leaves in retribution, and more whiskey numbed his frustration.

Wickham was sure he was born to enjoy a life of luxurious comfort, even though his father was a steward. His looks and demeanor gave him the right to live his life how he wanted. He deserved nicer clothes, even if he couldn't afford them. He did not need anyone to draw attention to the lies and inconsistencies in the stories that he told the women he was hoping to charm. If things had gone as they should have, he would have been tremendously wealthy by now. He simply wanted what he deserved. But right now, he was happy to drink his whiskey and plot.

***

KIERNAN PAUSED IN HIS imaginings to ask Elizabeth a question. "So William came to England and took over just because he won the fight against England's King Harold and killed him?" He was loving the bloodier parts of history. His walk that day was full of imaginary sword fights and grandiose battles. Branch in hand, he ran around the rocky terrain, vaulting off of moss-covered rocks and around the trunks of ancient trees. Elizabeth was ambling toward the peak of Oakham Mount, yet Kiernan was bouncing to the summit.

"He felt he had a right to the throne as well. He was the one who had the Domesday Book created," Elizabeth said. She drew crisp fall air into her lungs. She relished the earthy scent and its curative power. The beautiful vista of trees dressed in all their autumn splendor. The wind whispered through the leaves and sent them dancing to the forest floor. It was all a balm to her wounded soul.

"I don't understand why he thought that if he was from France. How could he think an English king could be from another country?" He hopped over a fallen log, only to have his foot slip on the decaying forest matter.

"Oh goodness, please do not fall." Elizabeth reached out to steady him. "As we get closer to the top, the edges of the path become steeper. What would I tell your family if you fell?"

"I will be careful," Kiernan reassured her, but it did not seem to stop his enthusiastic exploration.

"The first King George was not from England, he was from Hanover, Germany. Do you remember the name of his son?" Elizabeth gathered her skirts and climbed up and over another log that must have come down in the last rainstorm.

"That's an easy one. George, and he named his son George. The regent is the fourth George." Climbing a boulder to see how far they had left, he spotted two figures in the distance. "Miss Elizabeth, there are some people up ahead."

Elizabeth shaded her eyes and looked in the direction he pointed further up the trail. "Can you tell who it is from there?"

Something about the scene before Kiernan made him uneasy. "I think it's a soldier. It is someone wearing a red coat. The other person must be Mr. Darcy on Crumpet. I recognize Crumpet from here," Kiernan whispered.

***

THE SOUND OF SOMEONE passing on the nearby path startled
Wickham out of his doze. After another swig of his whiskey,
he grumbled with anger when he finished it after the second
mouthful. Wickham tossed the bottle further into the woods and
grumbled about everything conspiring against him. With unsteady
movements, he rose and looked through the trees, trying to figure out
the source of the sounds that had awoken him. He had to be careful,
especially as the world seemed to spin and refuse to focus when he
moved too quickly.

It seemed to be someone on a big dark horse, definitely not a soldier
in a red coat. No red coat meant he was safe. There was some reason
that he was afraid of the red coats. The realization that it was Darcy
on that great dark horse of his struck him like a bolt of lightning and
seemed to burn off some of the alcohol. The world liked him. It had
just brought him a gift, a world without that annoying Darcy in it.

Wickham stared in confusion at the layer of crushed leaves on his
trousers, but ignored that issue for the moment. He reached for the
pistol that he always carried. It only took a few attempts to pull it free.
It held a single shot, and he had often found it useful. He lurched
after Darcy, his alcohol-infused mind muddled, trying to concoct a
plan to get Darcy out of his life permanently. Darcy was not going
fast on his horse and seemed to take in the view. The addle brain fool.
The next time Darcy stopped to look out over the vista before him,
Wickham decided he would act. This was going to be fun.

***

Kɪᴇʀɴᴀɴ ʜᴇʟᴘᴇᴅ Mɪss Eʟɪᴢᴀʙᴇᴛʜ up on the higher ground so that she could observe what was happening. As Elizabeth gazed at the scene before her, she felt the peace she had gained that morning bleed away. Mr. Darcy did not seem to realize that Lieutenant Wickham was behind him. Wickham seemed to move through the trees to get closer.

The narrow part of the path was not much further on and he could not stay hidden for much longer. If Wickham was going to do something, it would have to be soon, which meant that she would have to hurry.

She knew what she had to do, and with a stern look, she told Kiernan to stay where he was. She clambered down from the rock, the rough surface of the stone scraping against her skin as she started to track Wickham. When he took aim with the weapon in his hand, Elizabeth knew she had to do something. She knew she did not have the strength to stop him with force, so Elizabeth would have to use cunning. "Lieutenant Wickham, I had not expected to see you on my walk. Are you enjoying the fresh autumn day?" Looking over his shoulder, it reassured her to notice that Mr. Darcy had heard her and was heading over.

"Why are you here? I was doing something and now you are here," Wickham drunkenly exclaimed. It had taken all of his concentration to hold the pistol steady, and now the impertinent one was here. The one who withstood his charms.

Elizabeth started inching her way up the path, trying to get closer to where Darcy was. Lieutenant Wickham had been drinking, and he was certainly not to be trusted. "I was walking up the path and saw your red coat. It would have been rude not to say hello." The path toward Darcy was rockier than she remembered. She needed to be careful of how she placed her feet.

Wickham's thoughts were in a jumble, and he knew he was forgetting something. "What are you doing here? You did not believe me. Why did you not believe me? Everyone believes me." He followed Miss Elizabeth's retreating form with a wavering shuffle and tried to remember what he had been doing before she distracted him.

"Believe you, Mr. Wickham?" Elizabeth realized that the man before her was not in his right mind. The weapon in his hand was waving wildly as he spoke, and he was making little sense. She hoped Kiernan had stayed where he was.

"The story has worked so many times and sympathy leads to so much fun. Why do you not believe me? I practiced!" Wickham moaned. He scratched his head with his gun barrel and moaned about his confusion. He was supposed to complete a task. As he trailed the woman out of the trees, he had trouble staying on his feet.

She was afraid to look for Darcy and risk angering Wickham, which would probably be worse than this odd confusion. "I am sorry that I must have disappointed you, Lieutenant Wickham." Elizabeth showed her sorrow for him and took a few steps back, attempting to get closer to Darcy.

"No, that is a lie! You are a liar. You laughed at me with your sister, the plain one who should have fallen for me too!" He stomped angrily up to her, his voice echoing through the air with his frustration.

"I am sorry. That was not nice of me at all," Elizabeth all but squeaked as she tried to stay out of his range.

"No, it was not. I was doing something before. I think you distracted me." He swiped at her and caught her wrist with his free hand. In his aggravation, he shook her and tried to think, but her loud yelping was making it hard to focus. "You need to keep your mouth shut. I am trying to remember."

***

Darcy had been enjoying the peaceful fall weather and the time away from Caroline Bingley. Now he was watching a terrifying confrontation unfold before him. He had been so absorbed in his love of nature he did not know anyone was in the area until he heard Miss Elizabeth. Wickham's unsteady movements and incoherent speech suggested he was drunk, if not insane. He wanted to step in, but with the pistol in motion, it was not yet safe to do so. He would have to bide his time.

He had chosen to stay put until Wickham had seized Elizabeth and shook her. He knew that Miss Elizabeth was often so animated and enthusiastic she seemed larger than life, but now, watching the encounter, he saw how small she was. Though taller than Miss Mary, she was still of a much slighter frame than a full-grown man. Yet she had, if his suspicion was correct, confronted him on her own. What had she said yesterday about her courage rising to the occasion?

Immediately jumping off his horse, he dashed to where Miss Elizabeth was in danger. Wickham had her by the arm and was shaking her back and forth. She seemed to have less substance than a rag doll he had once seen his sister play with. Knowing she could not withstand much more, Darcy knew he had to get Wickham's attention away from Miss Elizabeth so that she could get free. The pit of his stomach seemed to drop when he realized how close they stood to the edge. There was more at risk here than Wickham being drunk and dangerous. One wrong move and either or both of them could fall.

The urgent need to help Miss Elizabeth pushed Darcy to make his move and speak. "Wickham, were you by chance looking for me?" At the back of his mind, a gentle thought echoed that there was something beyond altruism at work here. But he did not have time to listen to that little voice. He had to make sure Miss Elizabeth was safe.

"Darcy, I was forgetting something, and I think it was you." Wickham forced his eyes to focus on the man who held so much of his hate. There had been a plan that involved Darcy. That was before the impertinent one had distracted him. Peering down at her and then at the gun in his other hand, he tried to connect the dots.

"I think you were looking for Mr. Darcy. I am ever so sorry I distracted you." Elizabeth uttered the lie, her jaw locked to keep the pain inside as his fingers dug into her wrist. When she looked over her shoulder, she noticed she was near the brink.

"That's what happened. I was trying to shoot Darcy and you... you impertinent one... You confused me," he growled.

"Wickham, I will talk with you, just the two of us, if you let Miss Elizabeth go. She has nothing to do with a quarrel between men," Darcy spoke up, hoping he would fall for this ploy. Elizabeth was dangerously close to the edge. Darcy did not know how far the drop was and did not want to find out.

"I did not want to talk to you, Darcy the Dull. I just wanted to do this." Bringing up his gun arm, he tried to shoot, only to be stopped by a blinding pain.

Elizabeth saw Wickham's intent, and everything seemed to slow. "No!" In desperation, she bit down on the hand holding her wrist, forcing him to let her go and causing enough distraction that the shot went wide and missed Darcy.

"Why did you do that? I had a good shot!" He reacted with rage, his gun hand lashing out and delivering a harsh slap across her face. The sheer force of the blow knocked her off her feet, and before she knew it, she was tumbling over the edge.

***

ELIZABETH EXPERIENCED THE ODDEST sensation of being weightless. The cloudy sky, a mix of dark blue and gray above her, filled her vision. Even though she tried to reach out and grab at something, anything, she seemed unable to slow her fall. Flashes of green interspersed with brown and everything moving so fast that her thoughts were as hard to grasp as what she needed to slow her plummet. Then there was a great flash of unbearable pain and then nothing.

***

Darcy's entire world seemed to freeze, and he saw nothing but the look on Elizabeth's face as she flew over the edge. Her green eyes, normally expressive and joking, had gone wide with alarm, her eyebrows raised high on her face. Her typical smile or smirk had no place on a face full of fright. It was a high-pitched wail from behind him that finally spurred him into motion.

"Where did she go?" It astounded Wickham that Miss Elizabeth had apparently disappeared. She was there, and then not.

"You knocked her off the edge, you drunken wretch. You are a blight on society and if I was not the man I am I would kill you where you stood." Shoving Wickham away from himself and the edge, Darcy tried to formulate a plan of descent. He thought he could see her blue dress about fifteen feet below where he was now. He would have to be very careful to not dislodge her or send debris onto her.

Wickham looked down at where Darcy knelt and thought of how easy it would be just to shove him over. His liquor-fogged brain had still not processed how the woman had disappeared or why Darcy was so upset. Before he acted on his thought, pain in his shin erupted and rattled his thoughts once again.

"Miss Elizabeth!" Voice hoarse with terror, Kiernan came running up the path from where he had been hiding. When he saw the soldier who had knocked Miss Elizabeth off the edge, lean over to push Mr. Darcy, he kicked the coward in the shin with all his might.

"Why would you do that?" Wickham fell over backward, away from the edge. With a deep breath, he pulled himself up from the ground and limped towards Darcy's horse. He made a grab for the reins that hung loose. It surprised him when the horse jerked them out of his grasp. With a growl of anger, he tried again, only to have the giant creature snap at him, just missing his hand. The horse made a show of his displeasure, his nose flaring and feet stomping. No one wanted to help him, not even the horse. Wickham tried to put as much distance between himself and the area as possible. His unsteady legs carried him away from the scene.

Kiernan ignored the man as he retreated and flung himself to the ground beside Mr. Darcy. He had stayed behind as Miss Elizabeth told him and he hated himself for it. Tears leaked from his eyes as he searched desperately for the woman who he viewed as his sister. He knew she was down there, but where?

"Kiernan, I wondered if you were here somewhere." Darcy tore his eyes from that scrap of blue cloth that he could see and to the boy beside him. Kiernan's face was awash in tears and he had gotten mud all over himself, probably when he hid. His breath was coming in quick pants. The poor boy had seen everything, and he cared so much for Elizabeth, such an event had to have terrorized him horribly. With just the two of them, they would have to work together to fix things.

"Miss Elizabeth told me to stay hidden and not to come out. You didn't see it but he was gonna shoot you and she stopped him, but now she fell. He was still here, but I kicked him. What are we going to do, Mr. Darcy?" Kiernan felt like his mind would not stop spinning and his heart was running as fast as Crumpet could.

"Kiernan, we are going to have to work together to save Miss Elizabeth. I need you to take a few deep breaths with me. In and out. Nice and slow." Darcy pulled Kiernan's hand to his chest so he could feel him breathing. For a few moments, it felt like time had stopped, but eventually Kiernan's breaths calmed and they could both concentrate.

"Alright, what do we need to do next?" He swiped his tears away with his sleeve, his attention now on the task they had to do. They would save Miss Elizabeth.

"We need help and a long rope to get Miss Elizabeth back up. I need you to ride to Netherfield and get Bingley and maybe some stable hands and we need rope." Darcy could not force himself to leave Elizabeth, not when she needed him. He could not let a child try to climb down to her. It would be too risky. He would do it himself once he got Kiernan on Cadmus.

"You want me to ride Crumpet? To Netherfield? What are you going to do?" Kiernan looked over at Crumpet. He had not wanted the soldier to ride him, but had been fine with him riding him before.

"Yes, you rode him before, and it was fine. He likes you and he knows the way back to Netherfield. Do you know your way to Netherfield?" Darcy got up and walked over to Cadmus, soothing him with a caress.

"I know the way. I will get help and bring it back. Tell Miss Elizabeth I'm coming back with help." With a determined breath, Kiernan stood and ran his hands along the velvety texture of Crumpet's nose. He was friends with Crumpet and together they would get help. Mr. Darcy hefted him onto the great, towering horse, and he grabbed chunks of the horse's luxuriant black mane.

"Kiernan, here are the reins. They help lead him where you want him to go. He probably will stay at a walk unless you try to get him to go faster. I do not want you to go too fast or else you risk falling off." Darcy looked the boy over. He had a good natural seat, and he prayed the boy made it to Netherfield swiftly and without incident.

"I will bring back the help, Mr. Darcy." Kiernan clicked his tongue like he had seen other riders do and was off.

***

DARCY CAREFULLY DESCENDED THE cliff, desperately trying to reach Elizabeth. Scrubby bushes clung to the cliffside, giving him handholds but obstructing his view. Cautiously and thoughtfully placing his hands and feet, he eventually reached her. He realized Elizabeth had landed on a small ledge and seemed to be at no risk of sliding further down. There was one worry solved, at least.

He inched his way closer, being careful to avoid any loose rocks and gravel, so he could get close enough to see what her condition was. She was not making any noise, and he found the silence disheartening. He wanted to hear her laughing voice tell him she was perfectly fine, but that was not to be. Finally, after what seemed like years of effort but was only a double handful of minutes, he reached her.

He looked her over, assessing her condition with his eyes first. There were various rips and rents in her once lovely blue dress, but there was not a lot of blood. That had to be good. He could clearly see her face, and it nearly broke his heart. It was so bruised. Because of the fall or the hit from Wickham, her face was swelling, turning a purplish-red. His fingers shook as he reached out to feel her slender throat, and he went weak in relief when he found her pulse strong, steady, and very reassuring.

Her hair had come free of its confines and was a riot of chestnut curls. It had gathered various leaves and twigs in her tumble. Shifting his eyes down her form, he noticed her left arm rested at an unnatural angle, most likely broken. Her right arm seemed fine beyond some scrapes and contusions. Darcy tried to convince himself she would be fine. Besides the broken arm, he saw no major injuries. Reaching out, he held her right hand, hoping it would bring them both comfort. He would feel so much better if she was awake. He was at a loss to explain why he had such a need to see her lips curl into a delighted smirk. Why would such desperation grip him over a pair of clear emerald eyes?

***

KIERNAN WAS GRATEFUL CRUMPET was such a smart horse. It had not taken long for him to realize that he did not know how to use the reins. Crumpet was heading back to Netherfield without direction. He was the best horse and Kiernan was going to ask to give him an entire bag of sugar lumps. They were moving as fast as possible without Kiernan falling out of the saddle.

They would be there shortly, and the help he needed for Miss Elizabeth was almost within reach. Kiernan worried about Miss Elizabeth but knew that Mr. Darcy cared about her too and would take care of her until he got back. Up ahead on the path, Kiernan saw the entrance to Netherfield's property. They were almost there, Kiernan letting go of the reins entirely before he reached down to give Crumpet a hug around the neck. In what seemed like no time, Kiernan had reached the front steps of Netherfield, but there was not anyone outside to help him. He would have to get off Crumpet and go inside to get help.

Holding on to the saddle, Kiernan swung his leg around and let his legs dangle. Looking down over his shoulder, he saw that the ground still seemed pretty far away. Despite this, he let go and fell to the ground, dropping like a sack of potatoes. Not even brushing himself off, he bounded up the stairs.

"Somebody, I need help! Help, somebody, is Mr. Bingley here?" Desperate, he glanced around, trying to find a person who could help. Where were all the servants?

Caroline Bingley had been relaxing in the parlor, perusing a fashion magazine and feeling intolerably bored, when a ruckus disturbed her. She flung her magazine to the ground, her temper rising as the servants had not yet tended to the disturbance. "How dare you!" There in the hall, a dirty waif of a boy was tracking dirt into her home, screaming with uncouth vigor. She may hate living here, but she would not permit her home to be invaded by filthy rustics.

"Ma'am, we need ..." Kiernan did not get to finish before a firm slap across his face knocked him off his feet. Looking up with wide eyes, he stared uncomprehendingly at the woman in a frilly mustard dress with a look of hatred on her face. Who was this horrible person?

"I did not give you leave to address me or enter my home, you disgusting urchin. You are not welcome here and will get out immediately." Outrage filled her that such a dirty being had had the audacity to come into her home. Caroline reached for his arm, and jerked him up and dragged him out the door, locking it behind him. She glanced down at her dress and realized it had been soiled. Who knew if it would come out? Frankly, right now she felt like burning it. She was in such a state.

***

HE RAN UP TO Crumpet and embraced him, his tears wetting Crumpet's fur. Not only had a hateful woman hit him, but now he did not know how he would ever get help for Miss Elizabeth. What was he going to do? He had to find help. He just had to!

Chapter Thirteen

GEORGIANA SAVORED THE SIGHT of the fall scenery from the window of her well-sprung carriage. It was so much nicer in the country than in London, at least in her opinion. "Do you think William will mind that we arrived early without informing him?" She questioned her cousin who rode his giant golden charger Achilles alongside the carriage. She smiled to see him riding today, as his injury in battle had prevented him from riding for some time.

Colonel Theodore Fitzwilliam had wasted no time in leaving London once they had completed the preparations. "Of course not! He is missing you something fierce, if my guess means anything. I think it is ruder that we have not informed our host, but Charles Bingley has invited me to come any time I wish. So, I am not regretful of coming when we did." He knew they were very close to Bingley's leased estate as they turned off to the property some minutes ago. He was getting sore and would be glad to walk around.

Mrs. Ansley was pleased to see her charge so enthusiastic. "Miss Georgiana, it is wonderful to see you so excited. I think this visit to the country will be an agreeable change for everyone."

"I believe so, Mrs. Ansley. Even accounting for Caroline Bingley, I think we will quite enjoy ourselves." Even though she knew her comment was not exactly polite, Georgiana could not remove the smile from her face. It would not do to lie, after all. She precariously leaned out of the window, her fingertips tingling from the cold air as she attempted to get a view of the residence they were visiting. Her cry of surprise had everyone looking at her in alarm. "Is that not Crumpet?"

There on the path before them was an admittedly grand dwelling that must be Netherfield. Yet the dignified building was not what had them all concerned. It was the fact that her brother's horse was there in front of it. There was also a little boy trying to get on the horse, struggling in vain as he was a small boy and the horse was rather large.

Theodore instantly became alert at the sight and spurred Achilles forward. He had helped to train Cadmus himself and he knew the horse would not let just anyone on his back, and could injure if necessary. That Cadmus was patiently waiting for the child to mount and not shying away meant something significant. Theodore dismounted his horse and approached the pair, moving slowly, not wanting to startle either of them.

"That is a mighty big horse to mount without help, little man." Theodore was close enough to see the evidence of tears and an injury on the boy's face.

Kiernan dropped to the ground from where he had been trying to pull himself into the saddle. He turned to see a man behind him, followed by a horse even bigger than Crumpet. "Oh! Help me! You have to help. Mr. Darcy sent me for help, but the mean lady kicked me out and locked the door. Are you Mr. Bingley?" Wiping at his face, he tried to hide the evidence of his tears.

"I am Theo, little man, Darcy's cousin. Did you say he needed help? What is happening?" His military mind was instantly alert and ready for action. He also looked over the boy, who seemed to be having a very tough time of it. Mud coated his clothes and his hair was in disarray. One side of his face was swelling from a blow, and his light brown eyes seemed wild with fear.

"The soldier hit Miss Elizabeth, and she fell off the edge of the cliff. Mr. Darcy said he was going to climb down to her but he would need a long rope and more men to get her back up again. I rode all the way here like he said, but when I went inside to ask for Mr. Bingley and to get help, the angry lady started screaming and threw me out of the house. We have to help them, we just have to!" Kiernan wailed.

He peered over the lad's shoulder and saw that the carriage had arrived and Georgiana and Mrs. Ansley had positioned themselves by the convenience. They would see to the lad while he did some yelling. "Do not worry, little man, we will help them. I will get the rope and some men and we will rescue your Miss Elizabeth. Can you wait here with these ladies for a bit while I gather what we need?"

"Yes, sir." Looking at the ladies, Kiernan was glad they both seemed much nicer than the horrible screaming one. A pale pink dress adorned the younger girl. Between her clear blue eyes and pale blond hair, he thought she looked like one of the princesses from the stories his Mam told. The other lady was older but not as old as his Mam, and her smile was so reassuring he almost felt like crying again.

Mrs. Ansley felt her heart go out to the poor thing. He had obviously had a time of it and yet was trying to be brave. "You have had quite the adventure today, it seems. What is your name, sweetheart?" Wetting a handkerchief from the canteen of water. She wiped some of the mud from his face.

"I am Kiernan Anderson, ma'am." Kiernan relaxed under the careful ministrations of the nice lady.

Once his face was clean, she could see the full extent of the fresh bruise on his face. A puffiness was forming near the corner of his eye, expanding down his cheekbone. It had yet to change from an angry red to the darker purple color that was sure to come. "It is nice to meet you, Master Anderson. I am Mrs. Ansley and the lady beside me is Miss Georgiana Darcy, Mr. Darcy's little sister. It sounds like you have been very brave today. How did you get this mark on your face? It looks very painful."

"The angry lady called me a disgusting urchin and hit me before she threw me out of the house." His voice was barely a murmur; his shame at being called disgusting hurt more than his face did.

Georgiana reached over to stroke his hair out of his eyes. "You are nothing of the sort. I find you gallant, much like a knight riding to the rescue of a fair maiden. Her actions were reprehensible." She glanced at Mrs. Ansley and noticed the fire snapping in her eyes before she quickly shuttered them. It would not do to upset the child, but Georgiana had a feeling Caroline Bingley would soon have an awakening.

***

Colonel Fitzwilliam marched around the outside of the manor house in search of the stables. Even if it had not been Darcy

165

requesting aid, you did not turn away those in need. Caroline Bingley had always annoyed him, but to throw out a child in need of help was beyond the pale. He quickened his pace when he saw a stable hand.

"You there, do you work for Bingley?" Theodore's air of command always prompted a quick response, which was what he needed.

"Jonah Moore at your service. I am one of Mr. Bingley's grooms, sir. How may I be of assistance?"

Theodore liked the ready way Jonah responded. "Darcy has sent for help. It sounds like someone knocked Miss Elizabeth off a cliff. We need rope, and Bingley needs to be alerted. Is there a doctor in the area?"

Jonah's mind flew over the number of things they would need to do to rescue Miss Elizabeth. "There is only an apothecary in town, Mr. Jones, but he is very skilled. I will send a boy to fetch him and bring him here. We have a suitable length of rope in the stable. I will gather it. Mr. Bingley is inside. I will have him brought out to you. Do I need to gather some men to help?"

"I believe if you get Bingley, the three of us should be able to accomplish the rescue. My cousin and her companion are in the carriage in front of the manor house. We had plans to surprise Bingley and my cousin Darcy by arriving early for our visit. I am going to speak with my men, if you could send Bingley to meet me there." He wished he knew how far the lady had fallen, because it might change how they needed to proceed.

"I will send him out to you at once." Jonah turned and rushed into the building.

***

THEODORE RETURNED TO FIND Georgiana encouraging the boy to drink from the canteen of water they traveled with. It looked like she had the food hamper open. The boy could probably use something sweet as well. He made eye contact with Mrs. Ansley in order to let her know he wanted her to meet him at his horse while he checked his saddlebags.

"How is the lad fairing?" he asked while strapping on his pistols.

"His name is Kiernan, and he is doing better after some reassurance and water. He rode all the way from somewhere called Oakham Mount. There, a soldier tried to kill Mr. Darcy but seems to have knocked a lady off a cliff instead. I do not quite have the complete picture, but it sounds dire. Upon reaching what he thought was help, an angry lady, who I assume was Miss Bingley, struck him and threw him from the house. This after calling the poor boy a disgusting urchin!" Mrs. Ansley did not hide how furious she was, even though she modulated her voice so as not to be overheard by the child.

"Mr. Bingley will meet us out here and the groom is gathering rope. I am going to leave Jacob and Hugh here with you and Georgiana. Please arrange with the housekeeper to have a room prepared for the lady. I do not know what condition she will be in when we return with her, but the apothecary is being sent for." He was grateful that Mrs. Ansley was cool under pressure, as they would certainly need it today.

"I suspect you will take young Kiernan with you so he can lead the way. I will make sure that he has eaten something before you go." Giving a quick nod of her head, she left to see to the child.

Theodore moved to whisper to the grooms that had once served under him. They doubled as guards and he felt comfortable leaving the ladies in their care. He had only just finished informing them of the situation when Bingley came hurrying down the steps.

Bingley was eager to help however he could. "Theo, I would say it is wonderful to see you and Georgiana, but we have an emergency. Jonah said Darcy had sent for help. What can I do?"

Theodore felt Bingley should know what a disgrace his sister was. "We have quite the situation, Bingley. It sounds like a soldier shoved a lady named Miss Elizabeth off a cliff. Darcy sent that little boy here on his horse for help. But when he got here and went inside calling for help, your shrew of a sister struck him, called him a disgusting urchin and threw him out. We ran into him trying to get help somewhere else."

"My sister did what?" Outrage rang out in his simple question.

"The poor kid's face is going to bruise," Theodore bit out tersely.

Bingley wished it surprised him. "That settles it. She is not fit to play any role in my household. But that is neither here nor there. What do you need right now?" Pushing back at emotions that he was unaccustomed to, Bingley looked at what had to happen right now. There would be enough time later to deal with his anger and frustration.

Theodore was glad that Bingley did not deny what his sister had done. "Georgiana and Mrs. Ansley will need rooms and there will need to be one prepared for the injured lady. I do not trust Miss Bingley. Will Mrs. Hurst be able to handle the task, or should Mrs. Ansley step in and collaborate with your housekeeper?"

Bingley wished desperately that his oldest sister was healthy enough and strong-willed enough to stand up against Caroline. "Mrs. Hurst has been unwell of late and has taken to her bed most days. If Mrs. Ansley could take over, I would be grateful. I will speak with Mrs. Nichols now and let her know to work with Mrs. Ansley. Do I need to gather any supplies?"

***

DARCY HELD HIMSELF IN place, trying to make sure he would not slip. He wished help would arrive soon. He hated that he had nothing to help Elizabeth with, but at least she was not bleeding heavily. Brushing her curls away from her face, he found himself fascinated by the spring in her curl. Of its own volition, it had wrapped itself around his finger, not wanting to let go. Its silken texture was soothing. It reassured him that some part of Elizabeth was well and acknowledging his presence.

"I wish you would open your eyes and smile at me, Elizabeth. Only then will I know that all is well. You have helped me so much. Did you know that?" Darcy spoke in a murmur, unsure if she would hear him or if his voice might hurt her head. She probably hit her head somewhere in the fall. He was unsure of their stability and did not want to risk it looking for a bump. He reached over and took her good hand in his own, feeling the warmth in their connection. All he could do was wait. He found he could not seem to tear his gaze away from her crumpled form. And then suddenly there was pressure on his hand.

The hand in his own was so much smaller by comparison, its nails dainty and smooth. Yet it was so powerful, for with just one squeeze, his entire world stopped. The slightest pressure on his hand by hers and he fought for breath. Looking at her face, his breath came back in a rush, for there on her face, once so still, her eyes were open and looking at him. Barely open, merely slits, her pain was evident in the lines around her eyes, but her eyes were open and he felt like writing an ode to their clear emerald depths.

"Elizabeth, you have taken a tumble and you are hurt. I do not want you to move, but can you tell me how you feel?" Darcy spoke in a hushed voice, as if raising his voice would ruin the enchantment.

"Arm hurts most, but..." Elizabeth moaned and seemed to grit her teeth.

"Do not speak if it is too much for you," Darcy urged, guilty that he had wanted her to wake and experience this pain.

"Where?" Elizabeth focused on Darcy, trying to fight back the pain and control her fuzzy thoughts.

"We are both on the side of the cliff. You stopped about fifteen feet down from the top. Kiernan went for help on Cadmus. He knows the way. Help should be here soon."

Elizabeth remembered what had started it all. It swirled in her mind and mixed with the pain, but it still appalled her. "Wickham tried to shoot you."

Even lying there, injured, on the side of the cliff, Elizabeth was worried about him. She left Darcy in awe of her. "I was wondering what exactly happened. I knew the moment I heard your voice that something was wrong, and that you were doing something courageous." He was trying to be grateful for her actions and not feel guilty about everything, but it was difficult. Guilt had no place here on the side of a cliff.

***

"Darcy? You down there?" an unexpected voice boomed.

"Theo, is that you? When did you get here?" Darcy questioned.

"The cavalry always shows up when needed. Have I taught you nothing?" Theodore lay on his belly, trying to spot them both below him so he could come up with a plan.

"Is Miss Elizabeth alright, Mr. Darcy?" Kiernan's tremulous voice called.

"She is safe and sound, Kiernan, a little worse for wear, but she is awake and talking to me. I am very proud of how well you did, bringing back the rescue party."

"Darcy, how are you situated down there? What are Miss Elizabeth's injuries? Anything we need to be concerned about?" Theodore's rapid-fire questions were something he reverted to when dealing with a crisis. He could see his cousin leaning near the recumbent lady and was curious about what other variables he needed to consider.

Darcy leaned back as far as he could safely, to see if he could spot his cousin above him. "I wedged my feet against one of these bushes and Miss Elizabeth is on a small ledge. She broke her arm, and she has several cuts and contusions, but nothing as bad as the arm as far as I can tell."

Well, it could be worse, thought Theodore. "I am going to send down a rope. I want you to tie it around your waist. Then I'm going to send a sheet down tied to a rope. I'm hoping you can get the sheet around her like she was sitting on a swing, and we can pull you both up." Several things could go wrong with his plan, but he felt it was the best option.

Sending the ropes down, he hoped Darcy could get the sheet around Miss Elizabeth. It seemed like forever before he heard what he wanted.

Darcy knew they had to get Elizabeth back on the path and that doing so was going to hurt her. How could he do it if everything in him was screaming to keep her from pain? "I am ready, I think. Miss Elizabeth is sitting up in the swing you rigged. I tied the other rope around my waist." Darcy spoke loud enough to be heard, but his focus was on the fact that Elizabeth's face had drained of color with every movement and sweat had broken out on her brow. Her poor eyes, which had been open, were now pressed tight shut, as if in desperation to blot out the pain of movement.

***

ASCENT UP THE CLIFFSIDE was a horrid business in Elizabeth's mind, full of sharp movements and a terror that she refused to acknowledge. Her pulse throbbed in her head, and the need to vomit was almost overwhelming. She would have screamed if she had not thought that the addition of such a sound would have been too much for her current fortitude. After they had clambered over the edge and gotten back on the trail, her only focus was on taking deep breaths to quell the thudding agony in her skull. The torment in her arm was acute, but she could think of nothing that would stem it.

When she finally managed to once again open her eyes, it was to see two faces looking down at her, one dark and suddenly dear, the other light and unknown. Mr. Darcy hovered above her, worry obvious in every line of his face. His chocolate eyes, normally so magnetic, now seemed almost mournful. Across from him floated a face that was also concerned, and his blond hair and piercing blue eyes were in stark contrast to Mr. Darcy's chestnut locks and warm gaze.

"Elizabeth, tell me what we can do to help." Darcy could see how hard she was struggling against the pain, and it was a dagger in his heart.

"I think asking for a new arm would be too much," Elizabeth ground out.

"I think I like you, Miss Elizabeth. Your arm appears to be broken, but we need to see if there are any other major issues. How is your head?" Reaching down, Theodore ran his fingers along her scalp, searching for anything that might show a major head injury. The woman had made a joke and her pupils both dilated normally, so he was not overly worried.

"I can feel my heartbeat in my head. I am sure you will pardon my confusion, but who are you?"

"Oh, I beg your pardon for my lapse in manners, Miss Elizabeth. Colonel Theodore Fitzwilliam, at your service. I am this one's cousin," he said, nodding to Darcy.

That would explain his knowledge of injuries. A military man would have knowledge of such things if he had seen the battlefield. "You excuse my not curtsying, but it is nice to meet you. Are you from the militia?" she whispered, afraid to raise her voice.

"As a member of the Regulars, I have the battlefield experience enough to help your arm in a moment. I will apologize now, but I am going to check you over before we head to Netherfield." Eyeing his cousin's frown, he was quick but thorough, checking for other broken bones or wounds. "Bingley, what do you have in the saddle bags you brought? Are there any strips of cloth?" he called out to Bingley, who seemed out of sorts.

Bingley's normal enthusiasm was subdued both by the situation and his disgust for his sister. "Yes, long strips of cloth and water and several other things."

"Would you be so kind as to bring the strips over? I would like to situate this break better before we move Miss Elizabeth," Theodore explained. "Miss Elizabeth, in a moment, I'm going to get Darcy here to help you sit up so we can strap your arm to your body. That way it doesn't move around as much on the horse. It should help with some of the pain."

"You sound like you have done this before, Colonel."

Theodore liked the lady's spunk, that was for sure. "Yes, I have. You do not get through as many battles as I have without having to learn field medicine firsthand. You are definitely prettier than the soldiers I helped patch up, though." He grinned, then nodded at Darcy to signal his need for help.

Once she was in her seat, Theodore carefully positioned her arm so that her palm was resting above her heart. They wrapped it around her, so that her damaged arm stayed put. When done, they lowered her back to the ground so that she could recover her breath.

***

"Miss Elizabeth, are you alright? I was so very worried. That soldier was drunker than a wheelbarrow and when he hit you, I did not know what to do," Kiernan quavered. His courage had left him now that Elizabeth was within reach. Crawling over to her, he put his head on her good shoulder and wept.

"I will be fine, Kiernan, back to myself in no time. You have been so brave. I just need a few minutes to catch my breath before we head back to Netherfield," Elizabeth comforted. Over his sobbing form, she could see Colonel Fitzwilliam gesture to Mr. Darcy and the two of them converse out of her hearing.

***

"THE WOMAN IS YOURS, Darcy. I will not poach." Theodore chuckled at his cousin's jealousy. He had never seen him so smitten, and yet he knew Will would not admit to it.

"I do not know what you are talking about. I am merely concerned with Elizabeth's welfare. We ought to bring her back to Netherfield, and hopefully the doctor can see her shortly thereafter." Darcy knew he had feelings he did not understand, but he was unwilling to analyze them right now in this setting.

"Right." Theodore quirked his eyebrow at his befuddled cousin. "Anyway, Miss Elizabeth has a knot on her head, but I do not see any evidence to imply it is more serious than that. The fall broke her arm in at least one place near the elbow, if I am not mistaken. She has a multitude of cuts, scrapes, and bruises, and I think she will be sore for some time. I can detect nothing more than that, though. I had the apothecary summoned before we left, so he should be waiting when we get there."

Darcy sighed and said, "It's as good as it could be." He reassured himself by looking over to see that she was still safe. Bingley and Jonah were talking quietly off to the side, presumably about Netherfield.

"I think I have been fairly patient, but what happened?" There was certainly a reason he had felt the need to strap on his pistols.

"It was Wickham, and he was more than a little bosky. What is more, Miss Elizabeth and young Kiernan came upon Wickham trying to shoot me in the back. She stopped him but paid the price for her valor." Darcy's forlorn tone of voice told almost more than his words did.

"That bounder! Can I assume he slunk away like the mangy cur he is?" Theodore fumed.

"You are correct, of course. I was too concerned about Elizabeth to give him any notice. Though I think Kiernan kicked him in the shin." Darcy smiled despite himself.

"He is a tough little mite. Would you believe Caroline Bingley struck him and threw him out of the house after she called him a disgusting urchin? I informed Bingley and he says he will deal with Caroline. Mrs. Ansley is in charge at the moment, as Mrs. Hurst is ill."

"I want to say I am surprised, but I am not. At least Mrs. Ansley has a good head on her shoulders and will help care for Elizabeth. We should probably head back. I would like to get her seen by the apothecary." Wearily, he turned and walked back to Miss Elizabeth. "Elizabeth, are you rested enough? I think we should head to Netherfield."

"Normally I would not hesitate, but I know this next hurdle will not be pleasant." Elizabeth grimaced. She had never felt this cowardly in her life. The pain was overwhelming, and she just wanted it to stop. Here she was, wrapped up like one of the mummies she had read about, but she was not foolish enough to think there would not still be pain riding a horse. Being brought up the cliff had been quick but incredibly painful, and she knew it would take much longer to get to Netherfield.

"We will be as gentle as possible, but I fear you are correct. Darcy, if you get on Cadmus, I will hand her up to you. You can ride with me again, Kiernan." Theodore waited for Darcy to get situated on Cadmus before carefully lifting Elizabeth and placing her in his arms.

Holding Elizabeth on his horse before him affected Darcy more than he thought it would. He could tell she was in pain by the way she gripped at his clothing with her good hand, clutching so tightly her knuckles were a stark white. Somehow her head had settled into the curve of his neck, and he found he never wanted her to leave his arms. Glancing around, he noticed everyone had mounted, and they were ready to head back.

"We are going to move now, Elizabeth. You must tell me if I can do anything to help you endure this." Darcy signaled Cadmus to go with a gentle tap of his heels. He was thankful for the horse's perfect obedience. Cadmus seemed to recognize his precious cargo and was moving with care.

"I rather find myself in need of a distraction, Mr. Darcy. Would you mind at all talking to me?" Elizabeth struggled to take the slow breaths she knew would help with the pain. She needed to move her thoughts away from the stabbing pain that flared every time she shifted.

"Is there anything you want me to talk about?" Darcy queried.

"Tell me about you, about your home. I have heard that Derbyshire is lovely," she responded, hoping for something to focus her mind on.

"Alright. Pemberley has been home to the Darcy family since Owain D'Arcy came over with William the Conqueror. They granted him most of Derbyshire for his service..." Gathering Elizabeth close, he continued speaking of his people and the land that he called home. It felt right somehow, holding her close and feeling her soft puffs of breath on his neck while he spoke of the place that he held dear.

Chapter Fourteen

Georgiana felt that if Caroline Bingley opened her mouth to complain one more time, it would force her to chuck her teacup at the woman. It had been nonstop since Caroline realized they had arrived and that all the gentlemen had left without informing her. She complained that everyone took advantage of her kind nature. No one appreciated how hard she worked to bring culture and style to the provincial hamlet she was stuck in. Georgiana glanced around, eyeing the style of which Caroline spoke and found herself not wanting to be part of her definition of style and culture.

"And Georgiana, darling, though I find your dress quaint, you will have to learn to keep up with the latest styles. Do not worry, we can go to the shops together and I can show you." Caroline hated to spend so much time with Georgiana, but she knew it would win her Mr. Darcy's gratitude in the long run. He had no thought to fashion, but he must be embarrassed to have a sister so inept at style and high-class social graces.

Georgiana had volunteered to keep Caroline occupied while the others went about their various tasks. Mrs. Ansley was working with Mrs. Nichols to prepare a room for the poor lady being rescued, as well as the surprise guests. They had all agreed not to bring up Miss

Bingley's churlish behavior or the rescue going on at the moment. She only hoped that the unfortunate lady would be well. "Oh, I could never aspire to have the style that you do, Miss Caroline. I hope Mrs. Hurst is alright. It is not like her to be keeping to her rooms." She tried to find a safe, natural topic to change the subject, desperate for an escape from fashion.

"She is decidedly ill-mannered of late. She has not been involved in any of my decorating projects and is turning her nose up at all the marvelous dishes the French chef has prepared. At least she is keeping to her bed instead of pestering me about treating the staff better. They are here to serve me and my wishes. I will tell you now, when you are mistress of a home, you must have a firm hand with the staff or they try to take advantage," Caroline huffed. Her sister was not at all supporting her as she should. Caroline was considering refusing to acknowledge her once she married Mr. Darcy. If Louisa did not help, she would not reap the benefits later.

Georgiana refused to respond to such a comment, so she simply took another sip of tea. A commotion in the entryway spurred her to set down her cup and rush to see if she could help with anything. There in the hall stood her brother, carrying a lady who had taken an obvious tumble. Her dark tresses were a riot of curls and coils free of any containment and littered with twigs and leaves. The lady's tattered blue dress shifted as her brother carried her and revealed the cuts and scrapes underneath.

There was something about the vivid green eyes glistening with pain, and the shaky smile she forced, that captivated Georgiana. "Brother, what can I do to help?"

Darcy completely ignored Caroline Bingley's disgruntled look and spoke to his sister. "Georgiana, I have missed you dearly, but you will forgive me if I delay our hug. I would like you to meet Miss Elizabeth Bennet. Elizabeth, my sister Georgiana. Do you know where they have put her?"

Georgiana rushed to show her brother the way, eager to be of aid. She guided her brother to where everything was waiting to help the unknown girl. "It is a pleasure to meet you, Miss Elizabeth. Mrs. Ansley has put her in the room connected to mine and across the hall from your room. She has asked Mrs. Nichols to heat water for baths for whoever may need to wash up. The apothecary should be here momentarily." Georgiana was glad to leave Caroline's screeching and complaints behind.

***

Caroline was indignant at the sight before her. Mr. Darcy was hers. He did not belong to that little strumpet. "Charles, what is going on? Why was Miss Elizabeth being carried in like that? She looks atrocious. She must have some kind of nerve to allow herself to be carried around by a decent gentleman with her hair down like that."

Bingley had become progressively more angry with his sister. To see her disparaging Miss Elizabeth, who had risked herself to help his best friend, was far too much for him to ignore. He might have developed the habit of ignoring some of the more unpleasant aspects of his sister's behavior, but no more. "Caroline, you will shut your mouth and follow me to my study."

Her brother ignored her strangled screech of outrage as he stomped to his study. She chased after him, eager to remind him of his place in her life. Only when he held the door open for her did she notice that his normally placid blue eyes had become something hard and unflinching. Only once she had sat in a shockingly uncomfortable chair did her brother begin. "Did you or did you not strike a child that came here looking for help?" Bingley's voice was cold and hard.

"There was a vagabond that had managed to enter the house and I had to make him leave. We cannot just allow trash into our home. How would that look?" Caroline could not comprehend why he was paying attention to this insignificant child she had just sent on its way.

"How could I have overlooked that my sister has no human decency? I have ignored your poor behavior for the last time. Darcy sent that child you just called trash here for help. That you had the audacity to strike a child who came to my home for help sickens me!" Bingley clenched his hands on the desk, his knuckles whitening as he spoke.

"I had no way of knowing Darcy sent him," Caroline argued.

Bingley refused to budge for his sister this time. "No child should ever have to endure such mistreatment. Your actions are inexcusable. Mother and Father would be ashamed of what you have become."

"What I have become is someone conscious of my social position as you should be. What would people like Mr. Darcy or his relatives think if they knew we mixed with riffraff?" Caroline rolled her eyes at his shortsightedness.

"I can say with confidence that they would not approve of your actions. As of right now, they do not. Colonel Fitzwilliam himself told me your behavior disgusted him." How could he make his sister see that her behavior was abhorrent?

It just could not be possible that anyone of rank would fault her actions. She had spent all of her time at that miserable school for girls copying the manners of the highest-ranking girls there. "That is ridiculous! He would not hold something like that against me."

"You can choose to believe what you want. However, you will abide by the restrictions I am putting in place. You are no longer to act as mistress of any home I am a resident of. Since Louisa is unwell at the moment, I have asked Mrs. Ansley to act in that respect."

Bingley had to pause to let the screaming subside.

"You cannot allow a companion to preside over your household. This must be a joke," Caroline screeched.

"Not only is she presiding over my home, but we are paying compensation to Kiernan and his family for your act of assault. I will take a full two hundred pounds from your pin money, your entire next quarter, to pay to his family. Do not think that this is something you can get around. I will contact all the shops you frequent to let them know not to offer you credit, as I will not cover it. Also, I have decided that I will begin deducting money from what remains if you act in any manner which I deem unacceptable." Bingley only hoped that his plan would work. He would hate to have to take more drastic measures.

Caroline was fighting the growing realization that her brother was being serious. "You would not dare give my money to that urchin. And why would you get to decide what is acceptable for me?"

"I get to decide because I have full control over you and your money until such time that you turn twenty-five or you marry. Which is something you often forget because I have always wanted you to be happy. Because I love you, but you only seem to love yourself. I want you to go to your room and stay there until they summon you for dinner." Bingley was proud that he had stayed the course. He only hoped it would be better next time.

Caroline glared at him before stomping out of the room. Her anger only increased when she realized her very fashionable slippers made not a sound and she was only hurting her feet by pounding her feet on the steps.

***

MR. JONES'S EXPERIENCED EYES swept over Elizabeth to gauge her injuries. "Miss Elizabeth, what have you gotten yourself into this time?" He spoke kindly to his patient. She had a break to her arm and several superficial injuries that he could see. She was in pain and weakened, but he hoped she could recover completely.

"I fear it was nothing good, Mr. Jones," spoke Elizabeth. Her head ached and her arm was a sharp reminder of what happens when you get knocked off a cliff. She was weary and worn and she hated that she had sticks in her hair. If she did not start feeling better soon, she was afraid she was going to turn into a whiny baby.

Mr. Jones reached into his bag and pulled out several things he would need and set them on the bedside table. "Then I will have to just take care of things." Miss Elizabeth lay atop a blanket that protected the bed from her soiled attire. He went to wash his hands in the basin in the corner. Cleanliness had always been important to him. He glanced back to his patient and saw Mrs. Ansley sitting beside Miss Elizabeth, her hands slowly brushing away dirt and twigs from her hair.

"I am very grateful for your coming out so quickly to help me," Elizabeth intoned.

"Mrs. Ansley, would you mind helping Miss Elizabeth sit up so that we can unwrap her and I can assess her arm?" Once Miss Elizabeth was upright, they quickly removed the bindings that held her arm still and Mr. Jones began his work. It broke in the fall, that was certain, right above the elbow. "Miss Elizabeth, I am sorry this may hurt, but I will need to assess the break to see if it needs to be manipulated and how to best set it."

A very painful interim later, Mr. Jones had her arm encompassed in a splint that he said would need to remain on for at least four weeks. It took no time to craft a sling, and the throbbing from her immobilized arm soon eased. Though the change could also be the effects of the laudanum Mrs. Nichols had put in her tea. Elizabeth hated the fuzzy muddled feeling she got when she took laudanum, but there was not much for it.

"Apart from your arm, Miss Elizabeth, how else are you feeling? That was quite the fall you took." Most of the scrapes she had received seemed fairly superficial, though her face sported evidence of a hard blow.

Elizabeth's pain was too intense to fabricate a lie to the apothecary. "My head aches something fierce. Almost all of me is sore, actually."

Nodding, he began inspecting her skull with gentle fingers. Probing and finding a lump on the side of her head that caused her to gasp at his light touch. Mr. Jones was glad that Miss Elizabeth was such an amiable patient. Any other lady would have been in hysterics after a fall off a cliff. "That is quite the bump you have there, Miss Elizabeth. But it is not bleeding, so as long as you are careful, I think it will go down on its own. All that you need now, Miss Elizabeth, is a bath and a bed. I will supply Mrs. Ansley with a salve to put on your wounds after your bath. I hope that a good night's sleep will set you on the right path." Sorting through his bag, he handed a jar to Mrs. Ansley and made his goodbyes.

***

EVENTUALLY, MAKING HIS WAY through the home to Bingley's study, Mr. Jones was met with three pairs of anxious eyes. Sometimes handling the family was worse than the patient. Looking into the three faces, he realized that even though these gentlemen were not family; they were just as anxious as a family would be, one more than the others.

Upon spotting the apothecary, Darcy stopped his pacing to stare at the older man with hope. "How is she, Mr. Jones? Do you think I should send for a doctor from London?" Darcy had been struggling ever since he had put Elizabeth down. He was frantic with worry.

"That is unnecessary, Mr. Darcy. I am perfectly capable of handling a broken arm."

"My cousin was not implying you lack skill. He simply cannot help but insult people when overwhelmed." Theodore chuckled.

Darcy ran his hand through his hair, letting out a long, frustrated breath. He wound a lock of his hair around his finger, unconsciously seeking solace. "Mr. Jones, my cousin, Colonel Theodore Fitzwilliam, is correct. I apologize for what I said. I do not doubt your skill. My top priority is to make sure Elizabeth has whatever she requires. The weight of my uselessness is crushing me right now."

"If you're looking for something to do, it may require some effort to keep Miss Elizabeth composed while she mends. She will have to stay here for a minimum of five days, as I do not want her to travel in a bumpy conveyance until her arm has started to knit together. Have you informed her family of the accident?" Mr. Jones knew her mother and sisters would be concerned for her welfare; her father would be another story.

"We wanted to hear from you before we alerted them," Bingley spoke up.

Mr. Jones watched the interplay between the friends closely. Miss Elizabeth had the tall, dark gentleman, Mr. Darcy, totally smitten if he did not miss his guess. "Her worst injury is her broken arm, which I have set and put in a splint. She will be significantly sore for a time, as she has several bruises and scrapes. The worst bruise I noticed was on her face and will take a long while to heal. She has had a hard knock on her head and might have a slight concussion. Mrs. Ansley is helping her bathe and get into bed. I have left a salve for her wounds and bruises and a supply of laudanum, though she is not especially fond of it. It would be best if she kept mostly in bed for at least three days. I will return the day after tomorrow, but please send for me if she develops a fever or anything concerning happens." Mr. Jones nodded to them all before leaving.

Bingley, too restless to wait for dinner, tapped his friend's shoulder in order to get his attention. "Darcy, do you mind if I alert Miss Elizabeth's family to her being here? I can also take young Kiernan home so I can speak with his parents. I would like to apologize to them and let them know I will give him Caroline's pin money for the next quarter."

"Of course not. Please send my apologies to Mrs. Bennet." Darcy watched him hurry out the door, and glanced around the room at all the awful chairs. These chairs were the stuff of nightmares.

"How are we going to deal with Wickham?" Theodore questioned.

"We can figure it out together, but not in here. Let us go to my sitting room. There is nowhere to sit in this room." Glaring at the chairs, he walked out of the room.

Chapter Fifteen

A DARK MIST OBSCURED her way. It clung to her, sapping her strength and leaving her confused. She did not have time to be confused. She had to save Mr. Darcy from Lieutenant Wickham. When she tripped, she heard a soft groan and saw it was Mr. Darcy. She felt her heart break as she collapsed beside him, her despair palpable at the sight of his broken and bleeding form.

It was too late; Wickham had shot Mr. Darcy in the back. She felt the warmth of the blood on her hands as she desperately tried to locate the source and stop it. She could smell the coppery scent of his blood as it pooled around them, filling the small depression they were in. With a shudder, she rolled Mr. Darcy over and saw the agony in his eyes. His labored breathing was raspy, and punctuated by the sound of wet coughs spitting up blood.

Knowing that there was nothing she could do, she drew his broken form into her arms, holding him close. He worked to say something, striving to get the words to cross his bloody lips. "Why... You could have stopped him... Why didn't you stop him, Elizabeth?" His accusations sent a chill through Elizabeth's body, making her stomach lurch. When Mr. Darcy's breath ceased, she sobbed despairingly. He died believing the worst of her.

Elizabeth's fear deepened when she realized the sticky, crimson pool that was slowly spreading around him had no end. She felt like she was being suffocated by the sheer volume of Mr. Darcy's blood. She felt the blood engulf her, warm and sticky as it crept up her body. A scream escaped her mouth and took her breath with it.

A soothing murmur entered her mind, and she jolted out of the horrible world around her. Jane's soothing voice called to her. "Lizzie, you must wake up. Come on, darling, open your eyes." Jane smoothed Elizabeth's hair back from her face, getting the curls away from her eyes.

"Oh, Jane, I am so thankful you are here. I was having such a dream." Elizabeth shuddered, then tried to sit up, only to grimace, fully feeling her injuries at the abrupt movement.

"Of course I am here. I could not let you suffer here on your own. You are going to have to accept help or you are going to hurt yourself. Would you like to sit up?" Jane helped Elizabeth to sit up and rearranged her pillows so she was more comfortable. "Mama would have liked to come, but Papa was in one of his moods and told her she could visit in a few days."

Elizabeth hated to be the one in need of help. "I hope she does not worry overmuch. I am mostly fine." She knew it was an untruth when the swelling in her face prevented her from smiling.

Jane tried to maintain her serenity for her sister's sake, but it was difficult. Between Elizabeth's broken arm and her face darkening as they spoke, Jane found herself becoming upset. "What happened? Mr. Bingley did not go into detail when he spoke of you falling at

Oakham Mount." She kept her hands occupied, trying to smooth the blankets around her beloved sister.

Elizabeth could recognize her sister's mannerisms and knew she was upset. "Kiernan and I were on our walk when we spotted Lieutenant Wickham trying to shoot Mr. Darcy. I could not stand by to see him harm Mr. Darcy and, in trying to stop him, he knocked me off the edge."

"Goodness, I never suspected he had that level of wickedness within him. What could have prompted him to do such an act?" Jane gasped.

"I think he had imbibed a great deal of alcohol, but his actions are still unpardonable." She spoke while remembering just how the alcohol had influenced him. "How long can you stay?"

Jane could not avoid the dreamy smile that graced her face as she spoke. "Mr. Bingley invited me to stay until you return to Longbourn. He was sweet about trying to reassure Mama that she could visit as much as she wanted to check on you."

"Though both Miss Georgiana and Mrs. Ansley were very considerate and helpful, it is ever so soothing knowing you are here. As nice as it is to have them caring for me, it is never the same as having your sister with you." Elizabeth would feel better with Jane helping her, as well as her healthful teas.

A soft knock at the door had them both turning to greet the visitor. Georgiana's blond head peeked around the door. "I wondered if you would be awake. How are you feeling, Miss Elizabeth?" she inquired. The lady was looking rather worse. Her bruises had darkened, but Georgiana hoped she did not suffer too badly.

"Tolerable, given I fell off a cliff, now that I am no longer jostling around and my arm is more secure. It is a bearable ache." Elizabeth was finding a damaged face annoying, as her customary smiles were becoming painful.

Georgiana could not help but giggle at her comment. "Would you feel up to eating anything? I am sure you need to keep your strength. I have arrived to inform Miss Bennet that dinner is about to be served, and if you will not be joining us, I can have it brought to you." She blushed at her presumption. She was not nearly as bad as her brother when talking with new people, but she did often regret how she spoke.

Already knowing that her sister would forgo eating downstairs to stay with her, Elizabeth spoke up. "Please go down to dinner, Jane. That way, you can entertain me with its description when you return. I can manage on my own. If I may just have some broth and bread sent up, I am not sure I could manage more. It is a good thing it was my left arm that broke, so I will at least be able to feed myself." Elizabeth once again caught herself trying to smile. She hoped she would not lose her humor waiting for her bruise to improve.

***

JANE LOOKED WORRIEDLY ACROSS the table at Mrs. Hurst. She seemed positively green. Every course of the meal had thick sauces and strong flavors which did not seem to agree with her. The poor thing needed a much plainer fare.

"Louisa, you did not even touch your squab. Really, your manners have fallen off since coming to the back of beyond," Caroline needled her sister while stabbing at the meat on her plate.

Jane signaled a maid and spoke with her briefly about bringing ginger tea and plain bread to Mrs. Hurst. It was not strictly her place, but she could not watch someone suffer when she could do something. She took a small bite of her meal, and when she tasted the bitterness of the sauce, she wrinkled her nose. She enjoyed a much plainer meal even if it was not a popular viewpoint of the ton.

As Caroline scanned down the table, she felt her heart flutter when Mr. Darcy looked up at her. "How was your sister when you left her, Miss Bennet?" She prompted the conversation she had been wanting to bring about. Caroline was always enthusiastic to prove her superiority in front of eligible gentlemen.

Jane put on her serene smile, almost grateful she had so much experience doing so. "She was doing reasonably well. She said that her arm feels better now that the splint is on it. Though I suspect it will be some time before she is pain free, she has always been one to push forward despite any impediment." The recollection of the fierce, dark bruise that had stretched from Elizabeth's eyebrow to her jaw disturbed Jane.

"Yes, I have often found Miss Elizabeth too forward. Needing to be rescued was a lot, but allowing herself to be seen in such a state was simply too much. Louisa, you were not there to witness it but her hair was down and it was full of leaves. I have seen nothing so disgraceful." Caroline smiled to herself, happy that she offered such a set down, but then realized the room had gone silent.

Jane preferred to interact with those around her with a gracious heart. However, Caroline acted with malicious intent, and Jane protected those she loved. "I beg your pardon, but I cannot but correct your mistaken presumptions. My sister became wounded while trying to help one of your guests and the gentlemen brought her here to receive succor. Any lady of the house would be honor bound to provide that care without the added burden of any cutting remarks or insolent thoughts. You should also be concerned with the care of your guests and family. However, you have left off that responsibility in favor of trying to impress Mr. Darcy. Abandoning your good sister to suffer this presumptuous meal when I am sure everyone would have been happy with something simpler. But maybe I am being too critical. As someone born apart from the landed gentry and part of a family in trade, you may not know how to act with civility and propriety. In case you did not know, your actions here are the definition of disgraceful, not those of my sister." Jane threw down her gauntlet with a small smile, her blue eyes unyielding. Too often she had to act with restraint around her father, but she was determined not to allow insults to stand here.

Caroline's anger swept away her usual inhibitions, and she acted without considering how it would appear to Mr. Darcy. "How dare you speak so? I received my education at an esteemed seminary in London. Charles, do something! I cannot stand to be forced to deal with the Bennets. I am certain that Miss Elizabeth is not so sickly that we could not send them back to their miserable abode." Caroline stood and furiously slammed her hands against the table, rattling the plates and causing her wine glass to topple over.

"I will do something, Caroline." Noticing the maid bringing Louisa tea and bread, he signaled to her and whispered a few instructions. "I will not force you to associate with anyone you do not wish. You are exempt from all meals until there is a marked improvement in your attitude. I no longer want to endure your pretension while I eat, nor will I allow your poor behavior around my guests."

"You are not serious!" Caroline scoffed.

When he glanced over at his sister, he saw her eyes blazing and her fists clenched tight. He realized he no longer felt fear at her rage. Today he had witnessed the actions of two women who had proved to him what ladies should be, no matter what the haute ton and his sister might believe. "Mrs. Nichols, my sister will eat her meals in her room for the time being. Could you see she has everything she needs?" Bingley spoke to Mrs. Nichols when she came into the room.

Caroline stormed out of the room, her body tense, not understanding why no one accepted her attitude. She trudged up to her room and collapsed onto her bed, the soft pillows muffling the noise of her frustrated screams. Why did things not go the way she wanted them to? Long ago, she had fallen in love with the comfort and grace of Pemberley and decided that it would be her home. Was that not how you went about these things?

Back when she had been at that horrible school, she had learned many things. How to paint and play the piano and host a tea. Also, how you always made those around you feel small if you were to maintain your own power and control. They taught her you did not look at marriage as a romance or a partnership; it was a business transaction. The older girls often spoke of how they went about choosing potential husbands by how comfortable a home they would provide. She had followed all the rules. Why did she not get what she wanted?

***

Louisa Hurst took a sip of the tea that Miss Bennet had suggested and was grateful for how quickly it was helping. "Please accept my apologies for my sister's behavior, Miss Bennet. I do not hold her opinions, but I have never had the energy to fight her on them. Even more so lately."

"I will not hold her actions against you, Mrs. Hurst. I hope you are feeling well enough." Jane was glad to see a little color returning to her face. Louisa had been so miserable of late and she was hopeful the tea could help her get some of her life back.

"The tea is helping ever so much. I am so grateful to have something that helps finally."

"I will suggest some dry toast in the morning with ginger tea should help mitigate some of your suffering." Jane suspected what the lady's malady was, but would not presume until she felt comfortable sharing her news. "I would love to sit with you longer, but I have been away from Lizzie for a while and I would like to check on her."

Louisa momentarily wished for her own sister to have as much consideration for her. "Please tell her I wish her a swift recovery," said

Louisa. Across the room, Miss Georgiana and Mrs. Ansley echoed her sentiments.

***

THEODORE SAT WITH THE other gentlemen in Bingley's sitting room, talking over their brandy. "So what are you going to do with Miss Bingley?"

Bingley stared gloomily into his glass. He had been living in a different world since his parents and brother passed away a year ago. As he reflected, he realized he had not made enough effort to be with Caroline before they lost their parents. His guilt over spending so much time away from his family had led him to turn a blind eye to many things. "I fear my sister requires a lesson that I am not capable of teaching. I can no longer allow her to reign over my home the way she does. After her actions this evening, I fear even removing her authority to direct anyone will not be enough. Seeing her behavior when held next to the likes of ladies like Miss Bennet and her sisters has shown me just how lacking she is."

Darcy saw the despondency in his friend's eyes and tried to come up with something to lift his spirits. "Do you have any family she might stay with while learning those lessons?" Darcy wished he could help his friend more, but had little knowledge of how to sort out difficult women. Plus, he was attempting to organize the tangled mass of emotions that had come up during the day.

"I have an aunt in Scotland who is extremely caring but does not cater to fools. There is another aunt from my mother's side of the family in Bath, but I fear Caroline would completely bowl her over. Maybe I should write them and see if one would take her on?" Bingley pondered his options.

Theodore took a sip of his drink before adding his two bits. "I say you leave the poor aunt in Bath alone for the time being. Start her off in Scotland. Maybe she can graduate to Bath before rejoining society. Who knows, maybe she will find a husband in Scotland and live in Edinburgh," Theodore chimed in, happy to help Bingley ship his sister off and away from himself.

"I believe that is a good plan. I will write to Aunt Guthrie in the morning. I believe she is visiting old friends in London, so I should receive her reply promptly." Bingley felt better at having come up with a plan.

"Darcy, will you accompany me to see the Colonel for the militia tomorrow?" Theodore asked. "I would like to report on Wickham's horrendous behavior. He needs to be stopped before he kills someone."

"I wish I thought about taking him in hand earlier, but I was too concerned with Elizabeth's welfare." Regret was one emotion Darcy was currently struggling with and the easiest to identify.

"I sent Hugh, one of the grooms I brought with me, after him once we returned. He is still upset with Wickham for his mistreatment of his little sister. Hugh is going to investigate and look and see if he can locate any of his usual haunts or potential spots to conceal himself. I think Wickham is probably sleeping it off somewhere." Theodore's gaze was thoughtful as he considered the possibilities.

"I should have thought of doing something like that," Darcy grumbled, upset over what he saw as a failure.

"Someone please enlighten me about these Bennet ladies. We have an example of a lady who was willing to confront a drunk soldier to protect my dearest cousin. Conversely, her sister's upbraiding was a thing of beauty. Her words were like daggers, yet her voice was still gentle. They seem remarkable."

Bingley welcomed the opportunity to talk about something less emotionally draining. "Yes, they are. Miss Bennet asks significant questions of me about many subjects. From how I am caring for the tenants to my opinion on the effect of the Luddite rebellion on the textile industry. I know Miss Elizabeth quite impressed Darcy. Do you realize, Darcy, you have called her by her name all day? You have completely dropped off the Miss." Bingley grinned at his friend, happy to joke around after a hard day.

"I would not do that without some kind of understanding. I... have been calling her Elizabeth since she fell off that cliff? How did that happen?" Darcy sputtered and slumped into his chair, his eyes wide.

Theodore loved the expression on Darcy's startled face. His cousin was normally so dignified and right now he was so undignified. "Darcy, the question is not how, but why. Why did you feel the need to use her name in such an intimate manner? I noticed it as well. Tell me about her. How did you meet?"

"I met her on the path to Netherfield. She was bewitching, her eyes glimmering with delight and her smile a contagious spark of joy. I froze and could not respond to anything she said." Ignoring the chuckles coming from his friends, he continued. "Then I showed poorly at the assembly. I was not handling the crowd well and made an insult about the ladies. When I apologized, she was everything that was generous and forgiving. She even suggested a tea that her sister makes to help with distress. It has helped me while dealing with crowds, and I think she helped more because she supported me with meeting all the strangers at the last gathering. Just knowing that someone was there who completely accepted me, problems and all, helped me.

"She is very intelligent and well read. In fact, she knew the meaning of Cadmus's name. Her own funds have gone into putting together a class twice a week for the children in the area because she knows it will improve their lives. She cares about the well-being of everyone she meets, including me. Did you know her father neglects to provide for the tenants, so the Bennet ladies had to resort to using their own pin money to pay for new roofs and other issues?" Darcy felt his chest tighten with emotion as he thought of Elizabeth. He had thrown his hands up in defeat, resigned to the fact that he could not keep the Miss attached to her name. It no longer felt right.

Bingley realized that the more he found out about Miss Bennet, the more he wanted to know her. "Somehow I am not surprised. They are all ladies to be esteemed."

"Well, I am happy you both met such wonderful ladies. I hope you can figure out how you feel about Miss Elizabeth. It is a pity there are only the two of them."

"Actually, Miss Bennet is the eldest of five girls," Bingley responded, laughing at the expression on Theodore's face. They did not realize how distracted Darcy had become.

"I think I am realizing that she is very important to me in a way I have never known before now," Darcy whispered only to himself. But the moment was coming when he could declare it to everyone.

Chapter Sixteen

"WHAT AN HONOR TO have you visiting my humble encampment, Colonel," Colonel Forester drawled off. He was a man who liked to be a big fish in a little pond. It was why he had established himself in the militia. He was decidedly not pleased to be visited by a big fish from a big pond.

Colonel Theodore Fitzwilliam took in his surroundings and the man who sat before him and found he did not like what he saw. The office, if you could call it that, was disorderly, papers scattered haphazardly and the remnants of several meals lay randomly around the room. Though there were two chairs, he did not ask them to sit. This told him a lot about the man before him. "I have come with my cousin to warn you of a wolf in your midst, Colonel."

"If your cousin is the revered Mr. Darcy. I can only assume you are here to complain about my Lieutenant Wickham." Forester expressed his displeasure with the gentlemen in words dripping with disdain.

Darcy kept his annoyance in check and didn't allow the officer behind the desk to offend him. There was too much at stake to be sidetracked. "Mr. Darcy, at your service, and yes, we are here to warn you of Wickham's most recent acts of misconduct. He has never been a man to act with integrity or prudence, but yesterday, I do believe he left all bounds of civility and goodness behind him. We must bring him to justice before he causes any more harm."

"You will understand if I do not bow to the whims of a man who has made it his goal in life to persecute one of my most charming officers," Colonel Forester chided his unwelcome guests, propping his feet up on his desk in a sign of contempt.

"Your charming officer tried to kill my cousin. We must bring him in for questioning and detainment. Do you even know where he is?" Theodore focused his thoughts on ways to circumnavigate the ineffectual officer and how to get him removed from his post. Men like him brought a bad name to anyone who served the crown.

Forester would not change how he operated because of two interlopers. "He does not have to report for duty until tomorrow morning. I do not care to curtail my officers' enjoyment. They go where they please and do what they please as long as they report to duty on time."

"I can see you have no wish to help look for Wickham and you have already fallen for his smiles and flattery. I would ask that when he does not report for duty, you reevaluate a few things. He has proven himself willing to murder and harm others and once he crossed that line, there is no telling what he may do."

"Your cousin looks fine. Were there even any witnesses to this murder attempt?" Forester scoffed.

"Two, in fact, a young boy and a young lady who were on a walk and came upon the attempt. Mr. Wickham injured the young lady when she sought to stop his endeavor," Darcy bit out, aggrieved by the man's attitude.

"Well, if that is the case and I find Lieutenant Wickham missing, come tomorrow, I will investigate your claims. Good day gentlemen, the Lieutenant will see you out."

Realizing the meeting was over, Darcy and Theodore left, glad to be done with the dunderhead. Theodore surveyed the camp as they left. It was in shambles; he had often been on the front lines, and this was still the worst encampment he had seen. He would be in contact with Colonel Forester's supervisors.

"And these are the men that are protecting England? I am instilled with such confidence," Darcy quipped.

"Rather, we should go through the town and see if we can gather intelligence on the way back to Netherfield," Theodore proposed while mounting Achilles and leaving the dissolute place behind.

***

"You were ever so brave to help William as you did, Miss Elizabeth." Georgiana spoke from the bedside of Miss Elizabeth, who rested by Mr. Jones's order.

Elizabeth settled more comfortably against the pillows that supported her. At her head, a cloth with ice chips rested against her bruised cheek; another lay at the back of her head where the bump was. "I found I could do nothing else and was quite questioning my sanity in the middle of it. I had no plan, only an impulse. It was not a sound action. Though I cannot regret it, even with the obvious consequences." She gestured to her confined arm with a smile.

Noticing that the cold compress on Elizabeth's face was both slipping and dripping, Jane removed it and put it to the side. She would get another one for her later.

"You always were one to run headlong into danger, Lizzie. Remember that time you climbed the tree to rescue Lydia's kitten? The branch snapped, and you both came tumbling down," Jane commented, laughing under her breath.

Despite the ache in her arm and various other body parts, she was having a relatively good morning. The room was pleasant enough in its pinks and roses, evidence that Miss Bingley had not tried to redecorate the guest rooms. Someone with actual taste did them. With a chair on either side of her bed, it was almost a sitting room. Or as close as she would get to one for the next two days under Mr. Jones's direction. "The kitten was out of the tree. What does it matter how?" Elizabeth kidded back with her beloved sister.

"Mother could have done without you coming home bloody and disheveled," Jane remarked as she took a sip of tea. Though her tone had been bland, her eyes danced with mirth.

Georgiana giggled at the banter. "If this is the bond between sisters, I have missed out." She was envious of their close relationship. She was close with her brother, but having a sister seemed different.

"I love having sisters, but we often have disagreements. It is not all laughs and giggles; sometimes it is screaming and stolen bonnets," Elizabeth warned.

Jane reassured the younger girl who she was growing to like. She seemed to need the warmth and comfort of a motherly figure, and Jane was eager to give it. "However, if you have a problem, they are all there for you. In fact, if anyone were to slight any of my sisters, all the others would see it as a call to war."

A quiet knock at the door signaled the entrance of another sister to the mix. Kitty had gotten the stable hands to take her to Netherfield by carriage. It was a bold move for her, but she could not wait any longer to see her beloved sister. "I just had to see how you were doing, Lizzie. I hope I have not come at a bad time," Kitty stated in a rush, nervous at her presumption of coming over uninvited.

"You are perfectly welcome here, sister dear. Miss Georgiana, may I introduce you to my younger sister, Miss Catherine Bennet?" Jane felt a swell of pride as she watched her younger sister take her first steps toward independence.

Kitty found it interesting to note how similar to Jane Miss Georgiana looked. Where Jane and Georgiana were both blonde with blue eyes, they could have been sisters. In fact, Jane was more like Georgiana in appearance than Elizabeth, with her dark curly hair and deep green eyes. Kitty executed a polite curtsy to the well-dressed blonde. "Though I would prefer you to call me Kitty; all my sisters do. It is lovely to meet you, Miss Georgiana."

"I will, but only if you call me Georgie. All of you call me Georgie. I honestly prefer it. The way some of my family say Georgiana makes me feel like it is such a pompous name. My Aunt Catherine, in particular, is so annoying when she says it. Well, anyway, I prefer Georgie." Georgiana blushed at her long-winded speech.

"I think we all have family members that we struggle to interact with. I would love to call you Georgie," Kitty reassured the girl she hoped to befriend.

"Well, then you can call me Lizzie if you wish," Elizabeth added.

"Lizzie, I did not know how bad you would look. Does it hurt so very much?" Kitty quavered from her spot, sitting on the bed at Elizabeth's feet.

"It has been unpleasant, but I have been managing, mostly. It has frustrated me that my face hurts when I smile and that I cannot do things as easily. Jane brought her teas to help me with the pain, but they are encouraging me to still take the laudanum at night to help me sleep." Elizabeth was not looking forward to more laudanum. It always gave her odd dreams.

Kitty looked at her sister's injuries with melancholy. Even now, in bed and injured, Elizabeth had a fearlessness that seemed to emanate from her very being. "I could never have acted as you did. Trying to stop Wickham all by yourself. You are so much braver than I am."

"I do not think it is so much bravery but the desire to act on behalf of someone else. The first time I did anything remotely brave and every time afterward, it was always to help someone that was not me. Your time will come, I am sure of it," Elizabeth reassured her little sister. With one hand, she tried to push herself into a better spot, but her muscles were too sore and exhausted to continue.

With each attempt Elizabeth made to move, Georgiana cringed, fearing she would further injure herself. "Lizzie, let us help you get more comfortable," she offered.

Jane noticed the pinch in Elizabeth's eyebrows and could tell she was in pain. "Actually, Lizzie, I think you need to rest, or more accurately, you need a nap. You have a lot of injuries that need to heal," Jane directed her sister. She cajoled Lizzie into taking a few sips of the bitter medicinal tea laced with laudanum. Once Lizzie finished her tea, Jane took away two of the pillows behind her and helped her get settled into a comfortable position for sleeping.

Elizabeth acknowledged she needed rest and did not fight Jane on her dictates. "Oh, I just remembered that tomorrow I was to teach the class. Who will go with Mary? I do not want her to do it on her own."

"I would love to help her in your place if you do not mind?" Georgiana spoke up quickly. She had talked with William at breakfast about the school and how they might try something similar at Pemberley. Often, she felt of little use at home. She was not planning parties or teas, she was not out, and had no one to go on calls with. If she had a project to work on, especially to help people, her days would have far more meaning.

"Not at all. I think you might enjoy it. They are all such dears. Please tell them I say hello," Elizabeth murmured with a yawn.

"We will leave you in peace, Lizzie. Do you want another cold compress while you sleep?" Jane asked from the doorway.

"I think that would be nice. Thank you for being so attentive, Janie." Elizabeth yawned once more before drifting off.

***

KITTY AND JANE'S FOOTSTEPS echoed in the hallway as they walked to the parlor, and Kitty murmured to her quietly, "I wanted to spare Elizabeth any distress, so I didn't mention the news from home while we were in there. Mr. Collins feels he has been very ill-used by our family and at Charlotte's invitation has been spending most of his time at the Lucases' home. By some comments he has been making, I think he will ask for Charlotte's hand before he leaves on Friday."

"I believe Charlotte will be happy to accept, though I fear she does not fully understand how much living with Mr. Collins will affect her life. Or how much his patroness Lady Catherine will affect her life, for that matter," Jane responded, genuinely concerned for the life her friend would lead if she made this choice. Choosing a seat that seemed comfortable enough, Jane greeted both of the other ladies while trying to ignore the horrendous colors in the room. Maybe Miss Bingley was colorblind; it was the kindest explanation she could come up with. Signaling the maid, she asked that someone bring a cold compress to Elizabeth.

"How are you feeling, Mrs. Hurst, any better today?" Georgiana queried from her spot next to Kitty.

"Yes, the tea Jane suggested has helped me so much. Being allowed to have the food I can stomach has also helped. Thank you, Mrs. Ansley, for being so considerate and asking me what would be helpful to serve. I love my sister, but she never took me into consideration." Louisa smiled, so happy to be feeling better.

Mrs. Ansley smiled back, happy that she had helped someone to feel at ease. "Oh, making sure all the people in a home are comfortable is the first obligation of a hostess. I truly enjoy making people comfortable. I believe that is why I became a companion, even though I was not obligated to, after my beloved Timothy passed away."

"Miss Bennet, please do not think me presumptuous, but I overheard your earlier conversation. Do you have a connection with a Lady Catherine?" Georgiana asked while smoothing her skirt nervously.

"You can call me Jane if you wish. Our father's heir, a distant cousin of ours, is a rector at the Hunsford parish, under the auspices of a Lady Catherine De Bourgh." Jane attempted to keep her distaste for the man out of her expression.

"I am not sure you are aware, but Lady Catherine is my aunt, my mother's older sister. I hate to say this, but she absolutely terrifies me. She is so critical of everything that I do, and the way she speaks down to everyone is just too much," Georgiana admitted.

Kitty grimaced, remembering one of his recent lectures over the dinner table. "Somehow that is the image I have in my head of her. Our cousin never seems to stop pontificating about her and how she condescends to direct his life and the life of every other person within her sphere."

"I have never met her rector, but if he is anything like the servile people she surrounds herself with, I can certainly imagine."

Though it was nice that the girls were bonding, it was not the best conversation to have in the parlor, so Jane changed the topic. "Mrs. Hurst, how long have you been married to Mr. Hurst?"

"I have been married to him for just over a year. It was a rather trying first year. I hoped that a stay in the country would be a bit of a respite." Louisa looked at the faces of the ladies in the room, remembering how Jane had stood up to Caroline. They all seemed so kind. Maybe she had finally found some people who would be friends despite her sister.

Jane felt her chest swell with compassion for her new friend. She also shuddered at the thought of having to suffer through Caroline's grievances during the early stages of a marriage. She refused to contemplate why this thought affected her so. "I am sorry to hear that it was a painful year, especially as you were newly married. Please let me know if there is anything I can do to help."

"I am not sure if any of you were aware, but I have just come out of morning for both my parents and my older brother. There was a carriage accident. All three were gone in the blink of an eye. It was such a blow that I was quite blue-deviled. Some days I still am. I only hope that things will continue to improve." Louisa was hopeful. She had had a frank conversation with her husband the night before and he promised to work on the marriage with her. It had never been a love match, but they had been friends until things went sideways. Maybe they could be friends again.

Mrs. Ansley's heart went out to the woman who seemed to be beaten down by the world. "You poor dear, I know well how hard it can be to deal with the death of a loved one. I am always here to talk if you need a listening ear."

"Yes, I am also available. Should you want to talk, I am certain my mother would be willing as well," Jane confidently spoke up.

Chapter Seventeen

"THERE IS A COLONEL Forester to see you, sir." A well-dressed footman interrupted Theodore's train of thought.

A slow smile spread across Theodore's face. Wickham had not reported to duty on time. "Do you know if Bingley is in his study?"

"I believe he is, sir," was his bland reply.

"Bring the Colonel to the study in five minutes. We should be ready by then. Oh, and could you arrange for these to be sent express?" Theodore handed the man a stack of correspondence.

"I'll take care of both tasks," he assured with a nod. With a respectful bow, he headed out of the room.

Theodore's footsteps echoed behind him as he made his way to Bingley's study, eager to put his plan into action. He pondered if Wickham's disappearance had motivated him to take action, or if he was still the same unbearable slug as before. They would find out soon.

When Colonel Forester entered Bingley's study and he glanced around, he noted the restrained luxury of the room. The stately fabrics and rich wood were far less ostentatious than the grand parlor.

Mr. Bingley sat behind the desk while Colonel Fitzwilliam leaned against the same desk facing him across the room as Mr. Darcy stood next to the fireplace.

He promptly took the seat offered to him and then regretted it. Though the room seemed to be decorated better than the other parts of the house, the chairs were certainly wanting. The silence stretched on until, so uncomfortable, he finally spoke up. "You let me know you thought Lieutenant Wickham would not report to duty. As he has not reported, I am left to wonder if you would detain him to prove a point. I also wonder about the witnesses that you spoke of. I am sure any of you would have the funds to secure false testimony." The longer Forester spoke, the more uneasy he became. He could not pinpoint whether it was the glares from the three influential gentlemen before him or the odd balance of the chair he sat in.

Still a slug, then. Theodore wished there were not so many fools so high in the ranks, but at least this man would never see combat. Or maybe he would. Who was he to say? "I would like to say that I am surprised that he did not show his face, but I am not. I marvel at the depth of your stubborn refusal to see what is in front of you."

"I suppose you can produce your witnesses for me to take their testimony." His deep, angry voice bounced off the walls, reverberating with a sense of defiance as Forester refused to accept defeat.

They had decided that he would be the one to speak while Darcy and Bingley would look upset and disapproving. No need to put all of their cards on the table just yet. Nodding to Darcy as he left the room to go see about Miss Elizabeth, he returned his focus to

Forester, keeping his expression bland. "We brought Miss Elizabeth here to assess her injuries and the apothecary, Mr. Jones, requested that she stay here to recuperate for a time. We can see if she is up to a short audience. As for the boy who witnessed the altercation, Kiernan is with his family, who are tenants on Longbourn land. I am sure we can arrange a meeting," Theodore said, his slightly jovial tone not revealing his irritation.

***

DARCY REGARDED ELIZABETH'S FACE in horror. Where her cheek had been puffy and beginning to discolor when last he saw her, now the bruise was a swirl of dark blues, purples, and reds that stretched that the length of her face. How had he allowed Wickham to do this to her when he was only an arm's length away? He was ashamed of his inability to protect the woman he found to be so important to him.

Even though a day had passed since her nightmare, she still felt the lingering feeling of dread; the vivid images were still fresh in her mind. When Elizabeth saw Mr. Darcy standing before her, well and whole, she felt a sense of calm. "Mr. Darcy, I am going to think I have food on my face if you stare so," she chided the gentleman before her. Had she not known him as she did, she might think his behavior rude, but now she thought it meant something else. She simply had to analyze what his penetrating look meant and why it made her heart flutter. If there wasn't something hidden beneath the surface, the dream wouldn't have had such an impact on her.

He berated himself for getting lost in his own head and attempted to bring his attention back to the present. "I came to see how you were feeling and ask if you were up to speaking with Wickham's superior officer." His words were no sooner out of his mouth than he became distracted once again. This time, it was her hair that held his gaze. The sight of her chestnut curls, unrestrained and full of life, made his heart ache. He reluctantly shifted his attention from her beautiful hair and back to her face, waiting for her response.

Elizabeth found confinement to be a bigger issue than other people might. She customarily spent a portion of every day being active, either on a walk or practicing archery. She would do almost anything to get out of being confined to bed, regardless of whatever pain she might be in. "I am doing well, especially as I have had the benefit of not having to lift a finger for the last two days. I would be happy to speak with the officer." Elizabeth was glad she had insisted on getting dressed, even if she was going to be in bed. She threw her blankets back, her feet searching for the floor.

Jane had watched the interaction between her sister and Mr. Darcy with a repressed smile. "What my sister may not say is that she is in pain, but she chooses not to dwell on it or let it stop her. However, if Lizzie is going to meet with an officer, we must make her slightly more presentable. Between Mrs. Ansley and myself, we should only be a few minutes," Jane remarked from her spot by the bed, completely aware that Mr. Darcy had not even noticed anyone else in the room.

"Come, brother, I will wait in the hall with you while they help Lizzie." The sound of Georgiana's laughter echoed in the hall as she pulled her big brother along. She had never once seen her brother so befuddled, and she loved it.

***

It was only a few minutes later when Elizabeth was ready and on her feet with the support of her sister. Walking to where Darcy stood, still looking a little flummoxed, she smiled up at him despite the pain it brought to her cheek. It was a rather endearing look on him, she decided.

"Would you help me down the stairs, Mr. Darcy?" Elizabeth requested.

"It would be a pleasure. You will say if anything is too much for you, will you not, Elizabeth? I would not have you overdo it." With her hand tucked securely in the crook of his arm, they began their journey down to the parlor.

Leaning on Darcy for support too much for her taste, Elizabeth still had the energy to engage in banter. "I cannot promise you anything in that regard. What if I am enjoying myself too much to retreat to bed?"

"What if I promise you more fun later on if you return to bed to rest after you speak with Colonel Forester?" When Darcy averted his eyes from Elizabeth's, he found he could speak more fluently. He decided that if he actually looked at the stairs, it would help him better navigate them.

"What kind of entertainment do you propose?"

"Well, I know you are fond of reading. We could discuss any of the Bard's works or your thoughts on the Greek or Roman classics. Unless you are fond of chess?" Darcy offered, unconcerned with what she chose, as he would be happy just to spend time with her.

Elizabeth had always wanted to learn to play chess, but would certainly never learn from her father. "I would love to discuss anything we might have read, though to be honest, my father would never teach me to play chess and I have always wanted to learn." Elizabeth bit her lip, wondering if Darcy would be patient enough to teach her.

"It would delight me if we spent our evenings playing chess together. We can start tonight after dinner if you are up to it." Darcy could just picture it, a crackling fire on a frosty night and the two of them chatting over a chessboard. They just had to deal with Forester first.

On the stairs behind the two, Jane, Georgiana, and Mrs. Ansley struggled to not burst into peals of unsightly laughter. It would not do to hurt Mr. Darcy or Elizabeth's feelings, but it looked as if both were entirely ignorant of their developing feelings. Jane met Georgiana's eyes and smiled. Who knew, maybe Georgiana would have sisters to enjoy before long?

***

"I am told you wished to speak with me," Elizabeth stated as she entered the parlor. Passing up the chair where Colonel Forester sat, she moved to sit across from him while Darcy took up the position beside her. Jane, Mrs. Ansley and Georgiana moved to the far corner in case they needed to be of assistance.

Forester knew they said Wickham had harmed the woman, but he was still shocked to see the woman so badly wounded. "Yes, Mr. Darcy has claimed that Lieutenant Wickham made an attempt on his life. He also stated that you would testify to it."

"I was prepared to step in and prevent your lieutenant from shooting Mr. Darcy. Why would there be an issue to disclose the information to you?" Elizabeth retorted. She did not know why, but she did not like this man.

"He pulled a gun on Mr. Darcy? I find it hard to imagine such a refined gentleman would do something without being provoked." Forester leaned back in his chair, his mouth agape in shock at the thought of such a jovial man acting so maliciously.

She sat upright in her chair, her regal posture a testament to her strength despite her bruised and battered countenance, and disclosed her facts. "Oh, Lieutenant Wickham may use fine words when trying to impress, but he is all flare and no substance. His story of being refused a church living was told in a way that made people feel pity for him. Anyone with a discerning mind could see the holes in his ploy."

"What do you mean, holes in his story?" He had found no issue with the history Wickham had disclosed to him.

"Mr. Darcy would be negligent if he granted a living to someone who did not even attempt to become ordained."

He found it difficult to believe this slip of a thing had figured out something he had failed to. "How do you know he never became ordained? It seems unlikely that a woman would have the knowledge to understand ordination."

"If my idiot cousin could become ordained and find a patron despite his difficulty reading and lack of comprehension of the holy scriptures. Someone as intelligent as Wickham could do it easily if he chose to. Especially as Mr. Darcy's father sent him to Cambridge. Frankly, if he became ordained, it would be far more rewarding for him to pursue a career as a rector rather than joining the militia. The money is better. But all of this is beside the point; you are here to question the possibility that Lieutenant Wickham attempted to shoot Mr. Darcy." Elizabeth was growing tired of dealing with the petulant colonel.

"Yes, I believe so. What can you tell me about the interaction between the two gentlemen?" Forester conceded the point and moved on. How was this conversation going so badly?

"I was walking the path to Oakham Mount with young Kiernan Anderson. We came around a curve and saw Wickham in a stand of trees seeming to follow Mr. Darcy, who was on horseback. We remained hidden until Mr. Wickham pulled out a pistol and I decided things were no longer safe. He was aiming to shoot Mr. Darcy in the back when I rushed forward and called to Wickham to distract him. Not until I got near him did I realize he was very intoxicated. After he complained for some time about the way things were not going as they should, including my not falling for what he called his well-practiced story, he grabbed me. Though Mr. Darcy drew closer to help, I heard a loud thud as Mr. Wickham's pistol hit my face, and I felt myself being thrown off the side of the cliff." Just talking about it all made Elizabeth's arm ache.

"I am astounded by your story. You are telling me you came out of hiding to confront an armed man by yourself?" he scoffed.

"I wonder what you are questioning, sir. Is it that a woman showed the courage to do what was right when called upon or that anyone would risk themself in order to protect another? I would never let someone suffer when I could help, and I pity those who cannot find that kind of humanity within themselves. Living only for yourself is a lonely way to exist." Elizabeth saw the man across from her for what he was: a coward who did not like it when someone did what he was afraid to do.

Suddenly, Darcy felt a rush of energy, and all the hairs on his neck rose, as if lightning had struck without warning. When he heard her speak with such conviction, it all suddenly made sense. All of his confusing feelings coalesced into understanding. Love. He was in love with Elizabeth. She was resolute but never rude, kind to others no matter their station, and understanding of his inabilities. She accepted him for who he was and helped him see the world in a better light. The thought of being alone with her made his heart swell. He was dreaming of reading books, playing chess, and feeling the crunch of leaves under his feet while walking with her in the woods. It did not matter as long as it was with her. He wanted to be away from the world, his fingers exploring her hair and feeling the warmth of her skin. Determination filled him. He wanted it all and would see if she did, too. He prayed she did.

Forester found he did not enjoy talking to this Miss Elizabeth. She made him feel small. He did not like feeling small. Despite his lack of bravery, he found some peace in knowing that he appeared to be more courageous than he was. He wore a military uniform, and he talked a good game, but here was this lady proving herself and being willing to risk life and limb. "I have the information that I need to proceed. I will contact you if I need further information."

Theodore was not about to let him slink away to lick his wounds without committing to some form of action. "May I assume you will begin a search for Lieutenant Wickham? With the aid of your soldiers – they may be quite interested in finding him. He has a great compulsion to engage in card games without the skill to back it up, which often leaves him in debt to others."

"Of course. Now if you will excuse me, I have duties to see to." With the slightest nod of his head, Forester quit the room.

"Lizzie, though I applaud your bravery for retelling your harrowing tale, I think if you want to eat dinner with everyone and learn chess from Mr. Darcy, you need to get some rest. Do not think I cannot see the pain in your eyes." Jane's mother hen instincts had kicked in and she was determined to get her sister on the path to recovery.

***

WICKHAM HAD WOKEN SOMETIME the day before with a pounding head and a mouth that tasted like a badger had climbed in it and died. Sleeping on the forest floor had given him a crick in his neck to accompany his hangover. His failure to end Darcy when he had the chance galled him to no end. He was unsure whether it was safe to head back into town. Wickham scanned the horizon, wondering if he would glimpse a search party. If there was any kind of search party. There was comfort in knowing that most of his fellow soldiers preferred him to Darcy, but that didn't give him full assurance. He had ventured out, desperately searching for a place to hide until it was safe. As he found the derelict cottage on Longbourn land, he could almost hear the gods' blessing spoken to him. Now he had water and a bed of sorts and if he was careful, he could get his hands on some food. His head hurt too badly to come up with a plan, so he lay back down to sleep it off.

Chapter Eighteen

"So the horse piece is called a knight, and it moves in an L shape pattern? Like this?" Elizabeth questioned. She picked up the white knight, and slid it forward one and over two, taking his pawn.

Darcy smiled at her and moved one of his pieces, curious to see what her response would be. "You are picking this up faster than I expected. It took me much longer to decipher things."

Taping her bishop in thought, she contemplated her options. She blocked out the sound of Jane and Mr. Bingley chatting with Georgiana and Colonel Fitzwilliam and concentrated on taking his rook. "You probably learned chess from your father as a child. It can be a confusing game for an adult."

"Yes, I was seven when I learned, but my father always said that it was no excuse to show a lack of understanding." He grimaced at the memory, but concentrated on dangling his rook in front of her.

"At least you can say you are a better teacher than your father. I am enjoying what I am learning." Confident, she took his rook with her bishop.

"I think almost anyone would be a better teacher than my father. I am glad you are enjoying yourself, though you still have much to learn. Check mate." His queen made a quick capture of her king, which was left defenseless when she shifted her bishop.

Elizabeth laughed, taking her loss in stride. Her clever mind took in the layers of the game and where she had left herself open. "Oh, I see what you did there. That is clever. I think I am going to enjoy this game."

"One thing to always remember is that your queen is your most important piece." He reached out and picked up the white queen, the ivory color standing out against the dark wood of the chessboard. He slowly placed it in her palm and gently guided her fingers around it. Holding her hand in his, he could not help but gaze into the emerald pools that were her eyes. Her eyes were so expressive, sometimes they said more than her words did. At this moment, they spoke of something new and exciting and yet tender. It was a conversation he wanted to be a part of.

She breathed and then looked away, a becoming pink creeping across her unmarred cheek. "I will keep that in mind." Something was happening, but she was uncertain of what it was.

Darcy slowly withdrew his hand from hers, allowing the moment to pass. "Do you think you would be up for a walk in the garden tomorrow morning? I know you are used to more time out of doors. I would not want you to fall into a decline because of a lack of nature's beauty." They would have the next day, he reminded himself. There was no need to rush, even if his heart wanted to beat out of his chest and join hers across the table.

"I would love to join you for a walk in the morning. I would hate to miss my daily need for fresh air; I..." A tremendous yawn broke off her continued thought and brought a warm chuckle from Darcy.

"I believe you may need to stop for the night so you can get your beauty sleep." Darcy loved the way she scrunched her nose at his remark. Now that he had realized what this elusive emotion was, he was free to treasure the little things that now meant so much.

"With the way my face looks, I will need to sleep for a month to reach beautiful. It will take at least that long to heal, I think," Elizabeth sighed.

"The bruise leaving your face will not make you beautiful." Darcy spoke but then felt that he had misspoken. He frowned and thought back, trying to figure out why that sounded wrong.

Elizabeth reminded herself not to get angry at the insult. The poor man could not seem to help but say the wrong thing. "I am sure that you did not mean to say that I am not capable of being beautiful, Mr. Darcy."

"No, that is not what I was trying to say. What I meant is I think you are beautiful right now, even with the bruise. I apologize that I cannot seem to say things properly." Darcy was upset that he just insulted the woman he loved.

"Well, I accept the sentiment and the attempt that you made to express it, even if it did not come out right the first time," Elizabeth reassured him. "I will bid you goodnight, Mr. Darcy. I will see you in the morning."

"Goodnight to you, Elizabeth." Darcy stood to watch her walk away, soon to be followed by Miss Bennet and the other ladies.

***

"So have you figured out the why, cousin?" Theodore spoke to Darcy as they all settled in with their port in Bingley's sitting room.

Darcy smiled begrudgingly at his cousin. That he was not the first person to know was disconcerting, but he was too happy to be upset. "I have realized that I am in love with Elizabeth. It took me a while to pin down what the emotion was. Now I want to know how you spotted it before I did."

Theodore looked at the grin on his cousin's face. Darcy so often struggled. It was nice to see him joyful. "I am happy for you. She is a remarkable lady, a veritable Boudica. Forester had no chance trying to go up against her logic." He knew that life had many obstacles and to have someone to help you over those hurdles was a genuine gift.

Bingley would not allow himself to be left out of the conversation. "You have some time while she is staying at Netherfield to make some progress with the lady. Darcy, do you have a plan in place?" Bingley knew his friend was very logical and would most likely have that carry over into his love life.

"I have asked her to walk with me in the morning, just in the garden. I have a feeling she would walk further, but I don't want to put too much strain on her healing body."

Theodore's mischievous grin was visible from across the room. "Will you be asking the lady a question? And if so, which question will you be asking?" he prompted.

"I think I will ask for a courtship. She deserves time to get to know me and the life she would lead should she join her lot with mine. What of you, Bingley, are you considering asking Miss Bennet anything?" Darcy was happy to turn the tables on his friend.

"I have thoroughly enjoyed our conversations, and she makes me want to be a better man. I think of the world around me more and how I can improve the lot of other people. My only question is what would I bring to the match? Is it fair to her if she helps me be a better person, but I offer nothing in return?" Bingley contemplated his hopes and some of the new concepts Miss Bennet had introduced him to.

Darcy paused for a moment, trying to think of ways to cheer up his dejected friend. "It may not be the way you want to help her, but you offer the stability that she does not have at home. I know she has the entailment hanging over her head. You have the finances to ensure that her mother and sisters would not suffer should something horrible come to pass."

"What I want to know is how things are going with your plan for your sister," Theodore interjected.

"My aunt in Scotland has agreed to help with my sister's behavior if I grant her control of Caroline's dowry. She married a landed gentleman and has been the mistress of his estate for some fifteen years, and can teach Caroline how to run an estate. My aunt said that she would like to come to collect Caroline herself. She said something about wanting to make sure she packed everything she needed and nothing she did not. Since my aunt is in London right now, she will be here sooner rather than later." He wished there was another way to restore the generous and loving girl she had been before her father sent her to that finishing school.

Theodore shuddered to think of spending an extended length of time with his Aunt Catherine. He was a battle-hardened soldier, but there were still things he would not do if he had his druthers. "I would never send Georgiana or anyone to my aunt to learn how to be a better person. You said your aunt had a good heart, right?"

"Yes, Aunt Guthrie is a dear. I spent some of my favorite summers staying with her and her husband, Callum McDougal. She treats everyone on her land from field workers to maids to visiting dignitaries the same. In fact, she demands that everyone else do the same, including the visiting dignitaries. I can only hope she reaches Caroline's heart." Bingley smiled, remembering his times with his aunt.

"I hope she helps her. That cannot be a comfortable way to live that your sister has chosen," Darcy said.

Bingley's grin grew at a sudden thought. "You know, Darcy, I have often wondered if we locked my aunt in a room with your aunt, who would come out on top. They are similar in disposition but diametrically opposed in worldview." When his comment made Theodore spit out his port and start choking, Bingley wondered if he had ever laughed so hard in his life.

***

ELIZABETH WATCHED THE TRANQUIL mist float along the ground, adorning the garden paths with pale gossamer grace. She could feel the beauty of nature to her very core. Bird songs played mysterious chords from their hidden retreats as they readied themselves for winter. Elizabeth stood still, absorbing it all. She was grateful that her injuries did not prevent her from witnessing this.

"I hope it is not too cold for you, Elizabeth," Darcy spoke up, concerned that the brisk weather would adversely affect her recovery.

She shook her head in mirth, loving the way her breath came out in puffs of white. "I rarely complain of the cold, and I would not miss this sight for anything."

He looked around the courtyard, and his eyes settled on Mrs. Ansley inside the morning room, her gaze surveying their actions discreetly. "It is lovely. I have rarely seen such a view, but please tell me if you feel the need to go inside. I thought maybe others would have joined us, but I see the chill has kept them away."

"I often find myself out of doors when my family thinks it is much better to be indoors. The sights I have been able to see when I do so have been worth the occasional red nose. We ought to walk the paths. It will help us stay warm," she advised.

"Elizabeth, I want to speak with you about something, but I fear I cannot do so without putting my boot in my mouth again."

Elizabeth found his confession so endearing she could not care less what subject he would bring up. "I am confident that I will decipher your meaning, even if your words may fall short. You may proceed."

"I know that people in my position in society, and the ton, have certain expectations and perceptions; they look down on everyone. You have no connections and no dowry, I am told. Most people I know would view this as completely unacceptable. Even members of my family will deride me for wanting to form a connection with you. Yet, I am struggling in vain to find the words to express the depths of my love for you." Darcy felt the weight of his inadequacy as he hung his head, knowing his words could never be called elegant or inspiring.

The touch of icy fingers on his chin brought his head up enough to look Elizabeth in the eyes. Ever expressive, their jeweled depths whispered to him of hope.

While Elizabeth questioned why he felt the need to bring up his domineering family's opinions, that was unimportant. What was important was that as she thought of his love, a feeling of warmth spread through her whole body, and her stomach fluttered with excitement. "Now, I know you did not mean to say that my family and I are beneath you. Or that you see my place in society is unimportant. Or that my dowry and family are not good enough for you. Could you be saying that you love me despite having a very judgmental family and connections?"

Darcy grabbed on to the possibilities he saw in her eyes and his heart seemed to swell in his chest. "Thank you for understanding my garbled declaration. I do not want you to decide without understanding the potential hindrances." Taking her icy hands in his, he held them to his chest, where she could feel the warmth of each beat of his heart.

"Are you asking me a question, Mr. Darcy?" Elizabeth felt her fear of having a marriage like her mother's raising its ugly head, though she tried to fight against it. She refused to tolerate the idea that Mr. Darcy was even remotely similar to her domineering father.

"Would you do me the honor of permitting a courtship? I would not want you to feel rushed into anything. I want to give you the opportunity to learn more about me and my family." He presented his heart to her, and as he stood there, the sound of his pounding heart echoed in his ears. He ardently hoped for an affirmative answer.

Elizabeth would take her future in her hands with her actions, but believed it would turn out alright. She decided she would dare to hope. "I would treasure the opportunity to be courted by you, Mr. Darcy."

After too short a time, enjoying the glory of fall and the delight of their burgeoning relationship, they went inside to the morning room. There they found Mrs. Ansley busily stitching on a project. "I know you are concerned about your family being an issue, but I am worried about my father being an issue." They had many things to discuss, and they were both becoming chilled walking in the garden. The morning room was comfortable, mostly because Caroline Bingley had not yet had the chance to redo it. Despite the slight signs of wear, Elizabeth enjoyed the warmth and comfort of the forest green settee by the fire.

"I have heard that he is not the best of men, but I did not want to pry into a painful subject." Darcy knew he had his share of memories of his parents that he did not like to think about. He wished that she did not have that pain, but knew that was unlikely. "How do you think he would react to my request to court you?"

"My father has never had to deal with interest in any of his daughters, so I do not know. I would think he would not be happy. He would jump at an offer if he thought you would make me miserable, but I really cannot say. I fear he might say yes, but forbid my mother or sisters any contact with me. Or something else like that."

"Would you think it would work to our benefit to request to court you before or after you get home?" Darcy wanted to go about things correctly. However, it might not be possible.

"I could say nothing with certainty. I can only tell you he will want to cause pain to more than just me." Elizabeth wished she could just take her sisters and escape from him. "One of the worst things about living with my father is how he feels the need to be critical of everyone and everything around him. Every time we eat at the dinner table, especially if he knows we have enjoyed something recently, he gets especially nasty. He likes to make us all live a bleak life."

"I cannot say how much it hurts me to hear you live like that. I wish I could help." Darcy found it harder than had imagined picturing her going back home to that man.

"I wish we were able to just leave, but my father has control over us just as he does the books in his study. He has the power by law to decide where and how we live. Frankly, he could cast us all into the fire as easy as he would a book." Elizabeth grumbled angrily at the situation they found themself in.

"But is not Jane of age? She could marry and lead a happy life somewhere." Darcy wondered why Jane was still at home if things were that desperate. She was very striking, and she had spent time in London, or so she said.

"Yet she cannot because she knows what it is her family is experiencing back at home. She also knows how terrible father can get when pushed." The thought of leaving the others behind filled both Jane and Elizabeth with dread.

"What is your father capable of?" Darcy questioned with a sinking feeling.

"When Kitty was maybe eight, we had a dismal and wet winter, and she developed a hacking cough that never seemed to go away. We feared for her health, and that is when Jane became so fascinated with the still room, as she was looking for something to heal Kitty. One morning Papa was suffering from a night of too much drinking; he had been in an argument about a blocked stream the day before and had not taken it well. I think his head ached something fierce and that morning at the breakfast table. When she could not stop her hacking for breath, he squeezed her wrist so tightly she cried out. By the time the screaming was over and he finally let go, her little wrist was so blue it was almost black. Mr. Jones had a salve that helped her wrist. Everything has filled her with dread since then." Elizabeth had felt guilty ever since that she could not protect her sister.

"Would it bother you if I tell you I think I detest your father?" Finding he could no longer remain still, Darcy stood and paced, drawing the attention of Mrs. Ansley.

"You may understand why I am always walking, or practicing archery. I have not the power to walk away or shoot him with an arrow, so I practice until I am ready to make a move." She stretched out her toes towards the fire, feeling its warmth on her skin, and hoping that a solution would soon present itself. Elizabeth had grown up knowing that knowledge was power. As much as she hated to disclose the nasty details of her past and her father, she knew it was necessary to be prepared for the battle she knew was to come.

"I would be the one to help you make that move if you will let me. You have been a great help to me. You have enabled me to cope with my struggles. It would please me to return the favor," Darcy soothed. returning to her side and taking her hand.

"If you want to help me stop my father, it is best to have all the pieces of the picture. I recall being around the age of eleven when I came to understand that my father had no concern for his tenants. He only cared for his port and his books and did not want to be bothered about leaky roofs or sick children or broken threshing equipment. Do not even ask about crop rotation or animal husbandry." Elizabeth spoke about her father while picking at a run in the settee's fabric with her thumbnail.

"If he had put the least effort into anything to improve the estate, he would have a greater profit margin. Why could he not see something that simple?" Such a lack of foresight confused Darcy.

"He knows that he could have increased dividends, but it was a matter of principle to him. My mother learned at the beginning of their marriage that my father was exceedingly angry about his lot in life. He was happy at Oxford and had hopes of becoming a fellow when there was an accident and that killed both his parents and his older brother. When his grandfather, who was still alive, summoned him back to Longbourn, he was furious. He did not want to leave the life he had built for himself at Oxford. When his grandfather forced the issue, he vowed to let Longbourn crumble as revenge." Elizabeth often found her father frustrating, but his need for revenge made him petty and small in her eyes.

"Well, that is a case of cutting off your nose to spite your face if I ever heard of one." Hardly anyone got exactly what they wanted in life, but it sounded like Mr. Bennet was acting like a cruel child.

"He picked my mother to marry because, as he later told her, she was the least suitable candidate he could find. She had never learned the skills necessary to manage an estate, as her father was the town solicitor. At sixteen, she was vibrant and naïve, believing she was in love when he showered her with affection. It was only after they were married that she saw his true nature. He wanted her to fail and to bring disgrace on the Bennet name, but he did not think his grandmother would take her under her wing. She helped my mother until her death, just after I was born. In remembrance of her, Mama gave Catherine her name." Elizabeth often wished she could remember the lady who had been so kind to her mother and had helped them all in such a way.

"I have always thought well of your mother and that is doubly the case now. Would you care for tea? I can ask for some to be brought up." Darcy could not imagine a young girl, only slightly older than Georgiana, having to deal with a petulant swine like that. He sounded much like Wickham, wanting the world to fall to his demands and causing problems when he did not get what he wanted.

"Tea would be lovely." Elizabeth smiled at Mr. Darcy sitting next to her. He was very considerate. Watching his interaction with the maid, she felt grateful, knowing that he was considerate of people from all stations. Not only had he asked for enough tea for Mrs. Ansley, but he was also thoughtful in asking after the maid's mother, who had been sick. "Though my father has great pride in his intelligence, he had a very limited field of study. My solicitor grandfather counted on this and wrote several things into the settlements that we ladies have used to our advantage. My father has suspected nothing and we can help our tenants when they require it."

"How so?" Darcy had heard that they supported necessary things on their own, but he had never figured out the details of such an endeavor.

"The interest from my mother's dowry goes back into the fund so that they reinvest it until my father dies or signs a form releasing the dividends to her. She will not be penniless on my father's death, which he often tells her, by the way. Her dowry has doubled during their marriage, providing her with enough money to live on if needed. Her pin money, which would normally come from her dowry, comes from his estate. He never asked for advice from anyone, so he did not know this was unusual. Also, the settlement states that her pin money increased by twenty pounds a year with every child she bore. After bearing him five daughters, her pin money has doubled. All of us girls have a stipulated amount of pin money too, all coming from the estate and larger than would be normal, not by much, but by some. Since my father feels he is above figuring his money, he has left the bookkeeping to his brother-in-law, the town solicitor. As long as his money for port and books stays the same, he does not much care what happens." She shook her head in frustration at how carelessly he handled his management duties.

"I would say he is certainly not as intelligent as he presumes." Darcy laughed and then prepared tea as Elizabeth liked it, as he had noticed she was having difficulty stirring the tea with a broken arm. Passing her the tea, he prepared himself for more of her father's tomfoolery.

"Mother should be here to see me this morning after breakfast. I hope we could talk to her and see if there is a plan we could come up with. Mama has spent most of her life learning to deal with my father's tantrums. She may have some words of wisdom for us." Elizabeth had missed her mother and was looking forward to being able to see her.

"Though I have enjoyed my time alone with you, I would hate to keep you from breakfast, and the others are probably heading down to eat now. What do you think of joining them?" Darcy suggested, offering his hand to help her stand.

"I would love to head to breakfast with you, Mr. Darcy." She stood, taking his hand, and walked with him to the door.

"I do not want to appear too forward, but would you consider calling me by my first name?" Darcy requested, yearning to hear his name on her lips.

"Fitzwilliam takes up a lot of space on the tongue. How do you feel about a more succinct version?" Elizabeth looked up at him, her eyes sparkling with mirth.

"I would not have any qualms about it, so long as I receive the same opportunity. Would you be against the idea of me giving you a pet name?" Darcy liked the idea of being the only one to use the name he chose. He also liked the idea of her doing the same for him.

"I think that is a brilliant idea." She placed her good hand into the crook of his elbow as they walked to breakfast. She tried out different variations of his name in her mind to determine the best option.

Chapter Nineteen

"You seem to do better than I thought you would, though that bruise looks atrocious. You would tell me if you were suffering too badly, right Lizzie?" Cupping her daughter's unharmed cheek, Mrs. Bennet looked into her eyes. The bruise on Elizabeth's face was ugly, turning green around the edges and purple at the center.

Holding her Mama's hand to her good cheek, Elizabeth tried to reassure her. "I am alright, Mama; my arm is much better than it was and Jane's tea is helping. Mostly I am just frustrated. I cannot do everything like I always do. Jane and the maids have to help me get dressed. I cannot even cut my food." She grumbled and then blushed slightly, remembering how Mr. Darcy had seen her dilemma and reached around her to cut her ham and eggs for her.

Fanny Bennet grinned at her flustered daughter. "That blush is new. Are you neglecting to tell your mother something?" She often regretted that her daughters had such solemn lives; they rarely flirted and enjoyed themselves as she had done as a girl.

Unable to meet her mother's eyes, Elizabeth looked down, studying the sling that she still wore. She tried to speak as if the words she spoke were not so very monumental. "Mr. Darcy spoke with me this morning and we have come to an understanding. He has asked for a formal courtship. I think he would be happy to have proposed, but we both seem to have family issues we are concerned about. He asked me to call him by his Christian name." She ended her comment in a whisper, slightly embarrassed to disclose this to her mother.

"I think that is rational. There is no need to rush. You have plenty of time. I am happy for you, my dear. He seems like a wonderful man. I will still ask your uncle to look into him, though." Mrs. Bennet hoped the first of her daughters had found her way into a happy future.

"We are both worried about Father. How do you think he will take it? Mr. Darcy wants to ask Father for his permission to court me." Elizabeth was becoming more determined to stop her father's reign of terror.

"He will not take it well. I know that much. I fear he may focus his anger on you. It might be best to speak with him now. Maybe he will have cooled off by the time you return home. He may even become distracted by new events. He does not know, but Mr. Collins has proposed to Charlotte and she has accepted. I have cautioned him not to let Mr. Bennet know, so the only way he'll find out is when the banns are read aloud in church on Sunday. If your Mr. Darcy is bold enough to ask your father about it today or tomorrow, his focus will not stay on him for long. I cannot promise he will respond positively either way." Mrs. Bennet was interested to see what her husband's reaction would be. He was too used to wielding his power and had not felt the pressure of a challenge in far too long. He would grossly misjudge Mr. Darcy.

***

"Do you think your aunt will be here soon?" Darcy questioned Bingley.

"Within a day or two, I think. Caroline has broken almost everything in her room. I have asked her maid to keep a tally of it all and I will subtract the cost from what is left of her pin money for the year. She is getting her meals brought up on trays. I let her know I have not confined her to her room. She can walk in the garden or even spend time with all of us, but she must be polite to everyone. She has stayed in her room." Bingley sighed. He loved his sister, but she drove him crazy.

"I do not know what is worse, dealing with a spoiled brat or a stubborn ignoramus," Theodore growled.

"Is the Colonel causing more issues?" Darcy guessed.

Theodore hated to see such inept behavior when he knew what needed to be done. He grumbled under his breath momentarily before responding. "Though he is now admitting that Wickham is not the upstanding fellow he had assumed, I find his idea of what makes up a search ineffective in the extreme." Rolling his eyes, Theodore tapped his foot rapidly in frustration, his annoyance bordering on anger.

"What is he doing that is so wrong? How complicated can a search be?" Bingley questioned.

"He has confined his search to checking all of Wickham's likely escape routes from the region and preventing him from leaving. He is coordinating with the stage and the hostler about refusing Wickham any means of transportation. I asked the townspeople to inform him if they came across him, after they tell me, of course." Theodore's tactician's mind saw all the holes in Forester's plan.

"I know you are not resting on your laurels because someone else is a fool. What have you been working on?" Darcy asked.

Theodore smiled knowingly at his cousin. Sometimes they could almost read each other with no conversation. "I have not been idle like some others who have spent the morning with their lady loves. I have been speaking with various estate owners and Hugh has been reaching out to the tenants, putting out the word of Wickham's dealings. If anyone sees something odd, they know to come to me and let me know."

"Do you think he is still in the area, or has he escaped the area and gone to ground again?" Bingley spoke while looking through the papers he had brought from his study.

"I think he is hiding somewhere, probably in an unused hunting cabin somewhere. It is like knowing a poisonous snake is living in the tall grass. He is going to come out and bite you at some point, but you cannot tell when." Theodore felt the need to deal with this snake sooner rather than later.

Bingley had never considered what it would take to search for someone. It involved more than he had imagined. "I can see how we do not have the manpower to search all the abandoned buildings in the area. He could even camp out in the woods, though he has never struck me as that kind of fellow," he asserted.

"If he rears his head long enough, we will be there to lop the snake's head off. Hopefully, it is simply a matter of time." Theodore grinned at the imagery.

"We may have two snakes to deal with." Darcy hoped they would help him come up with a plan to assist the Bennet ladies.

"I thought you were wooing this morning, not finding new enemies," Theodore ribbed his normally reserved cousin.

Darcy tapped his fingers against each other, trying to focus and devise a plan of attack. The anger he felt would not help him right now. "I spent a lovely interval with Miss Elizabeth. While I was concerned about how she would take to the madness of the ton and Aunt Catherine, she was concerned with her father. Though we are both happy to be in an official courtship, it is not quite official until her father approves." He practically growled at the word "father". That man did not deserve the term.

"I have never spoken with the gentleman. Come to think of it, we have been to their home several times. We really should have met him by now." Bingley realized the oddity of the situation.

"He is angry over inheriting the estate and in an act of petty revenge, and he is trying to drive it into the ground. He pays no attention to any issues, and he remains in his study, reading and consuming port, ruminating on his own superiority. People have long known of his cruelty to the ladies. Even though she was only a little girl, the memory of the injury he caused her still lingers in Miss Kitty's mind. Elizabeth said it affects her to this day. Elizabeth seems to fear he will retaliate against her sisters and mother, as he does not want them to have the chance of being contented." Such behavior confounded Darcy.

Bingley had no notion that things had been bad for Miss Bennet. Then again, he knew she took a lot on to herself. "You are right about him being a snake. That is despicable. Now we have two snakes to behead." Bingley wanted to rush in to help save the day, but did Miss Bennet want him to save her? She surprised him often.

"I am afraid that this snake will be more difficult to behead. It is one of the many things that my brother has tried to bring up in Parliament. Women have no power to protect themselves from ill-intentioned male relatives. If we are to take him on, we will need more information. Do you think you will ask him soon?" Theodore's older brother, the current Earl, had told him occasionally of the issues he was trying to bring up and how things kept getting moved to the side because of the war. It was one thing to hear that a girl he did not know was being taken advantage of by an unscrupulous family. It was another thing to know her and see the damage being caused.

"Elizabeth is speaking with her mother now to see if she has had a suggestion of how soon it might work." Darcy hoped the conversation was going well.

Theodore started thinking of some scenarios his brother had brought to his attention in the past. It was possible that one of them could help with one of the two snakes they were facing. "I would suggest that you learn as much as possible about him. We might have a few options if we know what he wants more than port and being a contemptible fool." Whatever happened, he had a feeling that Mr. Bennet would regret it if he pushed Darcy. Despite his unease in large groups, Darcy was undeterred and fiercely protective of those he cared for.

***

A QUICK CONVERSATION WITH Elizabeth and Mrs. Bennet had encouraged him to act sooner rather than later. Darcy soon found himself shown into the study and came face to face with a disgruntled Mr. Bennet. His life of indolent negligence had hastened him towards a well-stuffed form. His clothes looked as if a tailor had made them for someone much smaller than him. He sat at a desk littered with books of various sizes and colors, loose sheets of paper intermixed in the mess. Though it was slightly surprising to see that besides the copious amounts of books, everything was spotless. In fact, there was not a speck of dust on any of the shelves. There were bookshelves on every wall of the room; the only blank area was at the door where he entered and there was no chair for anyone but Mr. Bennet to sit in the room. Darcy supposed it was a statement.

"You have requested to see me, Mr. Darcy, and yet you are more fascinated with my collection. I would have thought a person of your standing would exhibit better manners." Mr. Bennet enjoyed watching how Mr. High and Mighty's eyes widened at his comment.

Darcy figured it would not hurt to butter him up if he needed time to gather information. "As a fellow bibliophile, I appreciate all the work you have put into your collection. I laud the work you have done here." Glancing around for further details, he spotted a polished chessboard on the corner of his desk, nearly obscured by the stacks of books. He recognized that several of the books were on chess mastery.

"I think it's an amazing accomplishment, considering I was working without the assistance of my Oxford peers. I have even collected most of Benjamin Striker's series on the importance of the Greek hero." Mr. Bennet preened under the acknowledgment of his success.

"That is an amazing coup, sir," Darcy replied.

"Yes, I am short only the third book in the set of seven. Regardless of your love of books, I would not have allowed you admittance if I knew you were going to stand there and gape at my library. Get to the point." Mr. Bennet grew frustrated and wanted to return to his study of Homer in the original Greek.

"I have come to ask you for your permission to enter a formal courtship with your daughter, Elizabeth." Darcy felt his palms becoming uncomfortably moist but did not want to show the weakness of wiping his hands on his pants.

"Has Jane turned you down? I would not have thought that of her. She has so few thoughts in her head, and all of them yearn to see people happy. I would not have guessed she would risk hurting someone like that." Mr. Bennet watched his opponent closely, trying to pick up on any signs of discomfort.

Darcy was used to dealing with family discord, yet this time, he was an onlooker, and the victim was the woman he loved. He expected to feel the familiar panic or anxiety that he dreaded so much, yet he did not. All he felt at that moment was outrage. His rage towards the person in front of him enabled him to push past his uneasy emotions and be able to do what he had to. "Though Jane has many positive traits, I have become enamored with Elizabeth and wish to begin a courtship and eventually marry her." Darcy knew Elizabeth said that her father was insulting, but to hear it himself was painful.

"Oh, that is not something you need to be concerned with. She is not worthy of marrying a gentleman like you. If you want to skip the whole courtship and marriage issue, you can take her as your bit of muslin if you think you can control her." He would not allow her to land in a happy castle that easily.

"I know I often mistakenly say things I did not entirely mean, so I would like to check that I understand what you mean. Are you stating that you feel I should take your daughter as a mistress?" Darcy was incredulous.

"Elizabeth has a modicum of intelligence, but I did not groom her to be the proprietress of a grand estate. I have refused to provide a dowry. She has no connections that would not embarrass you with your friends among the ton. Even her sisters should put you off. Take, for example, this painting I have resting on the floor. Her youngest sister Lydia painted it. There is no greatness in the art, and the subject is pedestrian. I am sure you would be ashamed if the sister I hear you have painted so poorly. That she gave me this painting is questionable. I have treated her and her sisters with derision for her entire life and yet she has not the intelligence to see it. You would be in a much better position if you opted to choose another bride. Take her as your mistress if you feel if you must have her." Mr. Bennet questioned the boy's intelligence. He could reach so much higher for a bride. His family was part of the nobility. As the grandson of an earl, he could get almost any woman he wanted and have a few mistresses besides. Choosing his daughter the way he had was not a smart move.

Darcy drew on his years of experience in dealing with troublesome people of the ton in an effort not to lose his composure. "Be that as it may, I have come to ask for a formal courtship with the intention of marrying her. Do you grant me my request for an official courtship?" Unable to look at his smug face any long Darcy looked over the painting. It was a picture of yellow carnations and orange lilies and petunias in a vase with buttercups scattered at the base. Suddenly, he remembered Elizabeth told him that Lydia was obsessed with the language of flowers. Even though the painting was simply done, he was sure that the message it conveyed would be remarkable once he figured out how to decipher it.

"My answer is no, you do not have my permission. She is not yet of age, so there is no way you can proceed for the next eight months. If you follow this course, I will cast her off and forbid her contact with any of her sisters and her mother. Good day, sir. I would like my study back." Ignoring the interloper, Mr. Bennet turned his attention back to his book.

Aghast, Darcy turned and left the room. Elizabeth had warned him that her father was not a good person, but his views and suggestions were astounding. What landed gentleman in his right mind suggests that his daughter become a mistress? Snake indeed; he was turning out to be a cobra, not a common adder.

Chapter Twenty

The Bennet ladies were finding themselves enjoying a congenial gathering in the Netherfield morning room. Once Mr. Darcy had departed, almost all the ladies had gathered to talk and do minor projects. The gregarious companionship thrilled Georgiana. She had just returned from helping to teach the class with Mary, and William had insisted they use his carriage and a footman, which enabled them to pick up Kitty and Lydia on their way back. It had been a splendid morning full of new insights and giggle fits. She had never had sisters, and she yearned to have these sisters as her own. Across from where she sat with Mary and Kitty, Lydia sat chatting with Mrs. Ansley and Mrs. Hurst, working on a project and seeming to have a good time. Lizzie and Jane sat with their mother by the fire speaking of something that had embarrassed Lizzie because her cheeks had turned a decided shade of pink.

"What do you think they are talking about over there that has Lizzie so pink?" Leaning over to whisper to Mary and Kitty to not be overheard, Georgiana's eyes danced with glee.

"I have a feeling that Mama realized Lizzie is rather fond of your brother, or possibly that he is fond of her. I suspect we may hear some kind of announcement about them soon." Mary grinned.

"I have suspected that my brother was fond of Lizzie for some time, but when did you realize Lizzie was just as smitten?" Georgiana asked.

"Elizabeth was walking in the garden with Mr. Darcy the other day. Mama and Jane were there, along with Mr. Bingley. Jane said that Lizzie and Mr. Darcy had been walking and talking when Lizzie said something so funny that he burst out laughing. Jane said she was so taken by his laugh and previously unknown dimples that she tripped and fell over her feet," Mary admitted with a straight face, though after a moment her eyes were dancing with humor. Kitty, sitting beside her, covered her mouth with her hands but could not prevent her giggle from escaping. Georgiana gave in to her mirth and joined her.

It was to this hilarity that Caroline Bingley entered the room. She had spent the last forty-eight hours confined to her room, not by force but by her choosing. Her indignant attitude grew with every minute. Who was her brother to say that her behavior was unacceptable? He had not clawed his way up the social ladder the way she had. He did not understand the way you had to fight to get what she had. She had screamed. Then she had raged. She had broken things and yet he had not come to apologize.

She came down this morning and sat in the parlor, determined to restore her authority in her family. Only she was alone. No one joined her to apologize for how they had not supported her. It was the peals of laughter that alerted her they had gathered elsewhere.

When she entered the room, she saw the three merry groups chatting. The younger girls were laughing so hard they were wiping tears out of their eyes. Mrs. Bennet and Mrs. Ansley looked on with indulgent smiles. Why did no one look at her like that? They punished her the last time she had laughed at finishing school. She had not laughed since. A lady never raised her voice and never laughed in public. Why did everyone flout the rules that she had learned?

Caroline grimaced, looking around the room with disdain. Why would anyone want to stay in such an unfashionable room? "Georgiana, dear, though commoners and peasants express emotions in unseemly manners, people of a higher class do not. I would have thought that your companion would have explained that to you."

The silence in the room was complete and abrupt. Expressions ranged from hurt to vexation. Around the room, eyes met, and they held silent conversations between one blink and the next.

A slight frown graced Mrs. Ansley's face. "Indeed, it is not correct to laugh excessively in formal settings. A contained giggle is acceptable in even the most formal of places, such as Almack's. Beyond that, in a private home among friends and equals, laughing is both acceptable and healthy." She spoke up to clear up what sounded like a horrible teaching at a finishing school. She did not want her charge to get the wrong impression or become overly reserved. Mrs. Ansley felt that the Bennet girls were a wonderful influence and most likely would soon be sisters to Georgiana.

Caroline stared, mouth agape. "Do you consider yourself our equal? You are a companion. What do you think you are doing to correct me?" She stared down at the older woman, though she was not bad looking. Her clothes were very plain, with practically no lace at all. The shades may have complemented her coloring, but they were not at all popular this season.

"As you have never asked, you do not know that I am the daughter of a baron. By birth, I am far above you, so no, we are not on equal standing socially. As a companion to Georgiana, part of my job is to inform her of socially acceptable behaviors for her to navigate her entry into society. I was merely correcting an untruth that you had exposed her to. For what it is worth, I question both the method and the lessons they taught you at that school of yours." Mrs. Ansley pitied the poor girl that stood in front of her. The life she had chosen would be very cold and lonely. Though there was still hope that she would see the light.

Caroline marched over to her sister and glared at the youngest Bennet chit. Lydia was in the spot that she would normally be in. How dare she be so presumptuous? Caroline turned her glare on her sister and all but shouted at her. "Louisa, sister, why are you not speaking up for me?"

"I have long allowed you to say and do what you wish. When Mother and Father died along with Nathan, I was so afraid. I felt the need to make sure all the family I had left were happy, so I supported you in what you asked. Only I am waking up to the fact that my actions have made no one happy. I have not been happy. My husband has been decidedly unhappy at my insistence to give in to you. Charles has not been happy and you, the sister that I love, are not happy. I will no longer bow to your wishes because I feel in the long run, you will benefit from learning some hard truths. One of those truths is that I will absolutely not support you in being snide and cruel. I like all the people in this room, and I will not let you act as you have in the past. If you would like, you can sit here with Lydia and I. We have been having a very pleasant conversation." Louisa had such relief once she had fished her speech. She had felt this way for some time, but had not felt up to the challenge.

Caroline stood in shock, unable to process this revelation. How had she never known that her sister held her views in such derision? Indecision rendered her immobile. If she proceeded as she always did, she would respond with some cutting remark and leave. But would that mean losing her relationship with her sister? She just could not understand it all. Why had everything changed when they came here?

"I am suffering from a headache. I will return to my room." Turning, she left to contemplate how her world was shifting. She needed to understand and find a way to proceed.

Mrs. Ansley felt pity for the obviously confused girl. Her work as a companion allowed her the experience to recognize just how miserable she was. Girls that unhappy often lashed out. "She seems very unsettled. I am hoping she will eventually recognize the value of kindness. It makes for a much more gratifying life." She knew it would be a hard road to travel.

***

DARCY ENTERED A MORE subdued morning room, not that much later. For as baffled as he felt from his interaction with Mr. Bennet, he was still remarkably glad to see the smile light up Elizabeth's face when he entered the room. He decided right then to save his thoughts about her father's problem for another time. For now, he was going to enjoy his time with a most remarkable woman.

"How does my lovely lady do in my absence?" Darcy queried, reaching out and taking her hand to kiss it with a flourish.

"Oh dear, I did not know purple and green were considered lovely or I would have tried a new beauty regimen long ago." Elizabeth's eyes danced, her pert smile in full use.

Georgiana giggled. She loved seeing his dimples on full display. Her brother smiling was a wonderful thing. "I see how it is between you two. Do you have something to tell us, brother?"

"Yes, but I think luncheon is ready. Maybe we can discuss it over our meal?" Darcy delayed the inevitable. He had no issue revealing the relationship but was uncertain how to keep from telling everyone about Mr. Bennet's awful behavior. Squeezing Elizabeth's hand, he raised his eyebrows, questioning her desire to explain things here or after a soothing meal.

"I would be delighted to have you escort me to my meal. I find myself quite famished." Standing, she wrapped her good arm around his and leaned her head on his shoulder. Though unaccustomed to having such positive male attention, she was finding it something she enjoyed. It would hurt nothing to leave everyone in suspense. It would surprise Elizabeth if they could not figure things out on their own with the way she and Mr. Darcy were acting.

"It would be my pleasure, my sweet. You never know. You may very well find yourself in need of my services once again," Darcy commented, enjoying the memory of the time they spent at breakfast.

"Do not become used to my current level of neediness. My arm will heal and then where will you be?" Elizabeth remarked.

"I think I will enjoy you keeping me on my toes," he whispered to Elizabeth, enjoying their banter.

***

THE MEAL HAD BEEN simple, but delicious. When Mrs. Ansley had taken over from Caroline, a lot of things had improved, and the food was one of the best.

Looking around, Darcy was glad everyone was interacting so well together. All the chatter was amiable and intelligent. The talk had ranged from the war on the continent to the latest thoughts on crop rotation, and the various literature people had been reading. He could not easily remember a meal that had been so enjoyable and intellectually challenging.

"Brother, you said you would say something at the meal and I believe the meal is almost complete," Georgiana reminded her brother, impatient to celebrate what she already suspected.

Darcy cast his gaze around the room, his smile beaming with delight. His excitement was contagious as he shared his news with everyone present. "I know everyone suspects as much, but I wanted to say that Elizabeth and I have come to an understanding and have agreed to court."

The tremendous squeal from Georgiana deafened him. She bypassed him though to hug Elizabeth, ever careful of her arm.

"Mrs. Bennet, would you be available to speak with Elizabeth and me before you return to Longbourn?" Darcy felt she had a right to know some adverse situations were coming up concerning her daughter.

"I have enough time to discuss matters with you." Mrs. Bennet watched the way Mr. Darcy seemed to communicate with Elizabeth without words. It certainly boded well for their future.

***

THERE WERE SEVERAL PEOPLE gathered to review a problem and find a solution. Looking around, Elizabeth felt a certain familiarity with the situation. It was not too dissimilar from the many times she had gathered to solve a problem with her mother and sisters.

"I am going to assume that your conversation with Miss Elizabeth's father did not go well," Theodore spoke up once they were all settled.

Darcy ran his hand through his hair, his frustration with Mr. Bennet visible in the way he paced. "I think that may be the largest understatement I have heard all year. I knew your father was not the best of men, darling, before I went over there and yet going over there was so much worse than I imagined."

"I will assume that my father was insulting to myself and at least one other of my sisters. It is nothing we do not hear spoken to us and of us regularly. What did he say about our courtship?" Elizabeth suspected he would refuse in a manner most severe.

Darcy's heart ached to hear Elizabeth's resigned voice as she spoke of her father's animosity. "Mr. Bennet refused to allow an official courtship or an eventual marriage. He went one step further to say that if we married, he would disown Elizabeth and refuse contact with any family still at Longbourn." He tried to avoid revealing some of the more sordid details of his interaction with Mr. Bennet.

"Mr. Darcy, I think you are very noble to protect our feelings, but I have been married to that man for nearly twenty-three years. I know that was not the whole. What did he say besides no?" Mrs. Bennet had known it would not go well. She wished to be prepared for whatever comments he made on her return to Longbourn.

"You know your husband, Mrs. Bennet; sadly, he was quite cruel. He suggested his daughter was not worthy of marrying a man like me and that he gave me permission to take Elizabeth as my mistress. His words implied she was not good enough for anything more." Darcy ground out the filth that Mr. Bennet had spewed in his study.

Bingley had never experienced such an intense feeling of disgust towards someone. "Excuse my candor, Mrs. Bennet, but I think your husband is a despicable human being."

"It is alright dear, I have known that since the beginning of my marriage to the man. May I assume we are all here so that we can unseat my husband and his delusions?" Mrs. Bennet had long dreamed of humbling her husband's smugness, and she could sense it would happen soon.

"Yes, Mrs. Bennet, that is the plan. Let me first start by saying you have my sympathy for having to endure such a man for so long. Though it proves that you have a core of steel that I think you must have passed on to your daughters. How else would Elizabeth have the gumption to take on a dastard like Wickham?" The more Theodore found out about Mr. Bennet, the more outraged he became. He found the opposite was also true. He was even more in awe of the Bennet women. They lived in a veritable war zone and yet they remained kind and amazingly strong.

"Oh, you do go on." Mrs. Bennet blushed at such a compliment.

Elizabeth realized how much she wanted a future with the man beside her. She would not allow her father to stand in the way of her happiness. "Though I would not be averse to waiting until we can marry, I am opposed to being cut off from my mother and sisters. Is there a way to force Father's hand?"

"Did you bring back any intelligence from the interaction, Darcy?" Theodore prompted. He had several theories on what they could do. Their next actions depended on what they could figure out about Mr. Bennet's desires and weaknesses.

Darcy concentrated on recalling the various details he could pick up on. "He is very proud of his extensive book collection. He even has all but one of Benjamin Striker's series on the importance of the Greek hero. He also appears to be a chess player."

"Yes, he has been after that one book for the last ten years." Mrs. Bennet remembered how angry he had become when someone outbid him for the last copy he had tried to purchase.

"I think he was the reigning chess champion back when he was at Oxford, though now he only plays himself," Elizabeth commented.

"Darcy, I think I remember your father talking about that collection. I think he purchased all of them. He got the last one about ten years ago." Theodore was not fond of his uncle, but he remembered him crowing about outbidding someone ten years ago.

Mrs. Bennet burst out laughing. She laughed so hard she had tears flowing down her cheeks. Hardly able to catch her breath, she struggled to compose herself. "That is just amazingly perfect." Accepting a handkerchief from Mr. Bingley, she wiped her eyes.

"Are you all right, Mrs. Bennet?" So far, Bingley had been of little help, but he had substantial feelings about the Bennet ladies' situation. He hoped that he would have a close bond with them. If Mr. Bennet acted so horribly about Miss Elizabeth, there was no expectation of a better response to a request for Miss Bennet's hand.

"Just fine, dear, I just realized that Mr. Darcy's father must have been the one to outbid Mr. Bennet. He had been willing to give up several of his extravagances for some time in order to get that book. When he lost the bid, he was furious. You will forgive me for finding an absurd kind of amusement in the situation's irony." She reached over and patted Mr. Bingley's hand. He was a very sweet boy and there were strong glimmers of his potential. She would wait to judge the possibilities of his being a match for one of her daughters.

"I think your humor completely justified, Mrs. Bennet." Darcy found himself startled to realize that her exuberance reminded him of Elizabeth's.

"Mama, you have given me the most astoundingly good idea. Mr. Darcy, what was that chess move you told me about? Where a player gives up a piece during the opening to win something greater?" As she looked into Mr. Darcy's eyes, she felt her heart flutter with the understanding they shared. Her father's reign was coming to a close. He just didn't know it yet.

"A gambit?" Darcy looked into the sparkling green depths of her eyes and grinned. She was right; it was a brilliant idea.

Chapter Twenty-One

Elizabeth was sitting with Mr. Darcy in front of the fire and was enjoying the ability to talk with him. Learning more about him was helping her to overcome her doubts about risking marriage. "I must admit that I have often wondered how you are so understanding of my connections in trade and my uncle, who is a solicitor. I thought that landowners often show intolerance towards different classes of people."

"I had always known I was second born, but had thought little of it until I was ten when I found out that my beloved cousin Theodore was not getting his own estate to manage. He was being told that he must make his way in the world. He had to choose between joining the church or the military or learning a skill." Darcy leaned back in his chair, watching Theodore talk to Bingley across the room. After Mrs. Bennet left with Miss Mary, Miss Kitty, and Miss Lydia, the remaining members of their party removed to the morning room. Even Mr. Hurst had joined the group, which was fascinating because he had spent most of his time at Netherfield napping in the understocked library.

"I know it is a normal practice to consolidate wealth and power. Younger sons must find their way." Elizabeth hoped if she ever had younger sons, she would provide better for them than was the custom.

Darcy watched one of Elizabeth's curls escape its confines and slide down her forehead towards her nose. He only felt slightly guilty that she did not have his undivided attention. After all, his attention was on her, it just was not all on her words. "Yes, it is very common. I went to school, and I met these second and third sons who were adrift trying to find a place in the world. I thought, if my older brother had lived, what would my choice be? What would I choose for my life?" He eased the curl back from her face, and she smiled in relief, as it no longer tickled her nose.

"What did you decide?" Elizabeth encouraged.

"I cannot tolerate crowds and speaking in front of them is impossible, so the church was not an option. I cannot stomach violence, so I would not head for the military. Though I am not opposed to trade, I do not have the connections or the business acumen. So I decided I would become a solicitor or a barrister. I like rules and order and there is a lot of studying involved. That is my long-winded story as to why I do not have problems with your connections. Had my brother lived, I would have been in the situation to have been part of one of those fields."

Elizabeth felt the warmth of a blush spread across her cheeks as she looked at Mr. Darcy. His adoring gaze and thoughtful gestures directed toward her made her feel incredibly special. "I think that is one of the most spectacular things about you. You do not contain yourself to the world in front of you; you explore other options, you acknowledge parallel paths and the feelings of others. You have proven yourself to be empathetic." Elizabeth loved the way her words caused a slight blush to highlight his cheeks. That he was allowing her to see him and not a front he put up to protect himself was significant to her.

"Would you be interested in trying to practice chess? We can set up a game in the corner." Darcy loved studying the way her mind worked. He thought that eventually, she would beat him regularly.

"I would love to practice chess some more. I find the game very intriguing." Getting up, Elizabeth moved to the corner Mr. Darcy had pointed out.

***

IT WAS MADDENING HAVING to take food and supplies from tenants the selection Wickham had to choose from was a degradation of his discerning palate. He slunk back to the defunct building he had adopted as his own after stealing a loaf of bread and some cheese. Once his head had cleared of the headache derived from his overindulgence, he had settled into planning a way out of his situation. He would have to leave the area, but that would take time at this point. Colonel Forester was not a man of action, but he was tenacious. He had posted guards around town that would prevent Wickham from getting on the post coach and from getting a horse. In a stroke of genius or accident, he owed money to all the men on the lookout for him. Eventually, they would become complacent, but until then, he had time on his hand to perfect his plan of revenge and he felt it was coming along nicely.

***

"Here, let me brush your hair out for you and braid it." Jane was tired of watching Elizabeth struggle, trying to do things on her own with her broken arm. Her sister was far too stubborn for her own good.

She moved to sit on the bed in front of Jane and let her begin her soothing task. "Thank you. Now that my arm is not aching as much, I am finding myself growing frustrated with my inability to do things."

"I noticed you did not have a problem with letting Mr. Darcy help you." Jane smirked at her sister's back. Mr. Darcy had not even asked. He had just leaned over and helped her when he realized she could not cut her meat.

"I will admit it has been a novel experience having someone dote on me as he does." As hot as her cheeks felt, Elizabeth was glad that she was facing away from Jane.

Jane grinned at her sister's slightly off voice. It was wonderful to see her so delighted. "Yes, I can understand that. I have had quite the opportunity to get to know Mr. Bingley, but it has been odd when compared to all I have known up to this point about how a man behaves."

"I find myself uneasy about getting married because of how badly I know it can go, but I also want to spend more time with Mr. Darcy.

I am even picturing our time together years from now. It is so very tiring, not to mention confusing." Elizabeth fidgeted with a ribbon on her nightgown.

Jane paused in brushing Elizabeth's hair. "Do you really think Mr. Darcy would act as Father does? Do you find him to be that kind of man?"

"No, not in my heart. He is kind and attentive. He often says the wrong thing, wording things in such a way that it is insulting, but now that I know him, it is becoming easier to decipher what he means. It is almost the opposite of being with Father. Where Father will say things in a way that you need to decipher how he is being cruel, Mr. Darcy has the best of intentions and truly is not trying to hurt anyone. He really cannot seem to keep his boot out of his mouth, but he means well." Elizabeth laughed, thinking of the things he had said while meaning the opposite.

"I have wondered about some things he has said, but I have never sensed the same malice I do from Father. If it means anything, I think he is a good choice. He seems upright, and he has shown evidence of a strong moral character. I know he has the finances to support you and any children you may have, but more than that, he will treat you well." Jane would miss Elizabeth when she married, but she could see how overjoyed she would be.

"That means something. You know I trust your judgment. How are things going with your Mr. Bingley? I can tell he is showing you special interest." Elizabeth wanted her sister to be just as happy as she was becoming. With her braid finished, she turned to face Jane.

Jane fiddled with the brush in her hand as she spoke. Though she liked him well enough, she struggled to let her heart go, but she would wait and see how things proceeded. "I find him everything that a true gentleman should be, though I wonder at his strength of character. He seems to lean on the suggestions of others, which could leave him open to suggestion."

"He has started to make some progress. I think he has stood strong on his stand with Caroline. Darcy said his aunt should be here tomorrow to take her in hand. It is something you can observe and see how things proceed." Elizabeth understood Jane's fears all too well.

"I think that is going to be something I can easily do. Something tells me we will be in each other's company for quite a while. I do not feel the need to rush." Jane would be content however things ended up.

"So your aunt should be here in the morning? How long do you think she will stay?" Darcy had met the lady once or twice before, but only briefly. He remembered a cheerful person who had been kind to him despite his awkward greeting.

"Yes, she should be here before luncheon. I know she needs to head back home to Scotland soon or else she will have difficulty traveling as winter sets in." Bingley understood that travel could be unpleasant if she waited too long to head north. At least she lived just across the border, so it should be better than going to the far north.

"She is kind to come out of her way to help you." Theodore had never met the lady, but appreciated someone willing to step in and help solve a problem.

"She is kindness itself," Bingley confirmed.

"Darcy, how bad was Mr. Bennet really? I could tell you did not want to reveal everything in front of the ladies." Theodore could read his cousin's quirks better than anyone, and he suspected it had been a tough morning for him.

"I do not know if I have ever met a more despicable man. Everything he said was an insult to those fine ladies. He had no compunction in suggesting that I take her as my mistress and even crudely suggested something about my preferences in choosing her. I suspect he spends all of his time in his little library feeling his own superiority and only ventures forth to harm his family and dependents." Darcy relished the burn of the whiskey as he swallowed it. It distracted him from the vile things that Mr. Bennet had said. He knew that Elizabeth would have to return home within five days and could not stomach letting her near that man ever again. He felt guilty letting Mrs. Bennet and her daughters go, knowing what they returned to.

"I think we have a good plan to stop him. We will put it into action after Elizabeth heads back to Longbourn, and no, you cannot run away with her to protect her from her father. She has survived him for twenty years and she will survive another two weeks. I even have an idea about how we can make sure that he gets what is coming to him. I just need to see a copy of the entail on the estate."

"Darcy is an upstanding fellow, but I can picture him running away with Miss Elizabeth clutched to his chest, protecting her from her father's sinister machinations." Bingley chuckled at the image in his mind.

"I do not deny I have that instinct right now. I cringe at the thought that she is in the same house as that man. At least Mr. Collins will be returning to Hunsford in Kent." Darcy pondered the ways he could ensure Elizabeth's safety.

"Why is that important?" Theodore felt like had missed something.

Darcy smiled at the thought of the man receiving what he deserved. "Before her injury, her father and Mr. Collins had schemed to have him creep into her room surreptitiously to compromise her. Her father liked the idea of her married to the smelly sycophant and instigated the whole thing. He knew she would turn the man down without pausing. Young Kiernan had overheard the two plotting, and he and his older brother surprised the man and broke his nose." He had been contemplating how he could add to the fund that Bingley had given the boy in restitution for his sister's actions. It would not do to embarrass Kiernan or his family, but he deserved so much for the aid he had given Elizabeth.

"Hunsford? Is he in any way connected to Aunt Catherine?" Theodore quickly understood how horrible the man could be if he was the type of person his aunt associated with.

"Yes, he is her clergyman. He is exactly like you might picture a man Aunt Catherine would choose to care for the spiritual needs of the people on her estate," Darcy commented.

Bingley shuddered to think of putting himself under the power of such a woman. It was a good thing Collins probably did not understand it all. "He left for Kent today, I think, so she should be safe from him. He is happy in the predominance of your loving aunt once again."

Chapter Twenty-Two

GUTHRIE MCDOUGAL DESCENDED THE stairs of her coach with regal dignity. Looking at her nephew, who waited on the stairs, she smiled at the boy. Her nephew was very dear to her. When she received his note, she had quickly put things in order to come and help him. After her brother passed, she had promised herself she would be there for his children. So here she was.

"Aunt Guthrie, I am so glad to have you here. Please come in. How was the journey from London?" Bingley jogged up to his aunt and hugged her, relishing the contact with someone he had always looked up to. After a moment, he stepped back and escorted her into the house, his arm around her shoulders.

Walking with him at her side, she was curious about how things were progressing. "I am happy to be here for you and your sisters. I have missed you all. How are things with Caroline? Is Louisa feeling any better?"

Bingley gazed at his aunt lovingly. Her strawberry blonde hair had a few streaks of gray, but her Bingley blue eyes still twinkled with the same life. Her beauty was still as undeniable. Guthrie was always practical. Her traveling clothes were subdued, but close inspection spoke of expensive fabrics and a tailored cut that was flattering. "I think Caroline is realizing that the world is not as she always thought it was. Louisa seems better; Miss Bennet has encouraged her to drink a special ginger tea regularly, and she has seemed much improved."

Guthrie smiled, happy to learn that Louisa was not truly sick per se. She would have to have a talk with the child. "I am glad that she found some relief. Did you say that there were guests in the home?"

Bingley could not wait to introduce the Bennet sisters to his aunt. He just knew that she would love them both. They had a similar zest for life. "Yes, Miss Bennet and Miss Elizabeth are here. There is an entire tale that I am sure you will be eager to hear and comment on, but first I would like to introduce you to Mrs. Nichols, the housekeeper." They had come into the highly polished entryway where Mrs. Nichols stood waiting, an inviting smile on her face.

"It is a pleasure to meet you, Mrs. Nichols. I can tell by the state of the entryway you are doing a marvelous job."

A few pretty wisps of graying brown hair peeked out of Mrs. Nichols' crisp white cap, and her intelligent brown eyes were smiling. "You are too kind, ma'am. I know London is not that far of a journey, but I was thinking you may enjoy freshening up before you join everyone. Would you like me to show you to your room?" Mrs. Nichols liked the no-nonsense look about the woman before her.

"You have read my mind! What time is luncheon? Perhaps I can join everyone then?" Guthrie yearned to remove the dust and sweat from her travels and slip into something refreshingly clean.

"That should be in about two hours, ma'am," Mrs. Nichols answered.

"I will look forward to introducing you to everyone, Aunt, but do not feel the need to rush by any means." Bingley kissed her cheek. He watched her follow the housekeeper up the grand staircase, relieved that she was here to help.

Guthrie followed the housekeeper through the house, glancing around as she went so she could find her way later on. "Splendid; show my maid to my room. I will leave my trunks to be stored at your discretion. I will not be staying long and will only need what I packed into my satchel."

***

GUTHRIE SPOKE TO THE lovely blonde her nephew was mooning over. Though she seemed to be very self-possessed for someone her age, she had a ready smile and keen blue eyes. "And when will you be returning to Longbourn?"

"The apothecary will come tomorrow to check on her progress. If his assessment is that her arm has healed enough for travel, she will depart for home the next day." Jane glanced at her sister playing chess with Mr. Darcy across the room. The bruise on her face had improved some, but still looked horrendous. Her arm was still in the sling she would most likely be using until the new year. Despite both things, she had never seen Elizabeth's smile brighter.

"You are a wonderful older sister to care for her so. Do you have any other siblings?" Guthrie noticed how she checked on her sister. There was affection between the two, and she was happy to see it.

Jane found the lady she sat with very sweet, though she had a lot of questions. "I am the oldest of five sisters, Mrs. McDougal."

"You must have a jolly time together. I only had one brother, but I would not have traded my time with him for anything. I would like to thank you for helping Louisa. Charles said that you had gotten her some ginger tea, and that she is feeling much improved. Thank you for being kind to her when you had your own sister to care for." Looking across the room, she smiled to see Louisa chatting with her husband. She was glad that things seemed they might be improving. Guthrie had been concerned for her niece. The last few letters she had received had been very concerning.

"I must admit that I cannot stand to see people suffer if I can help them. She was so miserable it was a simple solution to offer ginger tea to help her." On the settee near the fire, Jane noted Louisa's coloring had improved over the last few days and was glad of it.

"Has she confided in you?" Guthrie whispered, not wanting to draw undue attention to their discussion.

Jane shared a conspiratorial smile. "No, though I recognize the signs. I make various teas for all of our expectant mothers at Longbourn. Though it is my mother who attends the births if the midwife needs extra help. She seems to have improved, though she has not regained all her weight yet."

"I am reassured that she will have you and your mother near, as I cannot stay to aid her. It is possible I could be here for her confinement." Guthrie smiled back before turning her attention to Charles, who had been speaking with Theodore on the other side of Jane. "Has Caroline kept to her room for long?" Guthrie questioned her nephew.

"She stayed in her room for two days and after destroying nearly everything in the room, she came out yesterday. I think her reception surprised her," Bingley related.

"How was she received?"

Jane shared a conspiratorial smile. "She made a very critical comment that was incorrect in its essentials. Mrs. Ansley corrected her misconceptions and then, when Caroline asked Louisa to support her, she refused and told her she did not agree with her views. She returned to her room with a headache shortly thereafter."

Guthrie decided it was time to go check in on her other niece. "I hate to leave this enjoyable interlude, but I am going to check in on Caroline. I will hopefully return soon enough."

"I understand Aunt." Bingley gave his aunt a polite smile, but his gaze was irresistibly pulled towards Miss Bennet.

"Mr. Bingley, how has your review of the tenant homes going?" Jane prompted a change of a topic while Mrs. Guthrie McDougal left.

***

"Caroline, it is Aunt Guthrie. I am coming in." Guthrie looked around the room. She had heard from Mrs. Nichols that the maids had been told to stop cleaning up after tantrums. Entering the room, she glanced around with a critical eye, trying to gauge how things would proceed. At first, she did not see her niece, and then saw just the tip of her head on the far side of the bed. She had scattered the blankets and left them in disarray. Feathers were everywhere, evidence of at least one destroyed pillow. She had thrown clothes haphazardly around the room. Stepping into the room, Guthrie was startled to hear crunching; examining the floor revealed broken pieces of what once might have been beautiful figurines. Moving carefully, she came around the bed and crouched near where her niece sat on the floor in the corner. "Hello dear, are you ready to come out and talk? I find myself rather too old to sit on the floor."

Caroline did not even know where to begin. She was being told that everything she had set her foundations upon was wrong. She was unsteady and did not know what to do and where to turn. "I am so confused, Aunt."

"Well, you can be just as easily overwhelmed by confusion while sitting on the bed as on the floor. Up you go." Grabbing her niece's hands, she pulled her to her feet and shepherded her to the bed. She lovingly began pulling stray bits of down out of her curls. The poor child really had found her way into a smashing tangle.

"The way I act, the way I talk and walk, what I choose to wear and what I eat, I do so because they taught me to do it that way at school. The teachers and the other students showed me that life was a competition and that acting as I did was the only way to win. I always figured winning would mean finally finding happiness. But now I am unsure if that is what I am going to find." Running an unsteady hand through her hair, she came away with feathers. Groaning, she covered her face with both hands.

Guthrie hated to see her niece so lost, but thought it was encouraging to see her think. Putting her arm around Caroline, she drew her close. "What do you think your behavior right now will lead you to?"

"Probably more of the same. Not even Louisa agrees with me. I had thought that she was on my side and that she supported my opinions and actions. I realize now she just did not want to fight. But what can I do? I do not know how else to behave. Cutting down others to rise to the top is all I ever learned." Resting her head on her aunt, she let herself take solace. She had felt so alone for so long.

"You are not too old to learn new things. No one is ever too old to learn new things. The question is, do you want to learn a new way and, in my opinion, a better way?" Guthrie hoped she would make the right choice.

Even admitting that she might need to change went against all that Caroline held dear. Until this point, one guideline that she lived by was that you never admitted you were wrong. This smacked of admitting she was wrong. "I do not think changing that much of myself will be easy," Caroline mumbled in a small voice.

"Nothing of any worth is ever easy. Will it be any harder than always fighting? Of always striving after something you will never reach?" Rubbing Caroline's back, Guthrie tried to get her to come to the correct conclusion.

"I am embarrassed, Aunt. How can I tell everyone that I have been wrong all this time? How can I hold my head up while I learn a new way to be?"

"I would like you to come home with me. Stay with me until I come back in the spring to help your sister. It will give you a good start down your fresh path and you will not have to face those you know while you are learning your way." Guthrie held her breath.

"But there is not any society where you live, no entertainments." Caroline's instinct to complain was strong.

"All the better. You will not need distractions of that sort if you are learning a new way to be. It will give you a chance to discover who you really are without feeling the need to conform to others' ideas about who you should be," Guthrie reassured her niece.

"Alright, it has to be better than the way I am struggling here. Is there a plan on how we go about all this?" Caroline asked with a disheartened air.

Guthrie felt like she had stepped back in time to when her sons were little and she had to convince them to eat their vegetables. Some people never wanted to do what was right for them without prodding. "We are going to pack you up and make sure you have the clothes you might need for winter in Scotland. But before that, we take care of this room. It appears you have been very energetic in your fury." Guthrie braced for what she knew was coming.

"Well, do not try pulling the cord. No one comes. I swear the staff here are a disgrace." A disgruntled huff punctuated Caroline's complaint.

"The staff is not coming because it is not their job to clean up after a full-grown woman throwing a tantrum like a two-year-old. This will be your first lesson. If you break something intentionally, you will be the one fixing it. I will find a broom and some other necessary supplies for you, so that you can get to work right away. You should have enough time to finish before dinner. I think it is time you rejoined your family at meals." Standing up, she brushed off her dress, trying to free it of the feathers that seemed determined to cling.

"But that is their job, to do what I want them to," Caroline whined.

"No, it is not, and you are simply proving how very much you have to learn. I will return to show you how to do what needs to be done." Leaving the room and shutting the door behind her, Guthrie heard a shriek as she walked away. It was going to be a long year.

Chapter Twenty-Three

"Have you attempted crop rotation with turnip and clover, Elizabeth?" Darcy was fascinated by all the things that Elizabeth had been doing to benefit the estate without the aid of her father. There was a pleasant smell of coffee in the air as the servers brought out the dessert. Once again, Darcy relished the meal.

"Yes, though the land we work with is not large enough to show a significant increase in crop yields, it is enough to improve the lives of the tenants," Elizabeth explained enthusiastically, though she was stymied by the inability to gesture as she normally did. She had never realized how often she used her hands when she spoke.

The smile that spread across her face as she discussed her efforts to help her people mesmerized Darcy. "How so?"

"My father collects the same amount of rent whether they prosper or starve. Increasing the yields enables the families to get what they need when my father does not provide it," Elizabeth explained while eyeing the luscious-looking tart being put in front of her. The meal had been a simple roast and several side dishes, but all of it was good and the dessert looked to be amazing.

"How do you think he would act if the tenants left Longbourn? I know you have worked hard to make their lives livable, but if you and your sisters leave as you one day must, they would find the need to move to greener pastures, so to say." Theodore was toying with a thought of sending the man to the front in France. He did not like the idea of Mr. Bennet getting away with so much harm. He started to devise a plan for the Longbourn tenants.

"I would hate to see any of the families struggle. I do not think that Father would act until he found the problem interrupting his flow of port and books. He would soon find the estate insolvent and heading to bankruptcy." Elizabeth sat back in her chair, pondering the ramifications of the Colonel's point. How would she leave all of those families in her father's brutal grasp?

Upon seeing the panic on Elizabeth's face, Darcy rushed to reassure her, hoping to abate her fear. He reached over and squeezed her much smaller hand with his own. He knew how much all of those families meant to her and he would not see her fret over something he could easily amend. "You know, I believe Pemberley has several vacancies and could easily find a home for any families looking for a new start."

Blinking moisture from her eyes, she squeezed his hand in return. "I know that most girls would love jewelry from a man who is courting them, but I think your reassurance just now is worth more than any gems."

"Do not be so quick to turn down jewelry, Miss Elizabeth. He is bound to put his boot in his mouth again at some point. How else will he get himself out of trouble then?" Theodore cackled at Darcy's disgruntled look. He was going to have so much fun messing with his cousin now that he was in love.

*****

AT THE OTHER END of the table, Caroline looked around in confusion. The meal had been simple, with no excessive sauces or hard-to-get ingredients. There was nothing special about the meal and yet everyone commented enthusiastically about how good it was. While she admitted that the food was delicious, no one had ever complimented any of her fancy meals nearly as much.

Her aunt had convinced her she needed to join the meal and quietly listen to everyone. That was, of course, after she had to clean her own room. Sweeping up all the broken china and freeing her room of feathers had been a chore she had never attempted before. She even had to gather her clothes and put them away, though her aunt said they would review her entire wardrobe tomorrow.

The conversations that flowed around her were bewildering. Jane was discussing someone named Locke with her brother and Mrs. Ansley. It seemed like so much intellectual falderal. Miss Elizabeth and Mr. Darcy were discussing turnips and crop yields. How was he so engaged in talking about turnips? Louisa was laughing at something Georgiana said and smiling at her husband occasionally. Georgiana was bland. She knew nothing about style or the latest gossip. Caroline would often spend time with the girl, but she could barely bring herself to smile, let alone laugh. Even though it all went against the rules for how a proper dinner should proceed, everyone appeared to be having a good time. No one seemed to care at all that they weren't following any rules.

"Is there something wrong, Caroline? You seem confused." Guthrie had been monitoring her niece throughout the meal and easily saw her confusion.

"Why are they all enjoying themselves so much? They never enjoyed themselves like this at any of my dinners. I arranged everything so much better than this, and yet I could believe they would choose this meal over any of mine." Caroline stared at her plate, unwilling to admit that she thought the plebeian food much better as well.

Guthrie took a sip of her drink before responding. "Sometimes simpler is better. Not everyone has the stomach for more complicated meals and sauces. I know you were taught that you must serve the best to everyone in order to show your supremacy, but if the food is something they cannot eat, how does it show your superiority?" She guided her niece as kindly as she could.

"They are not even talking about any of the correct things. None of them are talking about any of the topics they taught me to bring up. In fact, I was told specifically to avoid intellectual discussions and talk related to manly responsibilities. Why are the gentlemen encouraging this?" Caroline heard a faint whisper of doubt in her mind as the truth of the situation came into focus. Everyone at the school had misled her.

"Rather than looking for a dull wife in order to satisfy their egos, these men want someone with whom to share life's joys. Everyone has their own likes and dislikes, and different groups will talk about different things. I have been to dinners with mathematicians and inventors who cannot speak of anything but numbers and angles and others where fashion was all that came up between the males and females. Accepting people as they are leads to better dinner parties, closer friends, and hopefully happiness." Guthrie thought of adding something about marriages, but thought that was a fight for another day.

Caroline looked down the table at all the cheerful faces and the bursts of laughter. She had never seen this much joy at this table before. "I think I have a lot to learn, or maybe unlearn."

"Do not worry, I have every confidence in your ability, Caro." Patting her niece's hand, she focused on the delicious fruit tart. It was superb.

The hard smack of a cane on the entryway floor was the first clue that they had a visitor. The level of anger conveyed by the simple act of striking a cane against the ground was astounding. Only those that knew the formidable lady suspected how bad the next interlude would be. Darcy, Theodore, and Georgiana all inwardly cringed against their memories of previous tirades.

The doors before Lady Catherine slammed open with the weight of the servant she shoved. She would have her way and no one would stop her. "I will not wait, you blithering moron, get out of my way!"

Bingley found that having confronted his sister on her behavior, it was much easier to confront someone with no hold over his heart. It really did not matter to him who she was, though he suspected even without an introduction that she was Lady Catherine. This was his property, at least for now, and he would see no one mistreated while under his protection. "Madam, I do not know who you are, but you will kindly treat my servants with respect or you will leave."

"I am Lady Catherine de Bourgh, and no tradesman's son will ever have the power to direct me. I am here to contend with what I can only assume are outlandish rumors." She scanned the room and spotted her family in various places around the table.

Guthrie studied the domineering older lady. She was wearing a poor excuse for a traveling outfit far too opulent and covered with ruffles to be comfortable to ride in a carriage for any extent of time. Her hand was clutching the top of her cane so tightly her knuckles had lost all color. The level of her indignation was obvious in every flare of her nostrils. "Nephew, Mrs. Ansley, would you at all mind my stepping in here? I am rather experienced in dealing with unwelcome guests." Noting their respective nods, she wiped her mouth, stood and stepped away from the table, facing the intruder.

"I know you cannot be implying that I could ever be an unwelcome guest. My goal is to make sure my nephew is safe from that social climbing harlot! I am also here to shield my other nephew and niece from her manipulative charm." After her conversation with her rector, Lady Catherine had rushed to put an end to the travesty taking place here. Yet no one seemed to value the effort she put into protecting the family.

"Oh, but how could you be anything but unwelcome? You did not receive an invitation from my nephew, who is managing this estate. I know neither of my nieces sent an invitation. So you cannot possibly be welcome. You are attempting to disparage one of his guests, who has been nothing but gracious and dignified during her recovery here.

Yet you stand here hollering like a fishwife with nothing but ill will and spite spewing from your small mind. Very most unwelcome, I would say, madam." Guthrie was careful to keep her voice soft and level. She had found that the key was to never raise her voice or escalate to match her adversary. It allowed her to maintain her control while the other person lost theirs.

Lady Catherine huffed. "I will have you know I am the daughter of an earl. My husband was a baron. My pedigree is beyond parallel. Certainly higher than anyone in this room."

"And yet you could not maintain even the barest of civility deemed necessary for society," Guthrie responded, her voice bland and unmoved.

Lady Catherine refused to be denied. Why was this nobody trying to stop her? "Nephew, I demand you do something. I will have my way!"

"Which nephew are you addressing, Aunt? I think everything is proceeding as it should. Carry on, Darcy, continue as you please." Theodore had never seen his aunt so provoked; it tickled him to see her so put in her place.

"I will be heard! Fitzwilliam Darcy, come away from that woman now. You do not know the sins she is guilty of. The abuse her family perpetrates," she exploded, spittle flying from her rabid countenance.

Darcy struggled to confront his aunt. Heightened emotions always made his struggles worse, and the stress of the confrontation threatened to steal his voice. "I know enough to know that her behavior is beyond reproach, unlike your own." To his shame, his hands shook. How could he hope to have a wonderful woman like Elizabeth if he could not defend her to his family?

Elizabeth's eyes narrowed and her mouth curled into a semblance of a smile as she looked at the older lady. "Now that you had your chance to speak, it appears you have done what you set out to do and you must be eager to be away from the people you find beneath you. I am sure we all wish you a safe journey." Elizabeth was furious that Mr. Darcy's own family had made him so overcome. Laying her hand over his, she encircled it with her own, hoping the comfort would stop his hands from shaking.

"Unhand him, you strumpet! I know of your manipulative ways. You connivingly arranged to be rescued, and it put yourself in my nephew's way, but I will not have your interference. You might have been good enough for my rector, but you let that opportunity slip from your grasp. You will never be good enough for a gentleman such as my nephew, flawed as he is. He is engaged to my daughter and has been since he was in his cradle." Lady Catherine advanced on the uppity girl, cane flailing in the air as she moved.

Guthrie McDougal forced her voice to maintain its passivity, but her eyes were blue steel. She had long ago figured out that being kind to everyone was as important as refusing to back down when it became necessary. "Now, madam, you would not be threatening one of my nephew's guests, would you? I have asked you to leave already and I will do so again now. Please take yourself home. What is going on here is not your concern. Your family has responded to your cantankerous tirade. You must have nothing more to say here. Know this: if you take one more step, I will have the groomsmen hold you until the magistrate can be summoned and you will be charged with trespassing and attempted assault."

"You would not dare. I am part of the peerage and above such petty actions." Catherine gasped at the audacity. She never had problems like these back at Rosings; people there knew to give her the respect she deserved.

"No, madam, you have an honorary title from your father the earl, but that does not make you part of the peerage. Being the widow of a baron does not give you any special authority either. You, madam, are a civilian and no better than anyone here. In fact your nephew Colonel Fitzwilliam, who has earned his rank is also the child of an earl; as such he ranks higher than a mere daughter. They can take you to the gaol just as easily as anyone else, so leave now or that is where you will end up." Guthrie had summoned the grooms while Lady Catherine was screeching at her nephews, and they arrived as she spoke.

"You would not dare!" Catherine brought her cane down on the ground with a resounding crash.

"The decision is yours." Guthrie allowed herself a small smile at the woman's disbelief.

"I will not be denied. You will unhand him and leave his presence." She reached out to wrench the hussy from her nephew, but a hefty and calloused hand clamped down on her wrist and stopped her.

Pulling her back from the couple, an imposing figure of a man removed her cane from her possession when she attempted to use it to strike at the siren. "Careful, ma'am, you would not want to harm yourself with this. I will just hold it for you."

"Unhand me!" she screeched.

"Thank you, Bennings. Take her to the stables. You may restrain her if necessary. I have every confidence in your ability. Oh, and see that you send for the magistrate. I apologize in advance. She seems to be especially vociferous." Turning back to the table, she glanced around at all the wide eyes and grinned.

Theodore was astonished and delighted at the power of Bingley's aunt. "Ma'am, if you were not already married, I think I would propose. You are magnificent!"

"I am not complaining by any means, but is she really going to be put in the town's gaol?" Bingley asked.

"Yes, most definitely. It will not hurt her and I am sure that she has long needed to learn that she is not above everyone the way she feels she is. Regrettably, I doubt the lesson will stay with her for long. Besides, I would not offer her a room for the night and I am sure she would refuse to stay at the inn. This way, her horses and groomsmen can get some rest tonight. If you excuse me, I will go make the necessary arrangements." Guthrie left the dining room to speak with the housekeeper.

Chapter Twenty-Four

"I ABSOLUTELY LOVE YOUR aunt, Bingley. She is amazing. She handled my aunt like a general directing his troops on the battlefield." Theodore piled his plate high with various breakfast items and headed to the table.

"Yes, I believe she is rather splendid." Grinning at his friend across the table, Bingley took a sip of his coffee. The night before had been both satisfying and highly entertaining.

"You gentlemen would not be talking about me while I was out of the room, would you?" Guthrie entered the room with a whirl of skirts and smiles. She made a beeline for the coffeepot, pouring herself a cup of its steaming contents.

Quickly standing, Theodore went to the sideboard and selected a plate for her. "Mrs. McDougal, let me get you a plate. What would you prefer?"

"Thank you, dear boy. A pastry and some eggs would be fine. You may call me Aunt Guthrie as Charles does." Guthrie inhaled the smell of her coffee as she sat; her eyes closed in contentment.

"I am honored, Aunt Guthrie." Theodore put a plate in front of her with a bow before returning to his chair and his breakfast.

"So, Aunt, what are your plans for Lady Catherine? Do we need to be concerned about a return visit, do you think?" Bingley dug into his breakfast after bringing up the question.

"I doubt she will be an issue going forward. I spoke with the magistrate last night and explained the situation. Miss Elizabeth is well-liked, and when he heard my explanation coupled with Lady Catherine's rant, he quite agreed with me." Guthrie took a bite of her pastry, enjoying the fluffy texture and sweet taste.

"What exactly did you agree on?" Theodore asked while spreading jam on his toast.

"I agreed we would not press charges if she would return home today, stopping nowhere near here on her way back to Rosings. One of my grooms will follow her until she is well on her way to ensure that she does." Guthrie smiled while staring into her cup contemplatively.

"I tip my hat to you. The way you handled the whole interaction shows amazing tactics. Do you play chess? I would love to match wits before you leave if you have time." His life as a tactician for the military was ending because of his injury, but that did not mean he would not find other ways to keep his mind sharp.

"Yes, I am rather fond of chess. I play with my husband regularly." Guthrie took a bite of her eggs before continuing. "I think I will have time to play a game with you this evening, maybe after dinner. That is, if we can pull Miss Elizabeth and Mr. Darcy away from the board; they seem to relish the opportunity to challenge one another."

Bingley smiled, thinking that it was nice that his friend had found so much happiness at Netherfield. "Yes, they seem rather fond of the pastime."

***

"I THINK YOUR ARM is coming along nicely. Your healing is progressing as expected. It doesn't bother you too much, does it?" Mr. Jones tried to judge the pain that Miss Elizabeth was in as he manipulated her arm. His patients either screamed at any little pain or they tried to out-stubborn the pain. Miss Elizabeth was the latter sort of patient.

Elizabeth tried to avoid a wince as Mr. Jones moved her arm. "No, it does not hurt too badly, and Jane's tea has been helping when it does. I dislike the way I feel when I take laudanum, so I have stopped taking it. The nightmares were becoming rather too disturbing." She hated the way her head swum when she took laudanum. Her arm did ache, but it was a bearable pain.

"Your face seems to have healed fairly well. Even though it still has a discolored appearance, I am happy that your cheek does not seem to be broken." Mr. Jones was relieved Elizabeth had come away from her fall at Oakham Mount with such little consequence to herself. Miraculously, she came away from the perilous situation almost unscathed. Mr. Jones felt it must have been the grace of God. She could have easily died. "I am confident that you should manage the return home tomorrow without further issues, as long as you are careful. I will come to Longbourn to follow up in about a week." Closing his bag, he smiled warmly at both the girls before he left.

Elizabeth felt guilty that she did not want to go home. Her home was where her mother and sisters were and she was allowing them to suffer without her there to help or act as a buffer. "I know this is not right to say, but I am almost sad I am healing so well. If I had been struggling, we could stay here longer."

"You have been enjoying your time with Mr. Darcy. I can understand wanting to stay in his vicinity." Jane soothed her sister's distress. She could see the joy in Lizzie's eyes when she spoke to Mr. Darcy. Anyone with that much affection for someone would want to remain close.

"I know that is part of it, but I also do not want to return and deal with Father. I will go home tomorrow, but it has been nice here, not having to endure the ongoing challenge of silently battling our father." Elizabeth was so demoralized by the fighting. She had been so free here that it only helped her to understand how draining her home was.

"I cannot but agree with you. It would be easier to never return; however, we know that there is a plan in place. It will not go on forever. Our tenure under his authority will end soon." Jane was determined to see the struggle at home come to an end. If the plan that they were putting in place did not work, she would come up with another, and another, until the suffering stopped. Staying at Netherfield had let her know just how tense she had been at home. She was having a wonderful time, and she was determined not to accept the dreary future her father had plotted out for her and her sisters.

Elizabeth linked arms with her sister and headed towards the delicious breakfast that awaited them. "You are right. Let us go down and have some breakfast. We still have one day of peace to enjoy before we return to discord."

Coming into the room, she spotted nearly everyone at the table and grinned to see Mr. Darcy hop up when she entered the room.

"Elizabeth, sit down. I shall get you some coffee and a plate." Darcy rushed to get her coffee just as she liked it, with cream and the smallest amount of sugar. She looked fairly well. The bruise on her face was healing more every day, though it was still very noticeable.

Elizabeth took the cup that he handed her, but when their fingertips touched, the most spectacular frisson ran up her arm. Looking into his eyes, she knew he had felt the jolt as well. Developing a relationship with Mr. Darcy was becoming a very interesting endeavor. "Thank you, Mr. Darcy. I would love a muffin and some of that delicious jam. What were you disusing when we arrived?" As much as Elizabeth desired to use a term of endearment for Mr. Darcy, she hesitated.

"We are disusing our plots and ploys to bring down the evil king," Georgiana spoke up from her spot a few seats down.

"Oh, have we set up his downfall yet?" Jane spoke while gathering her meal.

"There is a plan in place and everyone has their role," Theodore responded. He had been writing letters since Darcy and Elizabeth had come up with the idea.

Guthrie reached over and patted Jane's hand. She was a dear girl and even if things did not turn out as she suspected they would, she would like to keep in touch. "Now I want you to promise that even if things go wrong after you return home, you write to me; you have my direction."

"Yes, Aunt Guthrie, I promise, though I hope you will get the chance to say goodbye to us before you return home," Jane replied as she stirred her tea. She had enjoyed spending time with the woman she had grown to admire.

"Yes, I hope so too." Guthrie thought over the many things she wanted to accomplish with her niece and sighed. Things were moving along well, but if she wanted to get home before winter fully set in, she would need to leave soon. Stepping back from the table, she made her excuses and went in search of Caroline.

***

FINDING CAROLINE IN HER sparse but clean room, Guthrie knocked on the door to let her know she was there. Lost in thought, Caroline was gazing at the shattered mirror in front of her, and looked up at her aunt in surprise.

Guthrie spoke softly to her niece while moving to set next to her on the bed. "It looks like you are deep in contemplation. Anything you would like to share with me?"

"I once felt my life was in one piece, but now it's shattered into fragments just as much as the woman I am looking at. When I realized my plans on how to act and what to do were misguided, I felt a shiver of uncertainty run down my spine. As if I had lost my way and did not know where my path led. I do not think I know who I am or even who I want to be anymore." She continued to stare at her shattered representation, her life aligned in too many pieces to order.

"Who we are changes every day with every decision we make. Trying to take your identity on all at once can be very overwhelming. When you did your room, what did you think when you saw that mess?" Guthrie questioned.

Confused, Caroline looked at her aunt, her crystal blue eyes wide. "There were feathers everywhere and broken things. It overwhelmed me. I did not think I could do what you asked."

"Were you able to do it?" Guthrie prodded her niece.

"Yes, it took time, and you had to help show me how to sweep, but it is clean now." Looking around, she realized she was proud of the work she did and what she had accomplished. It was an odd feeling. She had done something she had always considered menial and yet, in the end, she had felt good and she was proud. She did not know what to think about it.

"In essentials, it is the same thing. You are overwhelmed at first, but then you get to work, taking it one piece at a time. You ask someone for help and keep working at it until you become satisfied with the results."

"What if I am never satisfied?" Caroline mumbled.

"It is a process that takes time, but I am confident you will find a way. For now, we need to go through all your clothes to find what to bring to Scotland. I have a feeling it may take longer than either of us would like. Do you have anything with warmer fabrics?" Standing, she went to the wardrobe and pulled out everything.

***

THEY CONDUCTED THE CARRIAGE ride back to Longbourn in near silence. Neither Jane nor Elizabeth felt much like talking. The tension in them both was a visible thing, measured in the relentless smoothing of skirts and constant knee bouncing. Bingley and Darcy rode outside the carriage for propriety's sake but were keenly aware of the strain on the Bennet girls. The last day they had spent at Netherfield had gone by in a blink and now the calmer times were over. They were all preparing for a pitched battle.

Darcy dismounted Cadmus and helped Elizabeth down from the carriage, squeezing her hand for support. Bingley quickly helped Jane down and escorted her to the house. Mrs. Hill stood in the entryway.

Mrs. Hill wiped at her eyes with her oversized apron, overcome with the sight of her sweet girl. "Oh, Miss Lizzie, I am that glad you are home. Even if you are rather worse for wear. Your mother is in the parlor with your sisters. Your father has stayed in his study. Now I know your beau is here, but you will go rest within the hour or I will know it."

"Thank you, Mrs. Hill. I will rest as you command." Elizabeth leaned in and kissed the older woman on the cheek.

"What would she do if you did not obey her edict?" Darcy questioned.

Elizabeth laughed while heading to find her mother and other sisters. "She would withhold Mrs. Allen's scones in the morning."

"Yes, a very horrifying punishment indeed," Jane attested.

Their sisters welcomed them with joyful laughter and enveloped them with unconditional love. Eventually, things settled but not before everyone received multiple hugs, and Elizabeth was shown to a well-padded chair near the fire even though she promised she had not caught a chill on the ride over.

"Now that I have delivered you into the warm embrace of your mother and sisters, we will leave. I will return in the morning so that we can go see Kiernan. I might even bring Theo so that he can spend time with all of you lovely ladies." Darcy bid her goodbye, only getting in a few whispered words of affection under the scrutiny of so many eyes.

Chapter Twenty-Five

A SLIGHT WEIGHT CRASHED into Elizabeth's side and clung with a fierceness that spoke of overwhelming emotion. Kiernan pressed his small face into the fabric of her dress and she felt the moisture of his hidden tears. Elizabeth gazed down into his moist brown eyes, her heart going out to him.

The last he had seen her, he had pushed past his terror. It was only after she had received help that his body shook, and he cried. At last, he could assure himself that she was well. "They said you were alright, but I have waited so long to see you." Kiernan's voice wavered with emotion.

"I am sorry that everything was so frightening. I wish that it had been possible to see you before now." Her love for him compelled her to smooth his hair back as she tried to comfort the wonderful boy.

Kiernan's shaking hand hovered near her wounded arm. "Your face is still purple and green and your arm is in a sling. Are you sure you are not hurting too bad?"

Elizabeth peered at him, observing him for injury. "Oh, it hardly bothers me, as long as I do not jostle it too much. How are you? They told me that Caroline was rather cruel."

"It weren't nothin'. I was more worried about you than anything." Kiernan stood tall, proud of how he had helped the woman he loved like a sister.

"Is your mother available to talk with Mr. Darcy and me?" Restraining her smile was a struggle for Elizabeth. Kiernan had been so focused on Elizabeth that he hadn't noticed Darcy standing there and the shock on his face was comical.

"How are you today, Master Kiernan?" Darcy chuckled.

"I am doing great now that Miss Elizabeth is home." Kiernan's smile was infectious. He took Elizabeth's hand and pulled her into his house. "I am sure Mam will be happy to see you. She is baking today."

Betty Anderson wiped her flour-coated hands on her apron and studied the young lady her son had in tow. It looked like her son had not exaggerated. "Well, it is good to see you up and about. To hear Kiernan talk, you got yourself in quite the scrape." Miss Elizabeth had always been a good girl, and it was sad to see her injured so, though she always was one to jump in without looking.

Elizabeth smiled at the kind woman who was raising four good boys and the sweetest little girl. "Thank you for taking the time to talk with us. I know how busy you are."

Mrs. Anderson eyed the handsome young man standing beside Miss Elizabeth. He stood with implied strength and dignity, his attention never leaving Miss Elizabeth for long. His outfit's cut and the fabric type spoke of luxury and expense. It seemed Miss Elizabeth had made a very wealthy conquest. "Oh, the dough needs another rise, anyway. Is there something you and your charming fellow needed to talk with me about?"

"I would like to introduce you to Mr. Darcy of Pemberley. He has an offer for your family." Elizabeth blushed, aware of the fact that Mrs. Anderson saw how Mr. Darcy gazed at her. She felt the warmth of his regard in his gaze. It made her feel warm even as the wind whipped her skirts around her legs.

***

"YOU ARE A FLATTERER, Mrs. Bennet. I am nothing more than a simple soldier, a second son, and nothing special. Call me Theo or Theodore, if you must. I do not care for stuffy pretension." Theodore grinned at the lady on the settee next to him. Her clear blue eyes were alert and understanding of his ploy.

Mrs. Bennet was rather fond of the young man who was part of the ploy to stop her husband. "Well, Theodore, have a scone with your tea. How have you been filling your time since your injury?"

"Mostly contemplating my future and enjoying my time with my cousin. I have spent too much of her life in France fighting in the mud. I have enjoyed coming to know her." Theodore watched his cousin laugh with the other young ladies across the room. She was an exceptional girl. It was nice to see her so joyful.

"She is a lovely child. I know that my girls have been happy to have her company. I know they would like to have a more permanent connection with her, but that is something we will leave up to different forces." Her eyes danced as she glanced at him over her teacup.

Mindlessly taking a bite of the scone that had found its way to his plate, Theodore froze in place. As his taste buds danced to the melody in his mouth, the complexity of the flavors left him wanting more. "This scone is worth fighting Napoleon's hordes for. I think I may have to find your cook and bribe her to come away to Pemberley. I shall have her set up as chief scone maker and will be happy all the rest of my days." Theodore only just restrained himself from licking the crumbs off his plate. His words were not simple flattery; it was the absolute best scone he could remember tasting.

"You are too kind, Theodore. I am sure that Mrs. Allen would be willing, should the enticements be adequate. She is a dear woman. Her husband was one of our tenant farmers when he passed, and she had no way of supporting herself and her young daughter. I set up for her to work here, given that the former cook was keen to move closer to her children in Bath." Mrs. Bennet smiled, eating her own scone. They were rather scrumptious.

Theodore stood, pulling down his waistcoat as he did. "I am sorry to leave your wonderful company, but I have to put the first part of our plan into action."

Mrs. Bennet felt compelled to speak to the man before he turned to leave to fight the dragon that was her husband. "I believe that you have given me hope, Theodore. I have long worried about my daughters' futures and now you and the other gentlemen have come. It is almost as if you have saved them already."

"Mrs. Bennet, we are endeavoring to free all the Bennet ladies. Not just your daughters." With a swoop of his arm, he took her hand and bowed over it with a grand flourish before turning away to find his target

***

"So this is where you are, Mr. Bennet. I had been hoping to have a word with you." Observing Mr. Bennet, Theodore could find nothing about the man to like. He was unkempt and slovenly. The eyes that turned to focus on him had an angry glint.

Mr. Bennet glanced at the interloper, unimpressed with his uniform and his lack of discretion. "I neither know you nor have I invited you into my study. Be gone."

"I will leave you to your peace. It was only I had hoped to help you, but if you do not wish... Well, never mind, I am certain you will find your own copy. Eventually." As Theodore spoke, he tried to remember how his commander's batsman behaved. The sniveling fool was indecisive and complimentary and was always getting under his skin. Theodore had decided that copying his mannerisms would keep Mr. Bennet off-balance.

"Stop blithering and be clear. What copy were you speaking of?" Mr. Bennet demanded.

Theodore regarded Mr. Bennet's reaction to the information and found it promising. "My cousin had told me you were looking for the third book in Benjamin Striker's collection. He must have forgotten his father had purchased the entire collection while he was in school.

I may be able to find a way to obtain it for you. That is, if you are still looking for it, sir?"

"I would be interested to see what condition the copy is in before making any arrangements." Thomas Bennet could not believe what had stumbled onto his path. He had been looking for that book for over a decade and here was an idiot just offering it to him.

"I sent for the book, as I had thought you might possibly be interested. I thought I might warn you, my cousin is rather keen on betting rather than payment. The book should be here tomorrow. If you do not mind my humble suggestion, I would suggest acting quickly before he comes up with a more elaborate game." Theodore set his bait and waited for his prey to go for it.

"I would be interested in meeting with your cousin to discuss securing the book for myself. What do you want in compensation for arranging this possibility?" Mr. Bennet asked, his eyebrows drawn together in question.

"I am but a second son with few prospects. Until recently, I have spent my time on the continent, but they cashiered me out of service, and now I must rely on my cousin for my bread and butter. Seeing him get what he deserves would make my day." Theodore did not lie. He thought his cousin deserved to be happy with the woman he loved, and this would see it happen.

"I am always happy to see a man who knows what he wants. Tell your cousin I will see him tomorrow. Have him bring the book with him," he directed and then waved him off, anticipating his easy victory the next day.

Theodore bowed and left the room, happy that things were going as expected. They would have the paperwork ready this afternoon and Darcy was speaking with the tenants at that very moment. Walking back out into the parlor, he smiled to reassure Mrs. Bennet of his success. Tomorrow would be the day they saved the Bennet ladies.

***

DARCY FELT THE MORNING had gone well. He had spoken to several of the tenant families and they promised to speak with the rest. Escorting Elizabeth back to Longbourn made everything that much better. He could be mistaken, but he hoped it was something akin to pleasure that had her grasping his arm so eagerly. Glancing back, he spotted the maid that had trailed after them the whole day. She was a quiet little thing, but she had kept up with Elizabeth's rapid pace. If they kept their conversation reasonably quiet, they had both privacy and propriety.

"When we started courting, you asked to use a shortened version of my name, but I have yet to hear anything like my Christian name pass your lips." Darcy did not want to feel disappointed, and yet he found himself almost desperate to hear something besides "Mr. Darcy" come from her mouth.

Elizabeth did not want to hurt Mr. Darcy's feelings, but knew that she needed to proceed at her own pace. "I have felt odd saying something like that in front of others. It is still so new. I am sorry if I have hesitated too long, Wills. I will try to use it when we are with our families at least. Though I would like to have a name for when it is just the two of us, I am not ready for that yet."

Darcy stopped the moment he heard "Wills" leave her lips. It was a little thing, but it somehow meant so much to him. Turning to face her, his smile tender, he cupped her unharmed cheek in his large hand, running his thumb soothingly along her skin. Slowly, so as to not frighten her, he brought his forehead to rest against hers, soaking in the elation he felt in the special moment. "Thank you." Darcy's breath puffed as he spoke, caressing her cheek. When she shivered, he brought his head up, his eyes concerned. It would not do to let her get cold. With a smile that involved both dimples, he turned them back on the path to her home.

"Thank you for being such a generous man. What you are doing for the tenants means so much," Elizabeth spoke up after struggling to clear her throat. Not wanting to reveal how undone that one slight gesture had left her, she tried to continue without pause. She was certainly glad for the cold weather because it would cool her heated face. Hopefully he could not see any evidence of the tingle that had gone straight down her spine, spreading warmth as it progressed.

"It is the right thing to do. I cannot see acting otherwise." Darcy glanced down at the top of her head where it nestled on his shoulder. "What have you thought of our courtship so far?"

"I must admit that I was unsure at first. All my experiences with my father had broken my faith in marriage and in relationships with men. But you have proven yourself true whenever an issue came up. Do not think I missed how difficult it was for you to stand up to your aunt. I am finding myself craving time with you. It does not matter if we are playing chess or going to see the tenants. I am enjoying my time with you more than I had thought possible." Elizabeth had not told him how he made her feel. She blushed at even the thought of expressing how she tingled when his hand touched her face or his breath caressed her cheek.

"I am glad that I am gaining your confidence. Hopefully tomorrow will go well and we can have all the time we want together." Darcy's tone reflected his hopeful attitude.

Elizabeth gripped Mr. Darcy's arm tighter in agitation. "Yes, so much rests on what happens tomorrow."

***

WICKHAM SIGHED AS HE sharpened his knife. He still could not find his way to sneak into the post coach. Signing up for the militia was a horrible idea. He had never been this dirty. Lack of care had matted his normally shiny blonde hair and his clothing had become stiff with grime. There was no way he could charm anyone into anything in the state he was in.

It was all Darcy's fault. If he had not been trying to get his revenge, he would still be clean and able to charm anyone he wanted. Except for that Bennet chit. She had seen through his beautiful illusion. It was not fair she was in on the whole thing with Darcy.

He needed to steal a horse. The punishment for horse theft was severe and so he tried to avoid it when he could, unless he knew he could get away with it. He had several estates that he could choose from, but his need for revenge focused his attention on Longbourn.

It was fortuitous that they had few servants and he could sneak about the property as he needed.

When a brilliant idea came to him, he was so startled that he cut his finger on his knife. Cursing and putting the knife away, he laughed out loud. He could get his revenge on everyone if he made one stop on his way to the stables. He decided to eat the last of his hard bread and rancid cheese this evening and set out when he woke up in the morning. Tomorrow was going to be a great day.

Chapter Twenty-Six

Darcy knew Cadmus sensed his unease. The poor horse kept flicking his ears this way and that, on the lookout for danger. He continued to settle his nerves before he faced Mr. Bennet by taking calming breaths. So much depended on the outcome of the conflict he was riding towards.

"When we get there, be sure to act like you are above Mr. Bennet, possibly even annoyed at his presumption to ask something of you as he turned down your request to court Miss Elizabeth." Theodore spoke from his charger, Achilles, his posture completely relaxed and unworried, his experiences in life having enabled him to remain collected even on the battlefield.

"So I should act the way you have told me not to act when in company. It feels like my life has come full circle. I finally come to a place where I begin to relax and feel close enough to someone to be myself, but to continue on that path, I must act as I did before. It is a peculiar sensation."

***

Mr. Bennet was happy to hear that his guests had finally arrived. He had worked himself into a frenzy, his heart pounding in anticipation of finally having the book in his possession. "So, gentlemen, have you brought the book in question? I do not want my time wasted by useless chatter."

"It is here, sir. If you would like to inspect it." Theodore produced the specially wrapped package containing the book he so desired.

Mr. Bennet grabbed it eagerly, unable to hide his glee at finally having the rare book in his clutches. His hands trembled as he pulled open the oil skin that had protected it. The binding was almost pristine, and the cover still had the embossing. A smooth finger ran along the words with the caress of a lover. It was destiny that they had finally found their way to one another.

"I suppose that if you would like to marry my daughter, you may have her if you leave the book with me." Mr. Bennet stated this without once removing his gaze from the book.

"No matter how you may view things, I am aware of the significance of the items around me." Darcy extended his arm and extracted the book from Mr. Bennet's clutches.

Theodore spoke up, hoping to move things along in the right direction. "I am sure you would be willing to make some kind of arrangement, Darcy. What if he upped the ante, so to speak?"

Darcy held the book aloft just out of Mr. Bennet's reach. "If I have something you want above everything, it is only fitting that you give me everything else that you have. I know the worth of this book and there is no way a man like you can afford it."

"I cannot give you Longbourn. They entailed it in such a way that I am unable to sell it," Bennet complained.

"It is so like you to refuse to see what is before you. You would not allow me to court Miss Elizabeth, and yet you would release her when you knew what I had. Now I say that is not enough. I want you to release them all. I know how much you enjoy the power you hold. That is the price I want you to pay." Darcy allowed his animosity to seep into his voice. He would never treat a woman in such a way himself, but he knew it was how Mr. Bennet would view things. Elizabeth had coached him on what to say to deal with her father.

Mr. Bennet's hand froze in the air, his mind too busy with indecision to contemplate motion as well. Oh, how he wanted that book, had wanted it for far too long. Yet he did not want to relinquish his hold over his wife and the girls. They were his chief form of entertainment, besides his books.

"Darcy, that does not seem very sporting. Don't take away the possibility of him experiencing the joy of being the victor." Theodore played his role as devil's advocate.

"What do you suggest, cousin?" Darcy questioned, as if they had not already planned every word.

"First off, I suggest we lower the stakes. What if you do not get the ladies? Maybe just removing them from his power is enough. They have an uncle in town. Perhaps he could sign something that would allow their uncle to decide for them and permit marriages and what not. As for your wife," he said to Mr. Bennet, "sign something granting her a separation and a release of her dowry to her. Second, you could get a chance to come out on top. What if you play a game of chess?" Theodore watched the wheels turning in Mr. Bennet's mind.

Darcy gave the appearance of vacillation. "That is not exactly what I had in mind. However, playing a game of chess against Mr. Bennet would satisfy me. It has been a long time since I played at Cambridge."

Mr. Bennet pondered the chance before him. He risked having to sign away control over the women in his life. How problematic would that be, though? His brother-in-law would provide them with a place to live, food and clothing, at his own expense. Having to scrimp and save was certainly a possibility. How much money did his tradesman brother-in-law have, anyway? Mr. Darcy would have to go through Mr. Gardiner if he wanted to marry Elizabeth. Their lack of connection to an estate would harm all of their standing. Was there a downside?

"I cannot recall. Which of us won the last time we played the game ourselves?" Theodore questioned.

"I believe you did, but has been quite a while." Darcy tried to sound bored when in reality he was exceedingly hopeful. Mr. Bennet was going exactly where they led him.

"I would receive the book if I win a game of chess, and in the slight chance that I lose, I would sign something to the effect of releasing the girls to my brother-in-law. Is that the agreement?"

"I would like that you sign the paperwork beforehand with the agreement that we cast it into the fire if you win. I would hate to cast you in an unpleasant light, but there have been those who do not follow through on their end of the deal when they are angry they lost." Darcy recognized the probability of Mr. Bennet being a very sore loser.

Mr. Bennet was unconcerned about the paperwork, as he had no intention of losing. "I suppose that is fair."

"I am carrying a contract with me now and if you give me some time to write the names, we can continue." Theodore cleared a small area of the cluttered desk to get to work. Once the contract was ready, he presented it to Mr. Bennet to review and sign. "There is a space at the bottom for you to sign, and Darcy and I will sign as witnesses."

Only glancing at the contract briefly, Mr. Bennet signed away all his rights where his family was concerned without a second thought. Darcy and Theodore both signed at the bottom as well, and it was complete save for the chess game. Taking the contract, Darcy waved it about to dry the ink before folding it up and placing it in his breast pocket.

"Let us proceed, then. I would like to read my new book." Mr. Bennet had every confidence in his chances of winning. He would relish this victory for years to come.

"I would be agreeable to start now," Darcy said, holding back his smile. He nodded at Theodore, who had moved the chessboard to the center of the desk and began arranging the pieces.

"Shall we begin?" Theodore allowed himself a small smile. He loved it when things went according to plan.

***

Head tilted, enjoying the peace, Elizabeth tried to absorb the serenity of nature and let her anxiety float away with the breeze. So much depended on this day. She had confidence in Wills, but her old fears surrounding her father kept creeping back like an ugly weed in an otherwise beautiful garden.

"At last you are alone. I have been watching you forever." A disheveled Wickham emerged from the bit of wilderness behind the archery field. His once spotless clothes were now stained and torn, giving him a squalid look.

Elizabeth's shock at seeing Wickham approaching her was considerable. The closer he got, the easier it was to note the sour smell of his unwashed clothes. She could sense a cold hostility radiating from his eyes, and it felt like it was chilling the atmosphere around her. Her heart pounded in her chest, but she refused to be cowed by his presence and held her ground. "What are you doing here?" she demanded.

"You will help me get one of your horses and get away. I hate this godforsaken town, and I am ready to leave." Wickham took the time to inspect his prize. He had pieced together what had happened after he had emerged from his drunken stupor. She had fallen off the cliff. Yet she only had her arm in a sling and a bruise on her face. It was not fair. With his luck, he would have broken over half his body. Why was luck so unequally shared?

"I certainly will not." Elizabeth stood trying to put the bench and distance between them.

"You and Darcy have conspired to ruin my life. He will not be so pompous when I take you with me, will he?" Wickham leered at her, admitting, if only to himself, that Darcy had exceptional taste.

"Did you lose your senses somewhere in the woods? Darcy has done nothing to harm you. He enabled those here to protect themselves from your manipulation and greed. If you lived an honest life, most of your problems would disappear."

"I want to get what I deserve. I am worthy of more, and I will do whatever it takes to get it. With people like Darcy standing in my way, how will I ever achieve it all if not by underhanded means?" Wickham made a haphazard grab for her arm, wanting to drag her towards the stable. If he could force them to let him take a horse, he would kill two birds with one stone. He would get away from his troubles. It would ruin Elizabeth when he took her with him. Uptight Mr. Darcy would not want a ruined woman.

Elizabeth ducked under his flailing arms. If she allowed him to capture her, she knew it would not be good. "If you got what you deserved, Mr. Wickham, you would be on the way to hang for attempted murder."

"Hold still. I am taking you with me. You are powerless to stop me." Finally grabbing Elizabeth, he sought to drag her with him but found his will impeded by her struggle.

Elizabeth's stomach twisted when his grimy hand closed around her delicate wrist. Instead of succumbing to defeat, a feeling of determination and strength surged through her. A spark of inspiration jolted her, and she acted on it without hesitation. "There is plenty I can do about it!" Kiernan had advised her exactly where to kick a man should she need to rescue herself. Kicking him with all her strength, she got him right where she needed to in order to make him shriek.

"I thought you were a lady. That is not playing fair." Wickham dropped to a crouch, his agony clear in the coarse string of curses he let loose. But despite his agony, he refused to release Elizabeth.

Elizabeth struggled in his weakened hold. Her injured arm was seriously hampering her ability to put up a fight. "Plenty fair, from my perspective."

"Why won't you behave?" Furious at her attack on his person, he reared back in to slap her, only to scream again.

Suddenly, Wickham felt the searing pain of an arrow slicing through his hand, leaving the arrow lodged in his flesh, sticking out of both sides. "My hand! What did you do?" Wickham cradled his injured hand, releasing Elizabeth to do so. His cries of anguish echoed through the air as he bemoaned his fate.

Kitty dashed up, panting and pale. She released the skirts she had picked up to run, drew her bow once more and aimed at Mr. Wickham. "Lizzie, are you alright? I was trying to wait until you were clear, but I could not let him hit you."

***

MR. BENNET STARED AT his tipped-over king, unable to fathom where it had all gone wrong. His bishop had taken Darcy's knight at the beginning. Things had been proceeding well. Where had that queen come from? He could not stop the attack that had left him completely vanquished, its force like a physical blow.

Darcy watched the shock and anger flit across Mr. Bennet's face. He had not even found the game to be that challenging. Darcy felt his jaw clench and his eyes burned with indignation as he watched the pompous man. He knew he was constantly tripping over his words, and it was worse when he was upset. Yet Darcy was trembling with intensity as he tried to find the words to say something of import to Mr. Bennet. "I believe you are an abhorrent person and not deserving of the kindness they could have shown you. I will advise the Bennet ladies to pack and prepare for their departure. It thrills me that soon they will no longer have to endure your company. My groomsman will stay here to assist them, as I want them to feel secure and safe as they go through this adjustment." He would not leave the ladies vulnerable to an angry Mr. Bennet. Darcy carefully wrapped the book by Mr. Striker and he left the room to allow Mr. Bennet to wallow in his defeat.

Theodore felt the need to add his own input before he left. "You thought your few years in Oxford playing chess against other boys would be enough to keep you at the top of your game. Staying in your library for the last twenty years has done nothing but encourage your unfounded pride in yourself. Let this be a lesson from a younger man with more experience in life: never underestimate the people around you. It may surprise you." Theodore placed a book about the language of flowers on the desk and left, closing the door behind him as he went.

Suddenly, a commotion in the entryway had them rushing to see if they could be of assistance. Lydia was leaning over, windblown and breathing hard, trying to catch her breath while asking for help. When she stood, she spotted them in the entryway and surged forward, grabbing at Theodore's sleeve.

"Mr. Wickham is on the archery field trying to take Elizabeth. You must hurry." Lydia pulled at the Colonel's arm, trying to direct him where he was most needed.

Theodore took off like a shot. Darcy followed, but at a much slower pace than his more athletically gifted cousin. A high-pitched scream caused the hairs on his neck to come to attention. Please, he begged in his heart, let her be alright.

***

"Why would you do that?" Wickham dropped to his knees, planting his forehead in the dirt. He was too overcome by the pain to flee.

"I would have aimed for your heart, but you do not have one," Kitty replied, not taking her eyes off the man threatening her sister.

"I came to assist a damsel in distress, only to find out she has already slain the snake." Theodore laughed at the scene before him. Wickham lay in the dirt, sobbing and cursing, an arrow stuck in his hand. Elizabeth's sister stood above him, another arrow cocked at the ready, an avenging Artemis in all her glory.

"I am glad you came, but I hope that this has not interrupted the goings-on with Father," said Elizabeth. Her words were calm, but her heart still fluttered in her chest. She tried to tell herself she was fine, everything was fine. There was no reason to fall apart from an attack of the vapors. Yet her hands were shaking and everything was going gray at the edges.

"Elizabeth!" Darcy cried out to the woman who possessed his heart. She appeared unharmed and still his fear persisted. She was looking at Wickham, who was on the ground crying and complaining.

"Wills, I..." Elizabeth found herself unable to continue. The world that had been graying at the edges faded to black.

Chapter Twenty-Seven

STARTLED, DARCY LUNGED AS he saw Elizabeth's face drain of its color and her eyes roll back in her head. Catching her as she fell, he scooped her up in his secure embrace. Her weight settled against him as he supported her.

"Elizabeth, sweetheart?" Darcy's voice strangled in his throat. Panic welled in his chest. He could not see any injuries. What was wrong with her?

Theodore noted the concern on Darcy's face. He was hopelessly in love with the woman in his embrace. It was a pity he was going to have to tease his cousin about it later. "Most likely it is just shock. It was probably too strenuous for her while she is still recuperating."

"If you bring her to the house, Mr. Darcy, Mama will help her," Kitty spoke up but kept most of her attention on Wickham, who was still crying on the ground. When she saw Mr. Wickham was threatening her sister, at first she had been terrified. The terror clutched her heart and made it tough for her to think, but then she remembered she had a weapon in her hand. She had always felt so powerless, unable to protect anyone, but that sensation vanished when she held the bow and understood her strength.

"I will take care of the snake while you care for your lady love," Theodore stated even as he laughed, his eyes narrowed at the miserable wretch on the ground.

"You call him a snake? My sisters and I have been calling him a weasel. His words and behavior make it obvious that he is not the gentleman he portrays himself to be. Whatever we call him, he needs to be dispatched. Did you have a method in mind?" Kitty asked the colonel beside her. She was at ease with her bow in her hand.

Theodore was having the best day. Darcy had beaten Mr. Bennet in a game of chess, and now he saw Wickham sniveling after being bested by two sisters. "Weasel? Yes, I think I detect weasel around the eyes. Has anyone ever said that you look like a weasel when you whine, Wickham?"

Wickham kept his eyes on his hand, seemingly fascinated by how the arrow stuck out of his palm. He sniveled and mumbled, snot running grimy trails down his dirt-covered face. "You cannot understand the struggles I have faced. Living in conditions not fit for peasants, and that other girl kicked me. Why is nothing fair?"

"When I take you to the militia, they will make your trial very fair. Now get on your feet; do not make me drag you. I swear you would not like the results." Theodore may have found the irony hilarious, but he was serious about forcing Wickham to see justice.

"Are you sure you won't need any help with him?" Kitty did not relish the thought of any escape attempts.

"Do not fret. Hugh should have arrived by now. He will be more than happy to help me get this one to town and his eventual trial. You might get to see Australia, Wickham." He grabbed Wickham by the arm and hoisted him to his feet. Kitty followed them back to the house, smiling as she went.

***

FANNY BENNET DIRECTED MR. Darcy to the settee in the parlor so he could lay Lizzie down. "Do not fret, dear, she will recover."

"She does not appear to be injured," Darcy said, reassuring himself and Elizabeth's mother.

"I know my daughter has been pushing herself further than she should. She may come around on her own before I return, but I will get my smelling salts. I am leaving the door open." She decided to take her time finding her smelling salts, and left with a smile on her face. Her daughter had found a kind and generous man.

He sat on the couch beside her, grasping her clammy hand in his own. Memories of her fall and waiting for her to wake plagued him. He told himself she was fine, but fear, in his experience, was never logical. When her nose scrunched in the most adorable way and her eyebrows drew together, he could tell she was waking up. When her emerald eyes opened and looked at him bewilderedly, his heart felt as if it could finally beat again.

"Please tell me I did not faint." Elizabeth closed her eyes in embarrassment.

A grin spread across his face, his dimples making another appearance. He loved her in all her moods, and this one was rare. He was grateful that she was well. "I will not tell you about how you fainted."

"This is ridiculous. Everything was fine, and we routed Wickham. I do not know why I collapsed." Sitting up with the aid of Mr. Darcy, she gave him a rueful grin.

"Theo has told me about soldiers in battle who collapse afterward. It is as if something tells them they are finally safe and they can deal with their injury." Darcy reached out to smooth a curl behind her ear.

"I am so pleased that particular skirmish has concluded. We will move ahead with our lives without him skulking menacingly in the shadows." Glad to have one fewer thing to worry about, Elizabeth allowed herself to relax.

"You are not worried that we will allow him to escape?" She had so much faith in him, and it gave Darcy a sense of pride.

"That is not one of my worries. With that arrow in his hand? I do not think so." She would have to commend Kitty later. She had saved her with that shot.

"He did seem rather pathetic. On the ground crying and complaining that you kicked him and asking why Kitty shot him with the arrow." He held her hand in his own, sliding his thumb along hers. It was a reassuring dance, his callused thumb dancing along her skin. Comfort settled over them both.

"Well, I did kick him rather hard in a very effective location." Though her eyes were laughing, her grin was almost wicked.

His bark of laughter burst out of him without restraint. "I wish I could have witnessed that."

"Well, I am glad to find you both so recovered," Mrs. Bennet stated. Sitting on the chair near them, she smiled maternally.

"I am sorry to worry you, Mama," Elizabeth fretted.

"It is alright, darling. Mr. Darcy was taking excellent care of you. I was not at all worried." Mrs. Bennet's fear of her daughters ever finding happy lives was fading away. She smiled at Jane as she came into the room, followed by Lydia and Mary.

"Lizzie, do you always have to get into scrapes?" Jane leaned over to kiss her sister's cheek before sitting next to her mother.

"Of course she does. How else would we find any entertainment?" Lydia said, laughing irreverently. Her youthful attitude and ability to find humor in the situation assisted her in bouncing back from the morning's escapades. She walked to the settee across from Elizabeth and Darcy, dropping in an ungraceful heap next to Mary.

"I do not intend for these things to happen. Do you suppose I throw myself into dangerous situations for your entertainment?" Elizabeth found herself unable to maintain a stern expression. She knew Lydia was not serious.

"Not truly. I only find it better to laugh than to give way to fear," Lydia said.

Elizabeth smiled at all her sisters and noticed that Kitty was not with them. "I would also rather laugh than cry, Lydie. Do not concern yourself. I was not upset."

"I speculate that Miss Kitty is accompanying Theo as he escorts the prisoner to the stables. She did seem rather assured that Wickham would not get away. He might end up with another arrow in him if he tries." Darcy's laugh was infectious.

As Kitty entered the room, laughter filled the air. Crossing over, she knelt down on the floor and embraced Elizabeth tightly. She had found her courage and felt that she would no longer be as fearful all the time. Despite that, she still required a hug.

"I am so proud of how brave you were, my sweet. I believe you are quite the archer." Elizabeth smoothed Kitty's hair in a soothing fashion. It was something she had done since they were both small.

"My heart felt like it was going to pound out of my chest when I saw him. When I realized there was something I could do to help, I became very calm. All his whining made me realize how small bullies really are." After a last squeeze, Kitty got up to sit by Mary and Lydia.

"Since you are all here, I would like to tell you how this morning went on another front. Do you think it is safe to speak here, or should we move to another room?" He watched the ladies silently communicate before they stood and left the room. He hurried to keep up with the swish of their skirts.

***

Glancing around the improved setting, Darcy said, "I'm pleased to report that things unfolded exactly as we had wished for. Your father did indeed lose the chess match against me, and he signed papers to release you to your uncle's discretion."

"Are we free then?" Mary spoke for all of them.

"Yes, in a fashion. You have many choices to make and I suggest you make them quickly. I have had one of Theo's groomsmen stay here for protection. I fear your father will not relish having you here if he has no right to control you." Darcy had sat by Elizabeth, holding her hand once again. The warmth of her skin against his did something to him that was quickly becoming addictive.

Fanny Bennet looked around the room at all her daughters. All of their hopes and dreams would soon have the chance to shine. "We will leave for London soon. My brother is prepared to receive us. We have never all gone to London together and I cannot help but look forward to it. Mr. Bennet always made sure some of us stayed behind. Almost as if his family were hostages to play with. We can pack quickly, right, girls?"

"It will not be a problem, Mama. We have warned everyone. They understand, and most have even encouraged us to leave," Jane spoke up, confident they could handle the situation before them. They would do it together as they had done everything else.

"Many of them have accepted your offer, Wills. Kiernan's family began it. Others followed suit." Elizabeth drew reassurance in the look of joy her words had brought to his eyes. She enjoyed the feeling of his hand in hers, her heart swelling with affection.

"You said that you would send your understeward to Netherfield to help coordinate their moving to Pemberley. When do you suppose he will arrive? We need to help expectant mothers as much as possible," Lydia asked for reassurance.

"I think he should be here in the next five days. He's assessing the open farms, ensuring they are ready." It filled his heart with delight when Elizabeth spoke his name as "Wills" once more. His gaze never wavered from her as he brought their entwined hands to his mouth, and the gentle brush of his lips against her skin sent a shiver down her spine.

The loving display she saw pleased Mrs. Bennet. "Well then, I assume you will want to remain close to my daughter when we make our way to London. Do you have a home there?"

"Yes, I do. My home in Mayfair has plenty of room. I know you would like to stay with Mr. Gardiner, but do not assume his home is your only option." He made the offer out of the goodness of his heart and his desire to remain close to his love.

"While I thank you for your generosity, I would like to accept your offer with a few changes. Mary, Kitty, and Lydia will stay with you and Georgiana under the supervision of Mrs. Ansley. Jane, Elizabeth and I will stay with my brother. If you are courting or engaged to my daughter, you will live separately. If you want to live with my daughter, you will simply have to marry her." Fanny Bennet laughed at the expressions on their faces.

***

His patience had worn thin, and Bennet knew that no matter how long he stared at the chessboard and drank port, nothing would change. More than twenty years of getting his way had not prepared him for a loss of this manner. He knew deep down that they had outmaneuvered him, yet he refused to admit that he had no chance of getting what he wanted. Even if he had signed something, he was sure he could convince the weak-willed woman that was his wife to remain. Stumbling away from his desk, he left his domain to make his frustration known.

"Can I help you with something, sir?" Hugh had been standing in the hallway waiting to see if Mr. Bennet would leave his library. He gave the man a cursory glance and was unimpressed by what he saw.

"Who are you? And why are you standing in my hallway?" Mr. Bennet blustered.

"I am here to help things to make sure things proceed smoothly while the ladies prepare to leave. I will, of course, help you while I am here. Are you on your way to your chamber? Let me help you." Theodore knew the man was attempting to cause issues, but he had no intention of allowing him to do anything. Taking the gentleman by the elbow in a firm grip, he guided him through the house. His grip on the man remained insistent as they walked.

Mr. Bennet had attempted to struggle when the man had taken him by the elbow but found that resistance was futile. He gritted his teeth as the grip tightened and he remembered just how much he hated pain. His failure brought home the point that he would not come off the winner if he attempted what he wanted to. He listened to the sound of his own heart pounding as he realized he would be better off staying in his library and sipping a glass of port. He would get some sleep and then his life would go back to how he liked it. Who needed those annoying women, anyway?

Chapter Twenty-Eight

THE LADIES OF LONGBOURN spent as much time as possible getting ready to vacate their estate. Sorting through clothes and belongings filled their days. They went around to the families in the area to say goodbye. Making sure they gave the Lucas family a proper farewell was especially important to them. They had been close for many years and wanted to explain the situation.

Unexpectedly, the interaction was quite uncomfortable. Charlotte was extremely proud of her engagement to their cousin, Mr. Collins, and was upset that they were not more delighted for her. She did not want to take any of their warnings to heart. When she implied they had treated their cousin poorly and should not expect to receive anything from the estate when he inherited, they left.

Despite their busy schedule, they also said goodbye to Mrs. Guthrie McDougal. They had a perfect moment to say goodbye when they gathered for tea. As the tea was served and conversation flowed, Caroline was unusually quiet, making only a few remarks, none of them being negative.

"I am glad that they will make him see justice. Leaving debts wherever he went, seducing young girls, attempting murder, and kidnapping. A man like that has no right to his freedom." Guthrie glanced around the room and smiled. Despite all the trauma these girls had gone through, they were on the path to recovery.

"Yes, he is a menace to society. I, for one, am glad that he is no longer free to threaten my girls." Mrs. Bennet was not at all upset that the man was on trial with the possibility of execution or transportation to Australia. Elizabeth still had remnants of the bruise on her cheek.

"Miss Kitty, how are you holding up? It cannot have been easy to defend your sister in such a manner." Guthrie eyed the girl, checking to see if shooting a man had adversely affected her.

"I could not allow him to hit her or attempt to take her away. I had to act. In the past, I felt like I had no power. It was quite liberating, realizing that I was not as powerless as I felt." Kitty said these words with pride.

"I am glad that you have gained confidence in yourself, dear."

"What time are you leaving in the morning?" Jane spoke up from next to Caroline.

"We will leave at first light. The sun sets so early now I would like to travel as far as we can before dark." They were ready to depart, only leaving out the necessities for tonight and tomorrow; everything else was in their trunks.

"I know we must leave soon, but before we go, I would like to apologize. The way they encouraged me to behave at school was not correct. I understand that now." Caroline was more subdued than anyone had seen her before.

Jane's love for people and the kindness at the root of her heart always led her to help those who were struggling. "Everyone has had the experience of being on the wrong track at some point. If you keep focusing on your relationships with people, you will certainly find the solution. We forgive you."

After reassurances of continued friendship and promises to stay in contact, Mrs. McDougal and Caroline left to return to Netherfield. It was nice to say goodbye to their new friends. They were all moving on to fresh paths and new possibilities.

***

DARCY AND ELIZABETH WATCHED the sun crest the horizon from the top of Oakham Mount, accompanied by the chorus of birdsong in the early morning. Kiernan had come along as well, happy to act as a chaperone. He wanted to make sure nothing happened to Elizabeth, as their last attempt to make it to the top of Oakham Mount had not ended well. From their vantage point, they could see the vista below them adorned with scarlet and orange leaves, sparkling with the mist from the chilly fall morning. It appeared as if everything was ablaze and glowing in the sunrise.

Darcy pulled Elizabeth into his strength, wanting to lend her some of his own. Entwining his fingers with hers, he watched as she said goodbye to her complicated childhood. "Do not think of it as an end,

Lizziebet. It is a beginning." His face lit up with a beaming smile as he referred to the woman he adored with the pet name he favored.

She lay her head on his shoulder, watching the sun rise above the horizon from the comfort of his arms. "I think it will be a glorious beginning if this sunrise is any sign. I have always felt that you should only think of the past as its remembrance gives you pleasure. There is pleasure in remembering the good things that happened. The good people who I knew here. Things were not all bad. After all, being here meant that I got to meet you."

"Mr. Darcy, do you have any horses like Crumpet at Pemberley?" Kiernan inquired from where he stood petting the magnificent horse.

"No, not exactly like him, but I was thinking of having him sire a few foals in the spring. I would like to continue his line." Darcy smiled back at Kiernan. He would forever be indebted to the boy. For every moment he felt contentment with Elizabeth, he felt the urge to add to his plans for rewarding Kiernan for all he had done.

"I am sure you will love watching all the young horses play." Elizabeth laughed at the glee in Kiernan's expression.

"Do you think he might enjoy further schooling? Maybe Eton?" Darcy whispered in Elizabeth's ear.

"He is a voracious learner. I think he would like it. Would they shun him for his position in society?" Elizabeth murmured back to Darcy.

"We could make it known that we are sponsoring him for his remarkable efforts on behalf of the Darcy family, and it might go well. Or we could say he has shown promise and he will be required to work for us for a few years to pay us back. Frankly, I think his character is so likable that he is bound to make friends," Darcy reasoned, enjoying the feel of Elizabeth whispering into his ear.

"I think it is a brilliant idea if he wants to do it," said Elizabeth, grinning. The idea of helping Kiernan to expand his horizons delighted her.

"Do you think I will like where I am moving? Will I be close to you and Miss Elizabeth?" Kiernan, like most children, was slightly apprehensive about change. He looked up at Elizabeth and Darcy, unaware of their discussion.

"I think you will love it. Your parents have asked to take over the opening at my home farm. It is very near where I live. However, Miss Elizabeth will not live with me at Pemberley unless we get married."

"Oh, that is just a matter of timing. You ask Miss Elizabeth to marry you. You say words at a church and you are married. Then you get to come to have fun with me at Pemberley." Kiernan's eager expression and innocent explanation of how the world worked were astounding to the two adults looking down at him.

"Of course, it is just that simple," Darcy said under his breath. When had the complexities of life taken away his simple view of the world? Had he ever viewed the world as clearly as Kiernan did?

"I know you love each other. It is not a question of if, it is just when," Kiernan continued, unaffected by the shock on Darcy and Elizabeth's faces.

"Just a matter of when?" Darcy parroted Kiernan's earlier statement. The gears in his mind whirring at impossible speeds.

"I guess so." Elizabeth was likewise engaged in a rapid analysis of her heart. Was there any reason not to want to be married to Wills? Her heart said no.

Without hesitation, Darcy made a bold move to grasp what he desired most. "Your mother has determined that Jane and Mary should experience a season. Is that something that you want for yourself?"

"No, having a season in the ton has never appealed to me. Now that I know what I want, a season would be useless." Elizabeth's eyes shone with hope.

"I had plans and a script. I was going to make sure I did not put my boot in my mouth this time. We were going to play chess at my house after dinner one evening and I was going to tell you about how you were my queen. You are the most important piece of my life. You make everything better. Everything is clear and good when you are near me. You see who I am, and what I mean, even when I put my boot in my mouth. I know am messing this up but I do not have better words right now, and I feel like now is the time to speak." The world dropped away from Darcy. Had someone transported them to the moon, it would have made no difference. All that existed at that moment was the woman standing in front of him and the way she made him feel.

"Are you asking for my hand in marriage?" Elizabeth asked. Tears of joy glimmered in her eyes as the morning sun illuminated her love. Her affection for the man before her was almost too great to bear.

"Yes." Darcy had every expectation of a positive outcome if her expression meant what he hoped.

Elizabeth raised up on her toes, attempting to bring their eyes closer together. "Do you remember me saying I wished I could call you something other than Wills, but I was too timid to let you know yet?"

"Yes, I remember. I am perfectly happy that you have been calling me Wills. Lizziebet, I am happy with anything you wish to call me." Leaning down to fill the gap between them, he nuzzled her temple, taking enjoyment in the warmth of her skin.

"Yes, Mr. Fitzwilliam Darcy. Wills, I will marry you. That way when we are alone together, I can call you mine." Elizabeth's cheeks grew hot in response to her brave declaration.

"Mine? I like that almost as much as yes." Darcy's lips descended to Elizabeth's skin, a smile tugging at his lips as he whispered his joy to her.

As Darcy's light kisses sent shivers down her spine, Elizabeth could feel her breath catching, and his gentle touches along her temple and down her cheek brought a whisper of, "Mine." She could feel the warmth of his breath on her lips when his feather-light kiss settled over them.

The weight of Kiernan's hug surprised them both when he flung his arms around them. "Can I come to the wedding?" He knew they loved each other. They were both just too stubborn to move forward without a push.

"As long as your parents approve." Elizabeth chuckled as she felt the tension leaving her body and echoing in the air.

Looking up at the pink and orange sky, Darcy blew a long breath out through his lips. This was not the time or place. There was plenty of time for more later, hopefully soon. Maybe he could arrange for a special license? "Kiernan, I want you to remember today when you court a girl you like."

"That is so far from now, I am not worried. Besides, I am Miss Elizabeth's chaperone. It is my job." The appearance of exaggerated responsibility replaced Kiernan's fleeting look of disgust. He was happy they had finally seen reason, but he was perfectly happy to avoid mushy stuff for as long as possible.

"I suppose it is. Let us head back. We do not want Miss Elizabeth to catch a chill." Gripping Elizabeth's hand tightly in parting, he moved to swing Kiernan back up into the saddle. Returning to Elizabeth, he took her hand again as he headed back down the path on the way back to Longbourn, Cadmus and Kiernan following meekly behind.

"I bet Mrs. Allen's scones will be warm from the oven if we hurry. Can I ride Crumpet all the way back?" Leaning over, he briefly hugged Cadmus in glee.

"Of course." Darcy moved to whisper to Elizabeth. "Maybe he will be so distracted that he won't remember to chaperone."

The sound of Elizabeth's joyous laughter filled the air, her arm around Darcy's as she nestled into his shoulder while they walked. She delighted in the view that had brought her joy in the past, and now it was even more special to experience it with the man she loved. With the vibrant oranges and reds of the fall foliage, the place she loved seemed to whisper a bittersweet goodbye.

All too soon they were back on Longbourn land and Elizabeth was saying goodbye to Kiernan. He would stay behind to help his family move to Pemberley. It only took a slight amount of convincing for him to accept that they would see him soon. They had decided on their walk down that they would marry from the Pemberley chapel. Hopefully Mrs. Bennet would host Georgiana for a time. They both loved her dearly, but felt that they could use some time to themselves.

***

BETWEEN THE WAY ELIZABETH was snuggled to Darcy's side, and the grin equipped with dimples that he was sporting, Mrs. Bennet soon guessed that their relationship had progressed. "Have the two of you set a date yet?"

"Wills suggested next week, but I insist I want my arm free of the splint and sling when we marry," Elizabeth responded with a grin.

"So, I have recommended she see a specialist in London to see exactly how quickly she can be done with them both." Darcy had never smiled this much in his life.

"I am so happy for you. Thank you, William, for giving me such a wonderful set of sisters!" Georgiana flung herself at the couple and after a brief hug, she darted over to Kitty and Lydia to dance around with them in glee.

"Congratulations, Darcy!" Both Theodore and Bingley were there promptly to slap Darcy on the back.

After the flurry of congratulations abated, they began overseeing the final preparations to get in the carriages and leave. Theodore, Darcy, and Georgiana were accompanying the Bennets to London. To avoid overcrowding, Bingley and Darcy provided them with the use of both carriages.

Suddenly everyone was getting in the carriages and Elizabeth paused, her foot frozen on the step. Looking over her shoulder, she took a last look at what had once been her home. Hundreds of years of Bennets had lived there, were born there, died there, and it all ended with her father. It abruptly made her very sad.

"Remember, think of this as a beginning. It is not an end." Darcy brought her hand to his mouth and kissed her palm tenderly.

"Yes, this is the start of our magnificent journey together." Elizabeth felt her heart flutter at his sweet display of affection, her face blushing in response. Her eyes were wide with anticipation as she scampered into the carriage and settled onto the seat. She found herself unable to sit still, abuzz with delight at the thought of planning her wedding with the man she adored.

Epilogue

Mr. Bennet's downfall was complete within six months. Forced to go into town to find staff to replace those who had fled, an angry shopkeeper confronted him. Without tenants, he did not bring the money he would need to pay anyone. The many letters he had been ignoring referred to the lack of funds and overdue bills. He was bankrupt soon after. Forced to find work, he left Longbourn and Meryton. No one who knew him saw him again.

Almost a year later, Mrs. Bennet received notice that she was a widow. After a scandalously short period of mourning, she remarried. The man she decided on this time was outstanding, and it thrilled him to have a woman like her in his life. She surprised her daughters by having a son ten months later.

***

Charlotte Collins, nee Lucas, realized that by choosing Mr. Collins for her husband, she had chosen a life of servitude. The illusion that she was the mistress of her own home was only the merest veneer. Lady Catherine dictated everything that she did, from what kind of meat they had on Tuesday to the size of the cut that was prepared. When the servants could not complete the useless tasks that Lady Catherine insisted on, Charlotte completed them herself. For a while, she looked forward to moving to Longbourn. However, that did not come to pass.

When Mr. Bennet became bankrupt, a clause in the entailment immediately transferred the possession to the heir. On discovering that it was a useless property with empty tenant homes and fields left fallow, Mr. Collins followed Lady Catherine's advice to sell it, as they designed the entail to prevent Mr. Bennet from selling the property, but allowed Mr. Collins to do so. He immediately invested the paltry sum in an investment scheme that Lady Catherine chose. The investment suggestion proved unsound. Not that Mr. Collins minded; Lady Catherine told him it was for the best. When Charlotte had daughters, she counseled them to make wise choices in marriage partners. It was not a lesson she had enjoyed learning the hard way.

***

UNBEKNOWNST TO THE COLLINS, or Lady Catherine, Mr. Darcy and Mr. Bingley, who was engaged to Jane by that time, had purchased Longbourn. By that time Mary was being courted by Mr. Goulding's second son, recently home from Oxford. It was gifted to them at the event of their marriage with the provision that he change his name to Bennet. He gladly complied with the proposal and worked with his new bride to help all the families returning from Pemberley to take up their old homes. Thus, the Bennet family continued at Longbourn, becoming wonderful stewards to its people and land.

***

WICKHAM'S STORY ENDED, AS it was meant to, embarrassing, cheerless, and a surprise to no one. The trial was swift and his rank stripped, yet despite his crimes, they granted him leniency instead of a death sentence. Put on a boat bound for Australia, Wickham found his powers of persuasion did not work on men more wicked than he was. After attempting to charm the wrong woman, he had a strange mishap that sent him tumbling overboard. When they could not save him, the man in charge simply shrugged his shoulders in resignation. No one had liked him anyway, and it was one less mouth to feed.

***

THINGS CONTINUED SPLENDIDLY FOR the Bennet ladies. Elizabeth found peace and satisfaction at Pemberley. Her love for her husband grew ever stronger, as did her chess game. She could soon best him regularly and often found herself able to beat Theodore. Regardless of how her skill developed, Darcy never stopped thinking of her as his queen. He called her his queen whenever he wanted to see her eyes sparkle. She was like a missing puzzle piece that fit together and made his life feel whole. She was the most important part of his life. At least, until the children came.

***

"SHE IS GOING TO be tiny. Be careful when you see her." Kiernan spoke in a whisper, smiling kindly down at his young charge.

"I wished for another brother." The tiny voice easily betrayed Artie's disappointment.

"A sister's love is irreplaceable. They give hugs you can feel to your toes, and they make the world brighter. As her big brother, it's your duty to look out for her. You get to help her stay safe." Kiernan watched as Artie's brows drew together and he tried to puzzle out these recent developments.

"I can protect baby Thea?" Something about that sounded right to Artie.

"Yes, you can protect baby Thea. I am sure you will do a wonderful job of it, too." Kiernan spoke reassuringly to the little boy despite the discrepancy in their sizes. He had grown tremendously in the six years since the drama that had brought Elizabeth and Darcy together. His relationship with the Darcys had only gotten closer over the years, and he was delighted to be there to welcome their newest child.

Elizabeth lay recovering in bed, cuddling her newborn. When they entered the room. Kiernan clasped Artie's small, chubby hand as they approached. At four, Artie was prone to throwing himself into his mother's arms with unrestrained joy, and Kiernan wanted to shield Elizabeth and the baby from his ardent hugs.

Though obviously tired, Elizabeth was glowing. It thrilled Kiernan that she had gotten the daughter she had wished for. Darcy kneeled on the bed beside the two, their two-year-old son Gilbert in his arms. His eyes overflowed with love as he gazed upon his wife and newborn daughter, tears streaming down his face.

"Thea is very red. Is she sick?" a little voice whispered to Kiernan. Tip-toeing, he crept closer. Arthur Theodore Darcy was a very caring child, and he loved his uncle Kiernan and trusted him to help.

"No, new babies are just like that. You were just as red when you were born," came the soft reply from Kiernan.

"Hello baby Thea, I am your big brother. I am going to help protect you." Reaching out, he ran a careful finger over her little clenched hand. He felt a rush of joy when he looked into her wide, trusting eyes.

***

Elizabeth and Darcy went on to have five children: Arthur Theodore, Gilbert Charles, Dorothea Frances, Kiernan James, and Catherine Mariana. Elizabeth cherished her large family. It was rare that they did not have some extended family member visiting.

Once a year, all the Bennet ladies gathered at Pemberley for a reunion. As they all married and grew families of their own, the number of people who came to Pemberley increased. While Darcy never felt comfortable in crowds, the people he loved understood how to interpret what he meant when he said the wrong things.

On one of these occasions, Kiernan met Marianne Gardiner, Elizabeth's younger cousin. During their long courtship, Darcy made sure he could act as a chaperone for Marrianne and Kiernan as much as possible. When Kiernan would glare at Darcy for his interference, Darcy would laugh and say it was his job as a chaperone.

After completing studies at both Eton and Cambridge, Kiernan used the funds he had been accumulating since Bingley started his nest egg to buy a horse breeding farm near Pemberley. His horses were renowned for their might, wisdom, and faithfulness. Though he had a diverse stock, his finest horses all descended from one sire, whom he had called Crumpet. After his first successful year of business, Kiernan married Marianne. When Elizabeth gave him a tearful hug on his wedding day, she told him he had long been part of her family. This would just force other people to recognize the fact.

Acknowledgements

Before you go, I would like to express my gratitude for reading Darcy's Gallant Gambit. It's been a joy to create this work of love, but without readers, it would be an exercise in futility. If you enjoyed reading this book, please consider leaving an honest review on your favorite site. It does not have to be very long, but I would really appreciate the feedback.

Cooming Soon

The act of writing has completely consumed me, and I cannot stop. I am currently immersed in writing another full-length Pride and Prejudice Variation, which is set to be published in May 2024. Coming Soon: Mary's Daring Demand.

Kitty's mother, Fanny, is the subject of my short story, Fanny's Strength. It tells the tale of how she found the strength to raise five amazing daughters and find her own happily ever after. By subscribing to my newsletter through the link below, you'll receive a free copy, as well as exclusive updates on my upcoming releases and other exciting content.

https://dl.bookfunnel.com/66ax5bftkb

About the Author

My journey with words started out as a painful one. The letters on the page seemed to taunt me, and I spent countless hours with my mother trying to decipher their meaning. Our reading journey started with Little House on the Prairie and continued with other books, mostly in the historical fiction genre. Slowly but surely, I started reading independently, advancing from historical fiction to fantasy and science fiction.

The stories I found in the books I read held me captive, and I often lost track of time. The realization of the true power of the written word inspired me to pursue writing. Unfortunately, I had to put it on the back burner in order to deal with pesky things like paying for food and housing. Then a dare from my sister brought back memories of my passion for writing in high school. It was a passion that I was determined to rekindle.

When I got back into writing, I turned to my latest reading addiction for inspiration, Pride and Prejudice Variations. My mind was fixated on the regency era and the romance of Elizabeth and Darcy, making it hard to write anything else. So I went with it and here we are.

I graduated from college and promptly realized that a degree in American Sign Language was not as helpful as one would hope.

Moving from working as a sign language interpreter to home health and hospice care and mental health services, I have had a diverse career.

349

www.ingramcontent.com/pod-product-compliance
Lightning Source LLC
Chambersburg PA
CBHW021209310726
48971CB00006B/1502